"ONE OF THE BETTER ENTRIES OF THE SEASON."

San Diego Union

"Fast paced, never predictable, yet always believable... The plot thickens to include broken marriages, several suicides, blackmail, homosexual relationships, a maniac killer, professional jealousy and racial tension."

Best Sellers

"Harry Stoner, a hard headed and soft-hearted Cincinnati private eye... knows his way around the nether-world."

Chicago Tribune

"Mr. Valin has a good feeling for pace, is a smooth storyteller, and has plenty of talent."

The New York Times Book Review

Other Avon Books by
Jonathan Valin

FINAL NOTICE
THE LIME PIT

DEAD LETTER

JONATHAN VALIN

 AVON
PUBLISHERS OF BARD, CAMELOT, DISCUS AND FLARE BOOKS

AVON BOOKS
A division of
The Hearst Corporation
959 Eighth Avenue
New York, New York 10019

The Dodd, Mead & Company edition contains the following
Library of Congress Cataloging in Publication Data:

      Valin, Jonathan.
      Dead letter.

      I. Title.
    PS3572.A4125D4   813'.54   81-3112
                                 AACR2

First Avon Printing, December, 1982

TO KATHERINE

1

The first time I saw Sarah B(ernice) Lovingwell she was sitting on the stoop of her father's home on Middleton Avenue. From where I was parked in front of the house she looked to be a pale, sober young lady with a sweet, demure face. She certainly didn't look like the sort of girl who would cause trouble. At least, not the kind of trouble I'd been hired to investigate.

Her father, Professor Daryl Lovingwell of the University of Cincinnati and Sloane National Laboratory, wasn't sure whether his daughter had caused the trouble, either. That's why he'd stopped at my office in the Riorley Building on a cold Monday morning in the heart of December. A dapper little man in his late fifties, he looked, I thought, like a polite, pallid George Bernard Shaw—high forehead, bald speckled flesh, trim white imperial cut to a satanic point, and white moustaches that exuded a faint odor of wax and of pipe tobacco. From the fine tailoring of his Harris tweeds and the trace of English accent that toned his speech like a silvery tarnish, he seemed to be a very proper gentleman, indeed. He seemed to be Lord Chesterfield in woolen bunting. But there was a wry gleam in his gray eye that suggested he wasn't blind to the slightly eccentric impression he made. And after we began to talk, I got the feeling that, like most eccentrics, the Professor only used his quirks and oddities of speech and of dress in the right company—which appeared to include me.

I'd pegged him for "family troubles" the moment I'd seen him come through the door. Maybe a wayward wife who, after twenty-odd years, no longer found Lovingwell's eccentricities all that winning. But I'd been wrong. The wife was dead—seven years. It was his daughter he had come to talk about. His daughter and the theft of a document.

"It would appear," he said almost apologetically, "that my daughter may be a thief, as she was the only person I can think of with access to my study and my safe. I mean, of course, the only person with reason to steal the damn thing."

He looked around my office with such a sweet, unstudied air of astonishment that I began to feel sorry for him. After a moment he swallowed that astonishment hard and eyed me candidly. "You understand I should have gone to the authorities as soon as I discovered the document was missing. I should have gone to my good friend Louis Bidwell at Sloane or to the FBI. But if I'd done that . . . I mean if Sarah should, in fact, be implicated." He shook his head and said, "I'm in a very difficult position."

There was no question about the legal bind he'd gotten himself into by concealing the theft. Under the National Security Act he was already liable to criminal charges. And, of course, that would mean the end of his career. To say nothing of the scandal it would create or the possible jail term he might face. And why had this odd little man done this I asked myself. Why had he jeopardized a lifetime's work? For love, Harry. What they will do for love. Only, deep down, I didn't think it was all that funny.

So, as I usually do when I'm not amused by the inequities of this unequal world, I tried to change the odds and the Professor's mind by suggesting that Sarah needn't be involved. But he wasn't having it. He smiled tolerantly, told me it was a "very decent" thing to say, and proceeded to explain the hard, unequal truth about his only daughter. "She's a Marxist, Mr. Stoner. An ardent, intelligent Marxist. And she's an environmentalist, to boot. An odd combination, perhaps—like an ivy wreath on a statue of Lenin. But potent, believe me. Sarah believes strongly enough in her principles to risk jail on their behalf. Indeed,

8

she has risked going to jail for them in the past. I wouldn't have come to you at all if I weren't certain of this and of the fact that she would lie to me if I were to ask her whether she was involved in the theft. You see, Marxists are a little like the Papists of the seventeenth century. They firmly believe that equivocation, as it used to be called, is a legitimate political tactic. Don't misunderstand—I love my daughter dearly and she loves me. But my work has become a political issue to her. And to her way of thinking, politics takes precedence over individuals."

"Even fatherly individuals?"

"Especially them, if they're scientists at work on breeder reactors that may pollute the environment and disrupt ecological balances. Good Lord, since Three Mile Island, she's barely spoken to me."

So much, I thought, for sentimental solutions. "The missing document," I said. "Why would she have wanted to take it?"

"I'm afraid I can't tell you that," he said with a pained look. "I know I sound ridiculous—rather like that dreadful little man, Nixon—but the document is a matter of national security. You'll simply have to take my word that Sarah would have found the contents interesting. Moreover, I'll have to insist for the same reason that, if you do recover the document or find out what Sarah's done with it, you neither examine it nor tell anyone else about this case."

I laughed out loud. "How the hell will I know if I've found the damn thing?"

"I might be able to describe the papers for you," he said after thinking it over for a second with that same touching air of perplexity. "I think that much would be safe."

"All right, Professor," I said. "What does this document look like?"

Lovingwell closed his eyes and pressed his hands to his face as if he weren't quite sure it was still *his* face. "It was thirty pages long. Typed in elite script on white, onionskin paper, with the imprint *Top-Secret Sensitive* at the top of each page. I stored it in a yellow manila envelope, at home in my office safe."

"Why there?" I said. "Top-secret stuff generally doesn't leave the premises, does it?"

9

Lovingwell dropped one hand from his cheek and opened a single, unhappy eye. "I was revising it. It was my work originally."

"Then you must have a top-secret clearance."

"I did have," he said mordantly. "Look, I'm afraid I'm setting you an impossible task."

I rubbed the nape of my neck and admitted, "It's a doozie, all right. I take it that all you want to know is whether your daughter's involved in the theft. If she is, I'm to recover the goods or find out how she's disposed of them. If not..."

Lovingwell lowered his other hand and smiled for the first time since he'd entered the office. "Then I can assure you that I'll turn this matter over to the FBI as quickly as I can. Of course, I'll pay you the going rate and any additional expense. If you find the document, I'll pay you a two-thousand-dollar bonus." He looked at me nervously. "Do we have a deal, then?"

It really wasn't my kind of case—espionage. It was too complicated from the start and it carried with it all sorts of unsavory possibilities. But staring at that proper, earnest little man with Shaw's face and the voice of a Cambridge don, I decided to make an exception. After all, Harry, I said to myself, if you leave the top-secret part out of it, it's just another domestic theft, just another kind of family trouble. And the going-rate was two-fifty a day. And, anyway, after hearing him out, I liked Daryl Lovingwell enough to want to help him.

"How long would I have to find this thing?" I asked him.

"Two weeks. I can get by for that long. Maybe for a week longer. But no more than that."

"All right, Professor," I said. "I'll take your case."

He smiled with relief and held out his hand. "I'm so very glad. You know I got your name from a colleague in the University who thinks you're a most trustworthy fellow. If you had refused me, I don't know where I should have gone."

"No need to worry about that, now. I'd like to take a look at your safe this afternoon, if you're free."

He pulled a worn leather pocket calendar from his coat. It was stuffed with loose papers and wrapped in rubber bands. He managed to open it without dropping an envelope and, after glancing briefly at one of the pages, said, "I teach at the University this afternoon and have an appointment at Sloane this evening. However, I do have some free time around three."

He looked back up at me and immediately caught what I was thinking. "She won't be home after three," he said with a slight blush. "She's going on an excursion at two-thirty this afternoon."

"Then I'll see you at three," I told him.

2

Sarah Lovingwell was sitting on the front stoop when I parked across from Lovingwell's house on Middleton at 2:30 that afternoon. It was a big, red-brick colonial on a winding street full of red-brick colonials, in that part of Clifton that could serve as the poster-child to suburban America. Its best season is late summer and early fall, when the maple trees that line the sidewalks begin to turn and the gray-haired householders go shirtless on their Lawn-Boys while their wives brown themselves on chaises in the backyard patios. In that dreamy season, Middleton and the other streets north of Wolper smell, night and day, of freshly cut grass and of charcoal fires, of coconut oil and of the pungent chlorine salts that the children wear home from community pools. In that season you'd have to be mad to dream of anything other than those lazy, S-shaped streets, full of tree filtered sunlight and of the men on their power mowers and of a kind of middle-American grandeur that is, itself, a piece of modern mythology.

But the street wasn't in season that Monday afternoon. And like something peculiarly disarrayed—like a familiar face seen in the wrong light or in an unflattering attitude—it looked its age in the winter sun and the glare of the snow chunked like thick white sod on the lawns and rooftops. The age, that is, of the American dream of which it was the most visible part. A dream that may be dying

13

if the Arabs and the Iranians and the oil companies and those other dreary conspirators of the dollar have their ways.

Sitting there, across from Sarah Lovingwell and the big, snow-capped house behind her, I had a vision of all the householders, standing shirtless on their summer lawns and staring aghast at the sheiks on their camels, who were bobbing slowly up Middleton—like some incredible Shriner's pageant—and turning all of that lawn green back into the unbleached flour of desert sand. What a world, the householders were whispering. What a loveless world.

What Sarah might be saying, I couldn't tell. From what her father had told me, she might have cheered. But, then, politics isn't something you can read in a face alone. To be perfectly honest, I thought that she looked like the last person on Middleton Avenue who would have applauded the decline of middle America. Sitting on the stoop, with her chin on her fists and her elbows on her knees, she looked perfectly innocent—not only of seditious thought, but of any thought at all. Now and then she stretched her arms in front of her, twisting her fists outward like she was stretching in bed. And her fists *did* stay clenched while I was watching her, but I figured that was because of the cold. Her face was long, pleasant-looking, and shy. A very English face, I thought. Small, sharp nose; small, very white teeth; thin lips; her father's high forehead; active blue eyes; and the sort of fine, straight auburn hair that looks lovely blowing free across a pale face. She smiled often while she waited and talked to herself constantly, a habit I find endearing since I do it myself.

Ten minutes passed and a blue Dodge van stopped in front of the Lovingwell home. The driver—black hair, full beard, checked tam pulled down to his eyes—honked once; and Sarah lifted one of those fists in salute, then jogged to the street. She got in the side door of the truck and off they went down Middleton. When they were out of sight, I took a fingerprint kit from the backseat, got out of the Pinto, and walked up to the front stoop.

Lovingwell arrived about a quarter of an hour later, in a powder-blue Jaguar sedan. It didn't look like the sort of car a physics professor could afford, even a celebrated physics professor. Daryl Lovingwell apparently had some money of his own. The Professor walked briskly up to the door, took a ring of keys out of his pocket, and fumbled with the lock. His face was pallid and nervous and, from the way his hands were trembling, I figured he wasn't at all happy about what he and I were about to do.

After a few seconds, he got the door open and we walked into a tiled hall, decorated elegantly with a cherrywood pew and a lacquered Chinese cabinet. "I'll take your coat," he said. While he was hanging it up, I took a closer look around. There wasn't any question that Daryl Lovingwell had some money of his own. What I could see of the house was furnished expensively and well. The living room alone—all buff calf and Persian blue and glossy burl— looked like a page out of *Architectural Digest*. Only far more masculine than their usual fare and, if possible, a little more expensive. Peering into that room was like peering through the door of a treasure house—it made me want to turn away and rub my eyes.

"So," Lovingwell said, "where do you wish to begin?"

"Let's look at the safe first. Then at Sarah's room."

He gave me another of those sad, astonished looks—as if to say, "how could I get myself into this"—and led me down the hall to the study.

The wall safe in Lovingwell's wainscoted study was concealed behind a small portrait of Madame Récamier. It was not an elaborate set-up—a Mosler with a dial lock and a handle release. There were no signs that the lock had been tampered with—no drill holes, no damage. Which wasn't at all good. I'd been hoping to clear the theft up quickly, hoping that I'd come in and find file marks on the tumblers. Then I could have told Lovingwell in good conscience that the theft was probably the work of a professional thief. Only that wasn't going to happen. From the condition of the safe and of the study, the robbery had all the earmarks of an inside job. Which led me to step two— what they call in the P.I. handbooks the "all-important" interview.

I sat down on a leather captain's chair for the "all-important," took a notebook out of my pocket to give me something to do with my hands, and began to ask those pert schoolboy questions that seem humdrum when you ask them and humdrum when you think back on them, unless you're very lucky and happen to ask the right ones.

15

"Who else knew about the safe?" I said to Lovingwell.

"Any number of people knew where it was, if that's what you mean. Only I knew the combination." He sat down across from me on the corner of a huge mahogany desk and smiled ruefully. "Of course, that can't be true, can it? Somebody else obviously knew the combination or I wouldn't be in this pickle."

"There are many ways to open a lock, Professor," I said. "Knowing the combination in advance is just the easiest. Was the safe open or shut when you discovered the theft?"

"Just as you see it," he said. "I opened it on Sunday morning to begin revision of the document and discovered that the damn thing was gone. I told myself I must have forgotten it or mislaid it at the lab. It's amazing the kind of lies you'll entertain when you're desperate. I put the document in the safe, all right. I put it in on Saturday evening when I came home from Sloane."

"Are you in the habit of taking papers home with you from the lab?"

"Oh my, no. As you might guess, they don't encourage that sort of thing."

"Since the morning that you opened the safe, has anyone but you touched the tumblers?"

"Not that I know of."

"No maid? No housekeeper?"

Lovingwell began to laugh. "Do you think my daughter would permit me to hire a maid?"

"She permits you to own this house," I said.

"If it's any comfort, Sarah shares your point of view, to the degree that she spends as little time as she can here."

"Was she here this weekend? On Saturday evening?"

"No," he said. "She was not here in the evening. She came in on Sunday morning and stayed through the afternoon. She goes on excursions quite often since she's become involved with the ecology movement. She belongs to a little club with a storefront office on Calhoun Street. The Friends of Nature. They take hikes and travel to parks. This afternoon, for instance, they've scheduled a trip to Whitewater Lake."

"She tells you where she's going?"

"We leave each other notes," Lovingwell said.

He opened the top drawer of the desk and pulled out a slip of paper. "This is our Saturday correspondence. I

16

have Sunday's, too. I thought they might be of importance, so I kept them."

I looked at the slip marked Saturday, December 13, 1980:

FATHER: Sloane in afternoon. Home at 7:00
SARAH: Miami forest in morning. Clifton in after-
         noon. Don't expect me home tonight.

"She's no longer a child, you know," Lovingwell said a little defensively. "She's twenty-four years old. When she says she won't be home for the evening, I don't interrogate her."

"She has a boyfriend?"

"More than one, I think," he said delicately.

"Does one of them have a beard and drive a blue Dodge van?"

"That would be Sean O'Hara. He's the son of a colleague. Why do you ask?"

"No reason, really," I said. "I saw him pick up your daughter and I was curious. It comes from the job or maybe the job comes from it. I've never been able to figure that out."

"That interests me," Lovingwell said. "Because I've never been able to figure out why I do what I do, either. Occupations are a little like childhoods, aren't they? They seem to be the most banal and incomprehensible parts of our lives. Do you know that I don't even like what I do! Isn't that remarkable? All this fuss about my work and I don't even care for it. It's my daughter whom I care for. If I wasn't in so bloody deep, if there weren't so many people and so much money dependent on me, I'd quit and go hiking with Sarah. There's a lot of that sort of thing in my soul. You see, I don't really like to sit in a room, solving dry little puzzles." He smiled at me pleasantly. "Your job must be a bit like that, Mr. Stoner."

I smiled back at him. "Not so dry, I'm afraid. If it were only a puzzle, if people weren't involved..."

"I'm offended," he said. "If you think what I do doesn't involve people, why would I need your services?"

"True enough."

"Sarah is my only child. She's the only thing in the world I care about. This is a very human problem, believe

17

me. I want you to save my life, Mr. Stoner. I want you to save Sarah. Can you do it?"

Could I do it? Could I rescue someone in love? I looked up at the Professor's long, Shavian face and shook my head. Under different circumstances we might have sat together in that plush, monied room and had a doleful chat about what we would and wouldn't do for love. But I was on his time; and I didn't know him well enough; and anyway I'd had that chat some ten thousand times that fall and winter after Kate Davis had left me for Berkeley and two years of graduate work in sociology.

"I'm not in the saviour business," I said a little bitterly. "At least, I like to think I'm not. But things may not be as bad as they seem." I took another quick look around the handsome room. "Something's not right here. I mean beyond the obvious fact of the theft. And frankly I haven't got enough information to figure it out."

He sat back on the desk and peered at me warily, as if he weren't quite sure he wanted to hear what I was about to say. "You can't help me, then?"

"I didn't say that. I don't know yet if I can help you or not. All I can tell you now is that something isn't right here."

He stroked the side of his nose with a single finger and his gray eyes lost their cautious look. "Explain," he said. And for a moment I felt as if I were in the classroom with the good Professor at its head. Staring directly into my face, with that finger beside his nose, he looked, for all the world, like a character out of a Dickens novel. I figured he was listening with his head now, as well as with his heart. So I made it as simple and complete as I could.

"Let's assume for a moment that your daughter did commit the crime. Let's say she came back to the house on Saturday night, after you'd gone to sleep, opened the safe, took the document, went back to Calhoun Street or wherever she was staying, then came home again on Sunday morning as if nothing had happened. For the time being that seems like the most probable hypothesis. The safe shows no sign of damage, which means that whoever opened it either knew the combination or picked the lock. Lock-picking is an art that takes years to master; so unless this crime was the work of a professional burglar—and I'm not ready to rule that out completely—it was certainly an inside job. Which fits your daughter. Your daughter had a motive or, at least, you've said she had. Since I don't know what the document is about, I don't know how it relates to her politics. But I'll take your word that it does. Now, here's the problem:

"Even if your daughter found the combination to the safe, even if she had sufficient motive to burgle her own house, why would she do it last Saturday night? How could she possibly know you were going to bring top-secret papers home with you on that evening? Unless you dropped a hint, either on the phone or in conversation, that you were planning to revise your papers on Sunday morning—"

He shook his head and said, "That's hardly something one would 'hint' about, is it?"

"Then she couldn't have known it would be there. Not without somebody's help—somebody at Sloane or the University. Somebody who can keep an eye on your research."

"A spy?" Lovingwell said incredulously.

I said, "That's one possibility."

"And the other?"

"That Sarah wasn't looking for the document at all."

Lovingwell lifted his finger from his nose and gawked at me. "But that's crazy."

"Suppose there was something else in the safe, something Sarah wanted to get her hands on. And suppose, by sheer accident, on the night she'd chosen to crack the safe, she also found a top-secret document along with whatever she was originally after. Stranger things have happened, believe me."

"There was nothing in the safe," he said firmly. "Nothing outside the document that would have been of the slightest interest to Sarah."

"All right," I said. "Let's go with the first theory, that she was working with an accomplice. Maybe the safe can help us with that. I'm going to try to lift some latent prints off the lock."

"Do you want me to open the safe, then?"

"No." I took a brush and a bottle of powder from the fingerprint kit and walked over to Madame Récamier—the courtesan who was so beautiful and mysterious that a color was named after her, which, when you think about

19

it, is about as rare a compliment as a man could pay a woman. I turned her face gently to the wall and began to dust the tumblers.

"I'm going to need your fingerprints, too, Professor," I said over my shoulder.

He said, "Fine."

Lifting a print is a little like trying to pick up a penny while you're wearing gloves. It took me ten minutes to get the first one onto the rubber stopper. There were two others on the lock but, judging from their location, they belonged to the same hand. Lovingwell watched me as I worked, peering over my shoulder with the sort of blank uncertainty with which he'd watch a mechanic repair his car. Toward the end of the job his presence began to bother me, but not because he was looking on. I liked Lovingwell in a mild way. I liked his accent. I liked his eccentric looks and the candor he'd shown about his job and about his daughter. I liked him enough that I didn't like what I was finding out from the safe. There was one set of prints on the tumbler and one on the handle. Just one. No smudges. No other prints anywhere on the safe. And that's what I didn't like. They were crystal clear prints, fresh as dew. Perfect and perfectly impossible.

"Are you sure no one has cleaned the safe in the last two days?" I asked Lovingwell as I packed up the kit.

"Lord, you're a suspicious fellow. I told you, no. But why do you ask?"

I looked back at the Mosler and said, "There are prints on here. Perfectly preserved. I don't know whose prints they are at this point. I'm not even sure I want to know."

"Well, I'm no detective," he said. "But it seems to me those prints would be a boon in helping you solve the case."

I shook my head.

"And why not?"

"This thing should be covered with latents. Even if the burglar wore gloves, your prints would still be all over the safe. Try to open a lock without shifting your hand and you'll see what I mean. Every time you revolve the dial, you grasp the tumbler in a new spot. There are

20

only one set of prints on this safe. And they're perfect."

Lovingwell pulled sharply at his beard and gave me a bewildered look. "What does that mean?"

"It means that someone took some pains to wipe off the safe and whoever did it must have done it between the time you last closed the safe and now."

"Why would anyone do that?"

"I don't know," I told him. "It's a damn good question."

"And the fresh set of prints?"

"Again, I don't know. Someone may have started to open the safe and been interrupted. Or it could have been an accident. The safe could have been wiped clean and then someone may have come along and touched it."

Lovingwell glanced back over his shoulder at the wall. "It's beginning to look as if my private study is about as private as a coach station."

"It's seen some curious use," I agreed.

At about five-thirty that afternoon, I solved the case. Or, at least, part of it. It was as easy as lifting those prints off the tumbler and just about as plausible.

It was on the floor of her closet. In the back, wedged between two shoe boxes. Hidden the way a child hides when he wants to be caught by his parents and whisked off to supper or to sleep. A yellow manila envelope with the logo "Sloane National Lab." printed on it. It was empty, but it was the one.

"That's it, all right," Lovingwell said as we sat over two cups of coffee in a dining room with red flock walls and cherrywood sideboards and a huge crystal chandelier overhead. "You've made quick work of this."

"Too quick," I said to him. "The whole thing stinks."

Lovingwell nodded half-heartedly. "It does seem careless of her to leave such damning evidence out in the open. Especially since she knows that I clean the house regularly."

"Careless isn't the word for it. I'm going to make you a bet," I told him. "I'm going to bet you that the prints on the safe are Sarah's."

"Meaning?"

"Meaning that someone's trying to set her up. Or that's the way it looks now."

"Then she's innocent?" he said hopefully.

"I don't know."

He ducked his head and said, "I wish you did. Well, at least you've made a good start today."

"I guess that depends on what I find out," I said to him.

3

Given the unusual nature of the evidence I'd come up with, Lovingwell decided to postpone his appointment at Sloane. I was to call him at home as soon as I found out whether the prints on the safe were actually Sarah's. I understood his anxiety—I was a little intrigued myself. And while I don't like to tailor my work to fit anybody else's timetable, I made an exception—my second on the case—for that exceptional little man. As soon as I got back to the De-lores—the four-story brownstone apartment house I've lived in for the last eleven years—I unpacked the kit, flipped on the Zenith Globemaster so that I'd be within earshot of a voice, pulled a folding chair up to my roll-top desk, got out the magnifying glass that came with the O.E.D., and went to work.

Reading fingerprints is like reading a road map—there are certain keys that tell most of the story. With a print you look first to see which of the three basis types you're dealing with: loop, whorl, or arch. That alone can often decide the question. If you find a whorl print on an item and your suspect shows up with loops, you've eliminated one suspect. It gets a lot more complicated if print-types match up. Then you have to analyze each one. If you're lucky and working for a police department, you can make slides and simply compare transparencies to get a match. If you're sitting on a folding chair and working out of an ice-cold apartment, you spend half an hour plotting bifurcations, hooks, dots, bridges, and enclosures. You also smoke half a pack of cigarettes and constantly remind yourself that it's really worth it because no two pairs of hands are alike.

At seven o'clock, with that last piece of conventional wisdom in mind, I rubbed my eyes, picked up the phone, and called Daryl Lovingwell.

"I finished checking the prints on the safe with the others I took from Sarah's room and from your study."

"And?" he said. "Were you right? Were they Sarah's?"

"You're not going to like this, Professor," I said. "But the prints off the tumbler are yours."

Lovingwell agreed to meet me at the Busy Bee on Ludlow at nine that night. I picked the Bee because I needed a drink. And if what I suspected was true, I figured Lovingwell was going to need one, too.

I hadn't been in the Bee in some months. Not since Kate Davis had left for California in July. It wasn't as if I'd been avoiding the place. I just hadn't had much use for a bar, even a bar as comfortable as the Bee. Bright and noisy on the lower level, if you like it bright and noisy, and dark and intimate on the bar floor, it's the perfect spot to listen to the bittersweet music of a cocktail piano and, if you're lucky, to share a drink with someone like Kate. Only I hadn't been having much luck since she'd gone. I hadn't wanted to.

When we made the decision to live apart for two years we'd agreed that there weren't any strings attached to either one of us. And maybe for Kate, with her very modern, very liberated sense of self, there weren't. Only I was sitting on the other side of a generation gap, and the longer we were apart the more lonely and vulnerable I'd begun to feel. Kate saw other partners as definite possibilities — possibilities that had to be consciously admitted, in keeping with her feeling that a secret, any secret, was a potential trap. I saw them as violations of a code. And best left untalked about. That's what an old-fashioned sense of morality will get you every time — an old-fashioned sense of guilt and shame. So, after a recidivistic fling or two that I'd indulged in mostly out of a sense of loneliness and frustration, I'd started staying out of bars and out of trouble. And scribbling off letters to her like a high school headache. And trying to keep myself from hopping on the red-eye flight to San Francisco. All the while telling myself that capitulating to the Puritan inside me was no way to live—it certainly wasn't Kate's way—that it would be better to do something impulsive, to hop on that red-eye flight or hop into someone's bed for more than a night. Anything to put a finish to a life that was being lived as if I were awaiting an important call. A call that I knew, deep down inside, probably wasn't going to come.

You always have your work, Harry, I kept telling myself. But that hadn't seemed as comforting or as interesting an alternative as it had once seemed. Or, at least, that's the way I was feeling when I stepped into the Busy Bee at eight that night.

Hank Greenburg was posted at the bar when I walked in. I marched straight up to him and ordered a Scotch.

"For chrissake!" he said. "Where have you been?"

Hank's a big, gap-toothed man, with a pencil moustache and a genuine fondness for his regulars. We'd always gotten along. He slapped a glass on the mahogany bar, filled it to the brim, and said, "On the house. And don't argue."

"Who's arguing?" I said.

He looked me over with that proprietary air that only worried mothers and bartenders can get away with. I was a little afraid he was about to ask me whether I'd lost any weight. But after he'd seen me come in with Kate for the better part of a year, I knew it wasn't me alone he was thinking of.

Hank bought me a second Scotch and we chatted for a few minutes. Then I took what was left of the drink over to one of the booths, sat down, and made ready for Professor Lovingwell—the man whose imperilled love I was going to save. After thinking that proposition over for a few minutes, I began to feel very silly and very low. And I probably would have stayed in that funk all night long, if another friend whom I hadn't seen in months hadn't clapped his big hand on my shoulder.

"Harry," he said. "Where the hell you been?"

I smiled before I looked up, because I knew from the deep, no-nonsense voice exactly who it was and exactly what was going to happen next. "Bullet" Robinson was one of those men who, when he claps you on the arm,

25

intends to pick you up and plop you down in *his* world. And I knew that that world was a cheerier place than the spot where I'd been living for the last ten minutes.

He sat down across from me at the booth. A big, coal-black man. Bigger than I was. With enormous shoulders and an enormous paunch that tipped the table a little when he leaned forward and a sleepy, oriental face that made him look rather like a six-foot, seven-inch B. B. King.

"Bullet!" I said.

"Harry, where you been keeping yourself? I ain't seen you up to the store in three months."

Bullet ran the Hi-Fi Gallery in the Clifton Plaza—a terrific place to browse, full of mellow sound and exotic components and a lot of laid-back young men and women who talked endlessly that special language of stereophiles while Bullet presided at the register like a cheerful black Buddha. I'd known him for better than fifteen years, ever since he'd been a tight end for the Bearcats and one of the few local talents who'd made it to the pros. He'd had seven years with the Lions, before he'd lost that battle with his belly for all time and been cut in training camp. He'd come back to Cincinnati after that, bought the stereo store with his nest egg, and grown cheerfully and loquaciously prosperous. He was always full of football stories and unsound advice. And I was very grateful for the company.

"What you mopin' around for?" he asked tartly. "You going to spoil your good looks. And then none of them ladies'll want you."

"How's business, Bullet?" I said to him.

"Oh, it's going."

"Not like the old days, huh? Pigskin glory."

"You ain't going to believe this, Harry," he said. "But I never liked football."

"I've heard this, Bullet."

"No you ain't." He picked up my Scotch and raised it to a waitress. "One more of these, honey. Straight up. I'm not kidding," he said, turning back to me. "You know that shit they feed you—how if you're black, it's athletics or nothing? Well, in 1965 it was true. I had a choice to make, Harry. It was a football scholarship or 'Nam. While nice white boys like you was trotting down to the allergist, I was earning my II-S by tackling dummies and pushing around blocking sleds."

26

"My II-S didn't do me much good," I said.

"Yeah, but you was a patriot. Anyway, I don't call no military police work servin' your time."

I laughed. "It got hairy enough on occasion."

"Bro', you sound like Larry. That po' soul don't know the war is over yet."

Larry Soldi was Bullet's hired man.

"Look at these hands," Bullet said. "They're a wide receiver's dream. But these hands are what's costing me four hundred dollars a month in alimony. You know about alimony, don't you, Harry?"

The waitress brought Bullet his drink and we sat quietly for a minute, sipping our liquor. I knew I was acting the straight man, but I just couldn't resist. "How did your hands cost you four hundred dollars a month?" I asked him.

"'Bout time," he said. "We were playing in Green Bay in early seventy. It was so damn cold that most of the guys were wearing gloves. Only I'm a wide receiver so I had to go bare-handed. Well, I'm walking up and down the sideline, trying to keep warm, when one of the Green Bay cheerleaders—a blonde girl with a shit-eating grin on her face and the devil in her blue eyes—comes sashaying up to me. She bats those eyes like a schoolgirl and says, 'I got a little bet going with the other girls?' She says it like that, like a question. I say, 'Yes, mama?' 'I bet those girls that there's a relation between the length and thickness of a man's fingers and the length and thickness of his...' She just looks down to the spot, not shy but conclusive. 'Uh'm,' I say. 'Why you pick me?' 'Well,' she drawls, 'you're the only one not wearing gloves, except for that boy over there.' She gestures to Bobby Lee Jackson, the quarterback. I take a look, and, shit, if his fingers ain't as small around as chicken bones. Then I look back at my own paws and up at her. Only she hasn't stopped looking down at that spot. Kind of like the game was being played down there and it was third and long?"

"I get the picture," I told him.

"I had more trouble staying on my feet during the first half than a hog on ice. Every time I looked over to the sideline, I saw her, one hand on her hip and her eyes narrowed like she was appraising a jewel. Half-time comes around and coach says to me, 'Bullet, you'd better start paying some attention to what's going on *on* the field, or you ain't going to be starting next half.' Christ, I wasn't pulling no attitude or nothing. I was just jinxed. I tried to get my mind right before we left the locker room, but the first thing I see as we start walking back to the field is that girl, standing up in the runway and staring at her hands like they was a map. When she sees no one but me is looking, she kisses one of those long fingers like she done burned it—a sweet little peck—and rubs her tummy with the other hand.

"I had the worst hard-on that second half I've ever had in my life. There wasn't a damn thing I could do about it, either. I couldn't walk. I couldn't run. I sure as hell couldn't go into the game, because it was a national broadcast and they go crazy if you touch your groin after you been speared. With that tent pole in my pants I would have been the laughing stock of the country."

I grinned at him.

"Harry," he said. "You're the most suspicious white man I ever met. Why don't you just be still and let me finish my story?

"It's getting to be the end of the third quarter and I'm still sitting on the bench, with a coat over my shoulders and my head bowed down like I'm praying. Every once and awhile one of the other players comes over and laughs kind of softly as he passes by. Finally coach walks up and says, 'All right, Bullet, what's it going to take?' I just look up, miserable and helpless. 'Well, fuck her then,' he tells me. 'But, for chrissake, get it over with. We're seven points down!' 'I would, coach,' I tell him. 'Only I can't stand up.'

"Harry, you're not going to believe this, but with the game close like that and with me out of the line-up, we just couldn't complete any of the long stuff. So coach calls time out and they bring a stretcher onto the field. 'Lie down,' he says to me. 'What?' I say. 'Just lie down.' So I do like coach says and they cover me with a blanket. I see one of those hand-held cameras poking around, so I turn on my side and, by God, they carry me off the field like I'm hurt. As I'm being carried off, I see out of the corner of my eye one of the assistants talking to that blonde tease along the sideline. And, sure enough, as soon as I get to the runway, she sidles off after me.

"Harry, I played the best fourth quarter of football you

ever seen. I caught 'em with my hands, with my feet. I caught 'em with my goddamn teeth. And we won that game, Harry. Afterward, coach comes to me and says, 'If she can do that between quarters, think what she could do before the game.' I didn't have to think about that. Only mistake I made was marrying the bitch instead of just using her to warm up with."

"Bullet," I said to him. "You're full of shit, you know that?"

"I got brown eyes, ain't I?" He laughed so loud the glasses stacked along the bar rang. "Let me see your hand," he said, swiping at my arm. "Oh, man, I can see from here what your trouble is."

"That's not it, smart-ass," I said.

"It's always that, Harry. That's about the only thing life's taught me." Bullet smacked his lips. "Pussy's behind everything. Pussy or money. Now, don't you want to tell me what life's taught you?"

"You're a strange nigger, Bullet."

He laughed again. "Well, at least you're smiling. And that's something."

It was indeed.

Between Bullet and the liquor I kept smiling right up until nine o'clock, when Professor Lovingwell, looking like Sherlock Holmes in an ulster coat and deer-stalker cap, walked into the bar.

"This isn't your idea of a disguise, is it?" I asked him when he sat down across from me.

He looked miffed and replied: "I wear this outfit every evening when I go out walking. Do I look that ridiculous?"

"Eccentric," I said.

Lovingwell sighed. "That word, again. It's been following me around most of my life."

"And all you ever wanted was to be one of the guys."

"Hardly." He glanced about the room as if the Busy Bee were not his idea of a good time and said, "I'm afraid we're going to have to make this fairly quick. Sarah thinks I've gone out for a walk—damn deception, again. If I don't return in an hour or so, she'll get worried or suspicious or both."

"All right," I said. "I'll come straight to the point. I told you this afternoon that someone might be setting your daughter up. Since I've examined the prints that analysis has changed."

"Now you think someone's trying to 'set me up,' do you?" he asked.

"Very good. You're starting to think like a detective."

He shrugged. "It's fairly obvious. My fingerprints on the safe. The empty envelope in my house. I've thought it through all evening and I'm a little afraid of my conclusion."

"Why would she do it?" I said.

Lovingwell threw up his hands in dismay. "I simply don't know. Our relationship isn't perfect. I don't know of a father's and daughter's that is. We've fought a bit lately. As I told you, she hates the work I'm doing on reactors. And I can appreciate her point of view. The hell of it is when you start arguing with someone, you say things you don't mean. It's hard to take them back later," he said with a grimace. "Let me be honest with you. I've been very critical of my daughter's lifestyle. Some of the criticisms were prompted by jealousy, some of them needed to be said. Sarah's the kind of person who can never do things halfway. She flings herself into every enterprise, whether it's politics, romance, or drugs. I didn't object to the boys— well, I did but I didn't say so. The politics I sympathize with. But the drugs. The night before the document was stolen we had a 'discussion,' as it's known around our household. I'd found some pills in her room while I was cleaning up. She accused me of snooping behind her back. I accused her of . . . well, of doing a stupid and illegal thing. Saturday morning she walked out and didn't return until Sunday afternoon."

Lovingwell stared darkly at the tabletop. "It doesn't look very good for me, does it? I mean if someone should, shall we say, 'blow the whistle'?"

"No," I said. "Not so good."

"I can't believe it," he said. "I just can't believe that Sarah would do this to me."

"It doesn't *have* to be Sarah," I said without much conviction. "After all, she hasn't reported you to the FBI, yet. Or turned the papers over to *Mother Jones*. We could still be reeling in a red herring. Think back—was there any time this morning or this afternoon that you put your hand to the safe without opening it?"

30

Lovingwell nodded. "It slipped my mind but this morning before I went to work I stopped to look at the safe. Just to look at it, the way a patron might look at a wallspot from which a painting had been stolen. I think I'd put my hand to the tumbler when Sarah called to me from the study door."

"What did she want?"

"Nothing, really. Just to know if she could borrow a few dollars."

It didn't have to mean anything and I told him so.

"I hope you're right," the Professor said. "Because this thing is beginning to frighten me. If it isn't resolved soon, I'm afraid I'll lose my nerve."

"You'll be all right," I told him. "I'll start tailing Sarah in the morning. If she doesn't lead me to the document or to her accomplice in a few days, we'll turn the case over to the FBI."

"Only if she's in the clear," Lovingwell said. "And remember—she's not to know that I'm having her... investigated."

4

Calhoun Street in Clifton is a crowded, urban road, lined on the south side with storefronts, fast food joints, and swart brownstone apartments and, on the north, with those university dormitories that look a little like sets of giant building blocks made of glass and steel. It was not, all told, a likely spot for a nest of conspirators or of spies. And yet, in spite of her demure good looks, Sarah Lovingwell seemed to be one or the other. Seems, not is, I told myself. Only it was such a strong case of seeming that I had trouble drumming up a healthy skepticism.

At ten o'clock that Tuesday morning I'd followed my seeming suspect up Middleton to Clifton Avenue, through the slippery side streets filled with dirty snow and drooping elder branches, to the door of the Friends of Nature Club on the south side of Calhoun. Judging from the flaky decal on the top of the front window, the clubhouse had once housed a shoe repair shop. There was an open lot to its west and on its east a used-clothing store, with one forlorn mannequin in the window, dressed like a befuddled flapper in a cloche hat and a silk chemise with a string of big white pearls on her breast. The poor mannequin looked so cheerless and out of place in the weather that I began to grow rather fond of her. But then she was the only thing I had to look at, save for the half-dozen collegiate-types bundled in fat, shiny parkas who passed her by without a second glance.

Sarah had pulled her tan V.W. into an alley beside the clubhouse and gone into the building through a side door. In and maybe out—I couldn't see the rear of the clubhouse from where I was parked. But then I didn't really care where Sarah went that morning. It was the Friends of Nature who interested me. For almost two hours, right up until noon, I sat in the Pinto with a candy bar in one hand and a Minox in the other. And every time someone went in or came out of the club, I stopped gnawing the candy and snapped a picture. It was a little like insurance work, which I don't like to do but which also happens to be the most common kind of job that this detective (and every other detective in the world) gets thrown at him since the courts have liberalized the divorce laws. So, you snap the picture, Harry. And scrunch up in the car seat like a bitter fetus. And maybe you come up with a face that the good Professor will be interested in. Not an insurance swindler—not this time. But somebody from the lab or the University who could have served as Sarah's accomplice. At least, that was the general theory I was going on. And, after all, it was only a matter of a couple of hours.

About twelve, I got tired of insurance work and general theories and decided to take a quick look inside the club. The wind was howling down the street, making the telephone wires snap like jump ropes on concrete and freezing me through my top coat as soon as I got out of the car. I ran across Calhoun Street—well, high-stepped it through the mire—slid up to the club door and ducked inside. At first glance, I thought the place looked vaguely like a political headquarters, which was an interesting point if my seeming suspect were indeed a spy. There were long folding tables scattered about the floor; papers, pamphlets and handouts stacked on the tables; Sierra Club posters on the walls; and hints of marijuana smoke drifting into the room from the rear office. All in all, it could have been a chapter of the Young Republicans. A few of the friends were warming their hands in front of an old Franklin stove by the front door; most were busy stuffing envelopes. So busy that they didn't seem to notice me. Which was just fine. I wandered toward the rear of the club, where a bulletin board was posted with the day's activities. For Tuesday the sixteenth it read: "Joint Protest with Friends of the Arts to save the Fountain. 2:30 P.M. at the Art Museum." The Fountain was Our Lady of the Waters on Fountain Square—once the cynosure of downtown Cincinnati. But since they've torn the Albee down and thrown up those huge steel towers about the square, the statue doesn't seem much more than another misplaced piece of memorabilia—the sort of monument that town councils love to bury away, because half of them aren't sure that anything more than a decade old isn't slightly un-American. I liked the fact that the Friends wanted to preserve the Lady from further attacks and I was also mildly amused by their enemies list, which was posted next to the bulletin board. Several ominous-looking, hand-drawn posters, made up to look like the wanted sheets in post offices, had been strung across the wall. The Mayor was number one, followed by the chairmen of the boards of Cincinnati Bell, the Metro bus system, C.G.&E., Proctor & Gamble. Most of the faces were predictable. The one that wasn't belonged to Daryl Lovingwell. Even in the drawing he looked alarmed, as if he were shocked to find himself in such company. The portrait was signed at the bottom—Sarah L.

I didn't see the artist around. But that was all right. I didn't want to see her or her to see me. I checked my watch, which was showing twelve-ten, and decided that if I left the club immediately I could drop off the film in time to get it back that evening, check in at my apartment, grab some lunch, and still make it up to Mt. Adams in time for the rally. So I picked up a few pamphlets from one of the folding tables, nodded to a blonde girl stuffing envelopes, and walked out the door.

I'd deposited the film at a Shutter Bug on Vine and was heading up McMillan to my apartment when I realized that the car behind me looked too familiar. It was a tan V.W., Sarah's car. Only Sarah wasn't driving it. I took a good look in the mirror when I got to the stop light at Highland. The man behind the wheel had a checked tam pulled down over his forehead and a big, bushy black beard. Sean O'Hara, I said to myself, Sarah's boyfriend. I'd never seen the guy sitting next to him before. He was high yellow, about twenty-five, sparsely bearded, wearing

35

a Big Apple cap, with a face that was thin, acne-scarred and mean.

I realized as I watched him watching me that I had been taking the Lovingwell case much too casually, treating it strictly as a piece of domestic theft, as "family troubles." From the look on that black kid's face, I decided damned quickly that he and O'Hara were just trouble, plain and simple.

I didn't try to give them the slip. Hell, I don't drive well enough to lose anybody. But I did take the precaution of pulling into the lot at the rear of the Delores when I got back home at twelve forty-five, and the extra precaution of parking between two burly old Cadillacs. I took a good look around before walking to the front of the building, but O'Hara and the black kid had driven past me, down Reading toward town. Which didn't really make me feel any better. Something was wrong or I wouldn't have been followed in the first place.

Once inside the apartment, I phoned Daryl Lovingwell at the University and got the Physics Department secretary on the line.

"He's not here," she said nervously. "He had to go home."

I didn't like the quaver in her voice. "What's wrong?" I asked her.

"You'll just have to talk to the Professor," she said and hung up.

I dialed Lovingwell's home, let the phone ring ten times—just like they tell you to do in the phone book—and was about to give up when someone picked up the receiver.

"Lovingwell?" I said.

"Who is this?" a man's husky voice replied.

I had the terrible feeling that I knew that voice, that I'd heard it before and not in any classroom.

"I want to talk to Daryl Lovingwell," I said.

"He can't come on the line," the man said.

"What's going on here? Tell him it's Stoner. Harry Stoner. I'm sure he'll want to talk to me."

"Oh, hello, Stoner," the man said affably. "This is Sid McMasters."

I had a heart-sick moment. McMasters was a homicide dick with the C.P.D. and I knew his voice because I'd

36

worked with him when I was on the D.A.'s staff better than a decade before. I didn't want to ask him, but I did—in a dull, weary voice that made me sound like my own father. "What's happened, Sid?"

"There's been an accident here," he said. "Lovingwell's been shot. At least, we think it's Lovingwell."

"Oh, Christ," I said softly. "Is he badly hurt?"

"He's dead, Harry. We aren't sure, yet, but it looks like he may have killed himself with a handgun."

It had happened to me before. Not often, but it had happened. I'd lost a client to suicide or to some stupid piece of violence, because in my business a good half of the people who come to me should have gone to a psychiatrist instead. The paranoid ones, tormented by creatures of conscience. And the bullies, looking for someone to hurt or to do their hurting for them. It had happened. But never so unexpectedly, so completely without warning. Lovingwell just hadn't seemed the type.

And, of course, what are you supposed to do? Pack it in and pretend that you don't care why a gentle, rather eccentric soul decided to kill himself? And even if you could do that, which I couldn't, what about the daughter and the untidy little secret the dead man entrusted to you? What do you do with it—after what it had cost him? Do you go to the cops or to the FBI, which is precisely what he didn't want to do himself? Do you turn it over to someone else? Probate it like another piece of property—one leather couch, one portrait of Madame Récamier, and, oh yes, one missing document that the Professor didn't want the world to know was missing?

Or do you get on with the business at hand? And add to it a bonus item—free, gratis, compliments of Harry the Sentimentalist? One dead man and the reasons why he died, to be produced along with a missing document that he may have died for.

It's hard to explain. In a way you have to be a bodyguard or a cop to understand the peculiar loyalties you feel to your charge. And when that charge dies, even by his own hand, you have to understand the mute, oddly professional grief a cop or a bodyguard feels. As if life itself were part of the job and death an outrageous violation of your contract. A personal failure. An insult to the profession. And

37

since it's your job, what you do well, you simply can't leave it at that. At least, I couldn't.

I went into that little cubicle that the realty company calls a kitchen, fixed myself a cup of coffee, and gave myself about half an hour to calm down. Then I walked out to the car and drove through the snow to the Physics Building on St. Clair—a great gray smokestack of a building with a crenelated top. In the afternoon light it looked like a lonely, abandoned battlement towering above Burnet Woods. The Professor's ivory tower. It was my first stop. And if I were lucky, I might find out why that secretary had sounded so grimly abstracted when I'd called at noon. Stop two would be the Lovingwell home. And if I were lucky again, the cops would have finished by the time I got there and I would have Sarah Lovingwell to myself.

5

The secretary of the Physics Department, Beth Hemann, was a thin, red-headed young woman with the pale, trembly, earnest face of a convent girl—one who had taken what the sisters had to say to heart. She still dressed for the schoolroom—tartan plaid skirt and plain white blouse. There might have been a smudge of lipstick on her lips and a touch of henna in her hair, but they seemed to mark the limits of her daring. The calendar on her desk listed the feast days in red.

The office in which we sat—she at her desk and me in a wooden chair across from her—was surprisingly old-fashioned, considering the streamlined exterior of the physics complex. The whitewashed walls were crowded with photographs of past chairmen and of departmental functionaries. The furniture was varnished oak—that spartan wood that breaks the undergraduate heart. With the exception of a 3-M copier humming mournfully in a corner, it was an absolutely lifeless place. And the red-haired girl looked very small and lonely in its center.

"This day has been unbelievable," she confided. "I hope to God I never see another one like it. Poor Professor Lovingwell. Poor, poor man."

"When I spoke to you at noon," I said to her. "You told me he'd been called home."

"Yes," she said absently. "I didn't know, then. He'd

39

gotten a phone call at eleven-thirty from Mr. Bidwell at Sloane. All the in-coming calls are routed through the office, so I'm sure it was Mr. Bidwell calling. Then Professor Lovingwell came down here to ask if Professor O'Hara was in. Professor O'Hara's the Chairman of the Department. I said he'd gone to the Faculty Club for lunch. The Professor told me he had a phone call to make and left."

"Do you know whom he called?" I said.

"No. We don't have anything to do with outgoing calls. But he looked very upset when he came back to the office. It scared me the way he looked."

"How?"

She tugged nervously at the collars of her white blouse and said, "I remember thinking he looked as if someone had died. I even asked him if anything had happened. Any family trouble."

"And what did he say?"

"He just said he would be going home for an hour or so and not to forward his calls."

"But you forwarded mine."

Beth Hemann ducked her head rather prettily. "I was worried. I thought someone should contact him. I even phoned his daughter."

"When was that?"

"At..." she looked at a yellow tablet on her desk. "At twelve-fifty. I made a schedule for the police. They asked me to."

She looked up at me expectantly and I began to think that she was a little glad of the attention. That this rather dull process of question-and-answer was a relief to her after the shock of Lovingwell's death. That she actually savored it—as if it were her modest way of flirting. It made me like her.

"What did Sarah say?" I asked with a smile.

"She said she'd go right home and look after him," Miss Hemann said. "Twenty minutes later a policeman came in. It's just been unbelievable."

"Do you think I could talk to your boss a moment?" I asked her.

She made a concerned face, and I understood that her boss had had a trying afternoon and that, like most good secretaries, she wanted to spare him any additional worry.

40

"I'll be gentle," I said and she laughed.

"All right, I'll ask him."

She got up from behind her desk, smoothed her skirt, walked over to the office door, and knocked once on the frosted glass insert.

"Yes?" a hearty baritone voice called out.

"A gentleman to see, you, Professor. It's about Professor Lovingwell."

"O.K. Show him in."

Michael O'Hara was sitting behind his desk and, when I walked in, he got to his feet and threw a huge smile my way, as if that were his version of a handshake. A tall robust man of fifty with a square, sallow Irish face, he looked more like a high school gym coach than a physics professor—all hail-fellow good cheer. But even at a first look, there was something phoney about his heartiness and his fund-raiser's grin. Maybe I just had trouble believing that anybody could be that cheerful without being a predator at heart. His office was large and nondescript, except for a wooden crucifix propped on the desk.

"So, how can I help you?" O'Hara said.

I sat down across from him and said, "You could begin by telling me if you know why Professor Lovingwell tried to get in touch with you this morning."

"Ah, Daryl," O'Hara said mildly. "What is your interest in this business? You're not working with the police, are you?"

"No," I said. "I was working for Professor Lovingwell."

"Doing what?" he said pleasantly.

"Investigating a private matter."

O'Hara snorted in disbelief. "He hired you—a private detective?"

I nodded.

"That was Daryl," he said, still smiling. "He was one of the oddest men I ever knew."

Smiling Michael O'Hara was beginning to get on my nerves. "Could you answer my question?" I asked him.

"Sure," he said affably and hunched forward in his chair. "I could tell you lots of interesting stories. But I'm not going to."

"Why not?" I said.

"Because the man is dead. And whatever job you were

41

hired to carry out died with him. You have no business asking me questions about Daryl Lovingwell."

He'd tried to say it with an impersonal scorn—the way he might browbeat a student or a teaching assistant. But some genuine anger had colored his voice. When I asked him what he had against private detectives, he started to smile again.

"Nothing," he said. "I just don't believe in telling stories about a dead man who happened to be a colleague. I'll tell you this much. He wasn't a happy man. I don't think he ever enjoyed his work, which was odd because he was very good at it."

"You think that's why he killed himself?"

"Oh, God, Mr. Stoner, how do I know? Why does anyone kill himself? It's an irrational thing. Now, if you'll excuse me, I have work to do."

I walked back out to the secretary's desk and told Beth Hemann that her boss was a difficult man.

She pinked and said defiantly, "He's a fine man. He's just had a terrible afternoon. He was close to Professor Lovingwell and he's not happy with the publicity about his death. The police and the newspaper people have been pestering him since the body was discovered. Come back in a few days. I'm sure he'll be more cooperative then."

Two squad cars were parked in front of the Lovingwell house when I drove up Middleton at four that afternoon. A camera crew was scurrying across the snowy lawn, and several other cars—including Sarah's tan V.W., Sean O'Hara's blue Dodge van, and Lovingwell's Jaguar—were lined up in the driveway. The place was busy, which was going to make my job difficult. I thought about going back to the Delores—O'Hara wouldn't be following me any more—and calling on the Lovingwell girl later in the evening. Only that wasn't going to make the questions I wanted her to answer any easier to ask; and then there was no guarantee she'd be willing to talk to me after a long, terrible day with the police and the reporters. I wasn't sure how to handle it. I wasn't sure how much Sarah knew about me and about what I'd been hired to investigate. Staring at that fine burgher's home, I realized that I wasn't sure of anything yet. Who was allied to whom? Who was a friend, who an enemy? Lovingwell's suicide had set the whole problem topsy-turvy, and it was like looking at a chessboard that somebody had bumped into in the middle game—pieces scattered everywhere and no clues about how to set them back up.

Well, one clue. Something had gone very wrong early in the day. So wrong that Lovingwell had killed himself. It was a big, vague clue, obscured by lots of mysterious doings—the theft of the document, the phone call from Bidwell, the second call, Sean O'Hara and his black friend. The police were probably on to most of it; but I had one advantage over them. I had been in on the case from the start and I knew what they did not—that Sarah Lovingwell was somehow involved.

I started up the walk to the front door when a police guard stepped off the porch and asked to see my I.D. I told him to call Sergeant McMasters outside. Five minutes later, Sid came out.

"Hello, Harry," he said.

"Sid. Can I talk to you?"

He tipped his fedora back on his head and ran a hand through his stiff red hair. Sid has the face of a prize doll at a county fair: carrot-topped, chubby-cheeked, with dull, unblinking blue eyes that are the only true indicators of his character—which is a cop's blend of thug and deadpan comic. I'd known him for about ten years and was as close to being his friend as any civilian could be, although you never know when a veteran cop's going to decide that you're one of *them*.

"I can use the break," he said. "It's messy in there. The daughter's all upset and the lab boys haven't quite finished. What's your interest in this thing, anyway?"

"Lovingwell hired me to look into a burglary that occurred over the weekend."

"Yeah? Why didn't he call us?"

"It was a personal thing. He didn't want to call the law in if he could get the items back without a fuss."

"What was stolen?"

"Some papers from his safe. Nothing you'd be interested in."

McMasters looked at me cagily. "You sure about that, Harry?"

"Sid," I said. "Would I lie to an old friend like you?"

"I hope not, Harry, because I wouldn't like it if you did," he said. "Not a bit. In fact, I'd hate it."

"I'm just an innocent bystander in this thing," I told him. "I came by to pay my respects and see if Miss Lovingwell wanted me to keep investigating the theft."

"Uh-huh."

"Do you know why he did it?"

"He didn't leave a note," McMasters said, "if that's what you mean. From what we can piece together so far, he'd been depressed about his work. The security man out at Sloane, Louis Bidwell, phoned him this afternoon. We're not sure right now—those federal boys are like clams—but Lovingwell may have been in some trouble at the lab. They have been having a problem with security leaks out there or so I've been told. Anyway, he called his daughter after talking to Bidwell, then went home and shot himself. She claims he wasn't upset on the phone, that it was just a routine call about when she was coming home today."

"Could I talk to her?"

"It's O.K. with me, if it's O.K. with her."

We walked past a knot of plainclothesmen into the living room, where Sarah Lovingwell was sitting on the buff leather couch. Sean O'Hara sat next to her holding her hand. From the expression on her face, he could have been holding a tree limb. O'Hara's eyes lit when he saw me, just a brief flare like an ember exploding in a dead fire; then his face went cold again.

"Miss Lovingwell?" McMasters said. "Harry Stoner wants to talk to you."

She didn't look up.

"I was working for your father, Miss Lovingwell. I wonder if I could talk to you for a minute?"

"She's in shock, man. Can't you see she's in shock?" It was O'Hara.

"I'm all right," Sarah Lovingwell said hoarsely. Her voice surprised me. It was deep and smoky, not at all like her father's Cambridge drawl. "You said your name is Stoner?" She blinked a few times as if she were awakening from a bad dream. "I'll talk to you." She got up from the couch. O'Hara stood beside her but she brushed him back. "It's O.K., Sean." He glanced at me nervously and sat down. "Let's to in the study. They're done in there, aren't they?" she asked McMasters.

"Yes, ma'am," he said.

We walked into the study, and Sarah closed the sliding panel door behind us. There was a chalk outline on the rug by the door with a dark wine-colored stain next to the head. I stepped around the outline as gingerly as if the body were still lying there. When I turned around, Sarah was staring vacantly at the marks on the rug.

"Don't look at it," I said. "We can go to another room."

"No," she said, waving her hand as if she were calming a child. "I want to get used to it. When my mother died, I almost lost my mind. I saw her dead in the hospital, but...it was different when I saw her in the coffin." She laughed bitterly. "What movie is it where the man looks at his wife in the coffin and says, 'What have they done to her face? She never looked like that'? That's how it was. I'd seen her dead, but I hadn't accepted it. And when I saw her in the box—she'd never looked like that. So..." She fluttered her hand again. "I want to get used to it this time. I want to know he's dead. That way, when I look at the thing in the coffin, I'll know it's really over."

"Why did he do it, Miss Lovingwell? I talked to him just last night and he didn't seem to be particularly depressed then."

"No, I'm sure he was charming. He could be very charming in his odd way. He prided himself on his eccentricities of look and dress, though he claimed he didn't. Why did he kill himself?" she said in a voice that was not quite under control. "To punish me."

"Does that surprise you?" Sarah Lovingwell said after a moment.

"Very much."

"You think I'm hysterical, don't you? In shock?" She gave me a cold, frank look. "My father hated me. I hated him. It's not a pleasant fact, but it's true."

"You hated him because of what he did? Because of his job?"

"Oh, no. I didn't like it. But there were far better reasons to hate Daryl Lovingwell."

I shook my head. "Do you mind if I sit down?"

"Surely. I wouldn't sit on that one though. Blood."

I walked over to the window seat and sat down on the cushion. "Do you know why your father hired me?" I asked the girl.

"No," she said without a trace of hesitation. I studied her face. It wore an ingenuous look, the look of someone awaiting an explanation. I began to feel very odd. "Your father hired me to find out whether you'd stolen a government document from his safe. That safe," I said, pointing to the wall.

"And why would I have stolen this document?"

"He said that you were a Marxist and that you hated his work."

"Both are true statements."

"Look," I said. "I'm very confused. Let me ask you bluntly, did you steal a government document from your father's safe?"

"No," she said.

I took a deep breath. "I want to be clear about this. I promised your father that I wouldn't turn this over to the FBI until I was sure that you weren't involved or until I'd recovered the document. If I go to the police now with what I know, you could be in a great deal of trouble."

"Oh," she said mildly. "So you're suppressing evidence to protect me?"

"No, I'm living up to a bargain I made with a dead man who claimed that he loved you."

Sarah laughed with genuine amusement. "Did he claim that?" she said curiously. "Did he really claim that? Oh, Papa, what a strange man you are." She stopped laughing and stared at me again with that same icy candor. "I hated my father," she hissed. "And I'm glad he's dead. He thought he could kill me by doing this"—she pointed to the floor—"obscenity. But I'm stronger than he thought and I'll survive. Is that all?"

I shook my head. "Just the beginning. Why did you hate him?"

"That isn't any of your business," she said abruptly. "Our talk is over. If you want to go to the police with what dear old Dad told you, feel free. If he owed you money, you can send me the bill. Otherwise I don't want to see you again. You remind me of him," she said with disgust. "And after this is over, I don't ever want to think of him again."

"I'm not dropping this case until I've solved it," I told her. "It would be easier if you'd cooperate. If you don't... call me if you change your mind. Harry Stoner. I'm in the book."

46

6

It's not that you expect other people's lives to be a little neater, a little less complicated than your own. You don't expect that with a crime, especially with a suicide. But you don't expect Gothic romance, either. And that's what Lovingwell family relations were beginning to resemble. I wondered if the girl was crazy or if I was. If Daryl Lovingwell had hated his daughter, he was the best liar I'd ever met.

I kept turning it over in my mind as I drove back to the Delores. One thing was certain. Somebody was lying to me, and it wasn't a little fib. It was a great big vicious piece of deception and it made me nervous to think about it. When I reached the parking lot at around seven-thirty that night, I just sat in the car for a minute and watched the wind eddying among the snow drifts. There wasn't a soul in sight in that big dark lot; the chill factor must have been twenty below; and I suddenly didn't want any more to do with Lovingwell "family troubles." Serves you right, Harry, I said to myself, for taking on families instead of their troubles.

I'd gotten out of the car and was working my way up the south row of the lot, skating awkwardly over the icy tarmac and now and then grabbing hold of a fender to steady myself, when I saw a tall, rather husky man standing in the shadows where the dogberry trees and rose-

47

bushes spilled down the hillside on the edge of the front yard. Now, there wasn't anything unusual about a man stepping out of the wind, especially on lower Burnet Avenue, on a bitterly cold night. Only this guy wasn't ducking out of the wind. This one was standing upright and staring at me. Which, in itself, didn't mean a thing. Only I'd gone through a very rough day, so for no good reason I didn't like the fact that a man in a gray herringbone overcoat with a green ski mask on his head was standing in my rosebushes and staring at me.

"What are you looking at?" I shouted over the wind and probably would have said some much nastier things if the man in the gray overcoat hadn't reached calmly into his pocket and then pointed his arm at me in that stiff, graceless gesture that is unlike any other gesture a man can make.

"Good God!" I said—make that shouted. The wind was so loud that I couldn't hear my own voice. Or the crack of the revolver that the man in the gray overcoat was pointing at me.

The windshield of a Ford parked about a foot-and-a-half to my left exploded as if it had been hit with a sledge hammer.

I dove blindly to my right and was damn lucky I didn't bash my head on the fender of a Buick. The man kept on firing—the gun tucked like a sachet inside his cuff. All I could see was the line of flame flying from his outstretched arm. Windshelds were popping all about me, exploding like light bulbs ground underfoot. And every once in awhile, a bullet would dent a grille or slam into a hunk of chrome with a sick-making crunch. And in spite of all of this, I couldn't quite believe it was happening. Couldn't believe that some madman with a pistol—and it was a major caliber judging from the way it had folded up that first windshield—was trying to murder me.

I stayed tucked against that front bumper until I'd counted three exploded windshields and ravaged grilles, then scrambled to the rear of the Buick, dug my foot into the snow like a runner positioning his leg in a chock block, and took off toward the basement door.

It was all right as long as I was behind the six or seven cars parked between me and the rear wall. But there was a good twenty feet of open ground between that last car and the building, and if the gunman were using an automatic he'd have at least one shot left. So I crouched behind the last car for a second, trying to catch my breath and praying that somebody in the building had heard that bang that sounds like an amplified hand-clap or the thud and tinkle of smashed glass. And, meanwhile, some not quite sane part of me was busy calculating odds—one of those "if you do this, if you don't do that" conversations that didn't sound quite real even to me. If you don't go down on the ice, Harry. If the son-of-a-bitch is really out of ammunition. And if he's not? Well, he'd have the snow to contend with, wouldn't he? And then there wasn't much light coming from the basement door. And he was an erratic shot. And the hard truth is that you don't stand a chance where you are now. I took a deep breath, wiped the sweat out of my eyes, and lit out.

It was a mistake. As soon as he saw me dash from behind that last car, he raised both arms like a man in a trance and began to fire again. Flames shot out of each coat sleeve this time. The bullets kicked at the snow in front of me, making it leap as if it were windblown and sparking brightly on the concrete beneath it. Jesus Christ! I shrieked to myself. And then I did the obvious thing—I shrieked it out loud, as loud as I could, and went barreling like a semi, with its brakes gone and its whistles screaming full-blast, through that little door and into the dark concrete hallway, where I went down hard on my butt. I'd practically taken the door off its hinges. And either the gunman had knicked me with a lucky shot or I'd put my hand through the glass insert in the door, because when I caught my breath I realized there was blood on my left arm.

I sat very still on that cold basement floor for a few seconds—counting my blessings—then crept back up to the window and peeked out at the lot. But the gunman was gone. So I said a little prayer to Whoever is in Charge of These Things, made my way to the apartment, and phoned the cops.

Even though there were only two other patients in the emergency room at General Hospital—a young black kid in a blood-spattered T-shirt and an old woman wrapped in a man's overcoat—it took the doctors over an hour to

49

get to me, which gave the patrolmen who had picked me up a chance to make time with the duty nurses. Between passes, they got my story for the record. I gave them as complete a description as I could of my assailant: a tall man in a gray herringbone overcoat, with a green ski mask covering his face, and at least three revolvers in his side pockets. But I guess I couldn't blame them for splitting their attention between me and the nurses. That kind of description is known in the trade as "male suspect armed" and isn't worth the paper it's written on. Once in a thousand times, a cop will spot a felon who's too stupid to change his clothes; and, occasionally, a guy will be pulled in on another charge and a gun or a mask will be found in his pockets. But my attacker wasn't going to be caught by chance, because my attacker was a killer whose only target had been me. He wasn't a professional killer or, if he was, he was a damn poor shot. I figured he was an amateur with a grudge. I figured he was either Sean O'Hara or his black pal. What I couldn't figure out was why.

I didn't tell the cops about my speculations. I had no proof to support them—only a feeling and the fact that O'Hara had been following me earlier in the day. Anyway, by the time the doctors finally got to me, the cops had lost interest entirely. When I came out of the examination room with a bandaged left forearm, a tetanus shot in my butt, and a bottle of Darvon in my hand, they'd already left. It took me another half-hour to catch a cab to the Delores.

I don't think I've ever opened a door more carefully than I did that night when I got back to my apartment. I'll be honest—I was really spooked. In fact, if some neighbor had hailed me in the hallway, I might have screamed. Regardless of what you may have seen in the movies, detectives just don't get shot at all that often. And the fact that I didn't know why I was being shot at made it that much worse.

It took me a week to satisfy myself that nobody was hiding in the apartment. I acted like a kid on a stormy night, opening every closet door twice. The nice part about being a kid is that you can do that sort of thing and feel good and safe when you're through. When I finished I felt distinctly like an idiot and not a bit safer than when I'd started. I went over to the liquor cabinet and poured myself four fingers and a thumb of Scotch. Then I turned on the Globemaster and tuned in a talk show on WGN in Chicago. Between the liquor and the soothing sound of a voice, I slowly recovered my sanity. "Someone tried to kill you," I said aloud. "That's all."

I kept saying it with different inflections, like an actor practicing a line from a play. "*Someone* tried to kill you; someone tried to *kill* you; someone tried to kill *you!*" After a time, I believed it. Then I asked out loud, "*Why* would someone try to kill you?" And when I couldn't answer that, I asked "Who?"

At the emergency room I'd been certain that my assailant was Sean O'Hara or his black friend. In my apartment that began to seem less and less likely. First, there was the time element. Before I'd left Lovingwell's home, I'd seen O'Hara sitting on the living room couch, glimpsed his Dodge van in the driveway as I'd walked up Middleton to where I'd parked the Pinto. It had taken me about a quarter of an hour to drive back to the Delores. Unless Sean had been following me in another car, he couldn't have known that I was headed home. And he would've had to have been moving pretty quickly to make it out the door, into a car, and over to the Burnet lot in fifteen minutes. Second, there was the physical evidence. The killer could have been O'Hara, but he couldn't have been the black boy, O'Hara's friend. I hadn't seen much of the kid in the rearview mirror. Just enough to know that he was a thin type and, if head size correlates at all with body size, not a particularly tall kid, either.

Thinking the problem through wasn't a complete waste of time; it made me realize that, while I might have had the wrong suspects, I had to have the right M.O. Whoever had tried to kill me must have followed me in a car to the Delores's parking lot—unless he'd been sitting there for almost five hours in the cold. He'd waited until I'd gotten out of the Pinto, then he'd popped from behind the rosebushes and taken ten shots at me. That meant that whoever it was had known that I was at the Lovingwell house. I began to feel unbalanced again—the way I'd felt in the study when Sarah Lovingwell had told me that she'd hated her father and that he'd hated her. I thought it

51

through one more time, but the facts stayed the same. I hadn't been followed once that afternoon; I'd been followed twice. And the second time, I'd been totally unaware that someone was following me.

7

First thing in the morning I called Louis Bidwell at the
Sloane Lab. I was in a delicate position. I didn't want to
tell him what I knew about the missing document; on the
other hand, if the document was the reason he had called
Lovingwell on Tuesday, I wanted to know what had been
said, especially if it had anything to do with an internal
security problem. Bidwell, who spoke in a thick Alabamian
accent—the voice of every second lieutenant I'd ever
known—was polite and not very helpful.

"If you want to come all the way out heah ta Batavia,
ah'll be more than happy to show you around. But you do
understand that my dealings with Professor Lovingwell
are confidential."

I told him that I understood and that I wanted to see
him anyway. We arranged an appointment for three. If
worse came to worst, I figured I could propose a trade:
what I knew for what Bidwell knew. I could temper it by
not telling him that Lovingwell had suspected his daughter of the theft; but, anyway you looked at it, I would still
be breaking my word to the Professor. Are you looking for
a document or a motive for suicide, Harry? I asked myself.
And the answer was, suicide or robbery, what choice did
I have?

As long as Sarah Lovingwell refused to cooperate with
me, I had no legal justification for pursuing any inquiry.

And she had made it very clear that she wouldn't cooperate. For a second I thought about chucking it all, just phoning McMasters or the FBI and letting them handle it. That would be the sane thing to do, I told myself. No more people snubbing you, or following you, or shooting at you. Especially shooting at you. I rubbed my arm through the bandage and wondered again why anyone would have tried to kill me. Obviously it had something to do with Lovingwell, because I wasn't the sort who had made a lot of bad enemies—sent killers up the river. So it was either the Lovingwell matter or a terrible case of mistaken identity.

Unless someone had been watching the Lovingwell house on Monday afternoon, the only time I'd been exposed was on Tuesday morning when I'd taken those pictures outside the Friends of Nature Club. I didn't think that anybody had been watching me while I was busy with the Minox. But I could have been wrong. If I had accidentally seen someone I wasn't supposed to see, that might explain why O'Hara and the black kid had been following me at noon. It might also explain my three-gunned assailant. I'd intended to show the photographs to Lovingwell on the off-chance that he might recognize a face—someone who had recently been in his home or, *mirabile dictu,* at Sloane. Now it seemed like the better part of something to show the photographs to Sid McMasters and the FBI.

I showered and shaved while listening to a Rossini overture and practically charged out the door at nine A.M., For a second I thought my car had been stolen, until I saw it tucked like a nettle in a Bible between a Buick and an outsized Caddie. I zipped down to the Shutter Bug—a little hole in the wall on upper Vine, hung like a delicatessen with all sorts of tasty items (Nikons, Hasselblads, Leicas)—and picked up the pictures. Then drove downtown to a sporting goods store on Elm.

I waited a second before getting out of the car. After the Ripper case, my handgun permit had been suspended for eighteen months—the State Board suspends you automatically if you're involved in a killing. Since the fall of 1979, I'd had no legal right to carry a weapon. In fact, I hadn't even handled a gun in several months, which had proved no hardship up until the night before. I'd no intention of being caught defenseless again. But before I break a law, I always like to think through the consequences very thoroughly. So I waited in the Pinto and thought them through again; and when my life didn't seem any less valuable the second time around than it had the first, I got out of the car and walked into the store.

An old coot in a cardigan sweater and baggy chinos was giving the woman behind the front register a hard time.

"That's where you're wrong, little girl," he said to her decisively.

"Take a calendar, John, for chrissake," one of the salesmen called to him from the back of the store. "Give him a calendar, Lois."

"What the hell do I need a calendar for?" John exploded. "I'm a happily married man. I don't need no new dates."

Lois, the register girl, laughed raucously.

I walked past the fishing tackle and camping equipment to a long glass display case on the west side of the store. The kid in charge of the gun display was still laughing at John's joke.

"No new dates," he said to me.

"Yeah, I heard it the first time. I'm looking for a gun."

"We got 'em. All calibers and makes."

"What's the most powerful handgun you stock?"

The kid went kind of glassy-eyed, as if this were a moment he'd been waiting for all his life. "Smith and Wesson Model 29 .44 magnum," he said dreamily. "This gun will cut a man in two at twenty feet."

"You do a lot of that, do you?" I said.

"Huh?" His eyes broke back into focus and he stared at me sourly. "Maybe you're looking for something smaller? To hunt rabbit or squirrel?"

"No," I said. "That'll do. I like my meat well-done, and this way I can kill it and cook it at the same time."

I bought the pistol with a four-inch barrel and a box of shells and walked out to my car. When no one along Elm seemed to be watching, I unwrapped the gun and stuck it in my overcoat. It felt like I was carrying a steam iron in my pocket.

It took me five minutes to drive across town to the Police Building on Ezzard Charles. I parked in the Music Hall Lot and walked through the snow up to that long yellow building that looks like nothing so much as a fifties high school. After getting cleared and tagged by a desk

55

sergeant, I took the elevator up to the second floor and Sid McMasters' office. I found Sid sitting behind a desk, peeling oranges with a Swiss Army knife.

"Fruit?" he said, holding out a section.

"Watch your language," I told him.

McMasters laughed noiselessly. "Heard you got shot at last night," he said in a mild voice. "Wouldn't have anything to do with Lovingwell, would it?"

"You tell me," I said.

"It might." McMasters speared an orange section with his knife and chewed on the fruit. "I got some news for you, Harry. That suicide. Well, it ain't quite kosher. In fact, it's *trafe*. From what the lab is putting together, it looks like your late client might not have done himself in, after all."

"Murder?" I said grimly.

"That's the ticket," McMasters said. "The position of the body wasn't right. He was shot here." McMasters put down his knife and jabbed his right temple with a thick forefinger. "We found blood and tissue on the safe, so he must have been standing in front of it at the time of the shooting. Somebody tried to clean off the metal, but they didn't do a very good job."

"Where was the gun?"

"By his hand. But that doesn't mean much."

"Prints?"

"His. But they're perfect. Just like somebody rolled each finger in ink and pressed it onto the butt."

"No smears or smudges," I said half to myself.

"That's right," McMasters said.

"Who do you suspect?"

"We don't have a clue."

"What about the daughter?"

"That's a grim little thought coming from you," he said. "You were working for the family, weren't you?"

"I still am."

"Well, unless you know something we don't, she's in the clear. The O'Hara kid swore up and down she was in the nature club office until one P.M. yesterday."

"He did, huh?" I threw the package of photographs onto his desk. "I'd like you to have the FBI take a look at these. See if they can make any of the faces. Tell them to check the local subversives file—Marxists, Weathermen, stuff like that."

McMasters fingered the envelope and looked uncertainly at the snapshots. "What's this about?"

"They're members of that little club that Sarah belongs to. The Friends of Nature. It's possible that the club is a communist front."

McMasters' eyes lit up. "Yeah?" he said happily. "That could be a help. Thanks, Stoner. I'll have this checked out."

Traffic was heavy on the expressway because of the weather; so I spent almost half an hour getting back to Clifton. I took the Hopple Street exit to the Parkway, the Parkway to Ludlow, ground my wheels up that long, lazy hill that flattens out at Resor, then picked my way among the side streets to the Lovingwell home. I pulled into the driveway behind Sarah's V.W. and Lovingwell's Jaguar and stepped out into the white glare of the morning sun.

Sarah Lovingwell answered the front door on the first knock. She looked less haggard than she had the previous afternoon, though her face was still pinched with fatigue.

"I thought I told you that I never wanted to see you again," she growled.

"That was yesterday. I thought you might need me today."

"Why? Nothing's changed. You still remind me of him."

"Plenty's changed. Your father didn't commit suicide. He was murdered. And your boyfriend lied to the police about being with you at the time of the Professor's death."

"Murdered?" she said with what seemed like geniune surprise. "Who says he was murdered? How do you know that? The police haven't told me that."

"I was just with the police," I told her. "It kind of blows your theory about why he killed himself. Or was that a fib, too? Like the alibi?"

"What do you want?" she said in an ugly voice. "Money? Is that it?"

"I'm getting sick and tired of people treating me like low-life because of my job," I said angrily. "I came here to help you, because I promised your father I would. And what I want is to find out what happened to that document and what happened to him."

57

"I don't care what happened to him. Whether he committed suicide or not, he deserved to die."

I shook my head. "Are you sure we're talking about the same man? Amiable, eccentric Daryl Lovingwell?"

Sarah Lovingwell smiled for the first time since I'd met her. It wasn't a pleasant smile, but it was a damn sight better than the dark looks I'd been getting up to that point.

"I feel like Cary Grant in *North by Northwest*. Remember the scene when he says, 'Forgive me. But who are those people living in your house?' I think I'm owed an explanation."

She shook her head.

"A cup of coffee?"

"All right," she said. "But that's all."

As Sarah and I walked through the living room and down a narrow hall to the kitchen, I was taken again by the elegance of Lovingwell's home. If houses tell you anything about their owners—and they invariably do—this one spoke clearly of a man who loved luxury. It spoke of old money glittering in a hundred different knick-knacks—crystal animals, glazed porcelain statuary, the sorts of things you see advertised in the back of architectural magazines and wonder who on earth ever buys. Daryl Lovingwell had bought them. The brocade loveseats with inlaid burl, the silver tea sets, the bronze baskets and dull pewter ornaments. I spent a moment admiring a Swiss clock I had seen advertised for years in *The New Yorker*, while Sarah looked impatiently at the dial.

"He had fine taste, your father," I said to her.

"He grew up with money," she said with almost clinical dispassion. "He liked it the way other people secretly despise things. To him, it was a deep, ugly obsession."

The kitchen was big and white and comfortable. We sat at a butcher block table set in a small, glassed-in alcove that looked out on a rolling lawn which swept up to a huge, leafless oak and then down to a hedge of rosebushes. Sarah said nothing. Her hands played at the coffee cup, at the spoon. Her prim, pretty face was restless and self-absorbed.

"Do you want to tell me why O'Hara lied to the police?" I said to her.

She shook her head slightly. "What makes you think he was lying?"

"Because he was following me in your car at 1:00 P.M. He and a black kid in a salt-and-pepper beanie. And I think you can tell me why."

She looked uneasily out the window toward the oak. "He planted that in 1949. The year he got his appointment here."

"Why do you always talk about him in that tone of voice—as if he were a character in a book?"

A spark of amusement lit Sarah's blue eyes. "You're a smart fellow, aren't you? I thought detectives were supposed to be plodding, dim-witted types. Muscles with speech."

"That's the second time you haven't answered my questions."

"And who are you to ask me questions?" she flared. "Just because my father hired you to do a job for him doesn't give you the right to harass me and grill me like I was some derelict in a police line-up."

"There was a murder committed in this house," I said, "and a theft. You may think the police fit your description of a detective, but don't count on it. They're going to find out that the O'Hara boy is lying. And they're going to find out, from Bidwell, that a government document is missing. They're going to find out you're a communist, too. And the whole world knows how you felt about your father. One fine day those dumb cops are going to plod their way right up to your door."

"I didn't kill him," she said serenely. "And I don't know anything about a government document."

"That may be true. But that's not going to stop the police from investigating you and your friends of nature."

Sarah Lovingwell eyed me distrustfully. "Why do you care what the police do to me?"

"I told you before. I promised your father I would look after you."

"That's very noble," she scoffed.

"It's not," I said. "Your father left me in a tight spot. Technically, I'm withholding evidence right now. For all I know, evidence that would help the police tie up this case or help the FBI stop an important secret from falling into the wrong hands."

"Communist hands?" she mocked.

"Look, I'm apolitical. You can start as many revolutions as you want, once I'm in the clear on this thing."

"We don't start revolutions. The people do."

"Fine," I said. "You tell the people it's all right with Harry, once this case is settled. All I'm asking for is a little prerevolutionary cooperation."

"What kind of cooperation?"

"Now we're getting somewhere. I want you to hire me."

"For what?"

"Let's say . . . to look into your father's death."

"I've already told you, I don't care who killed my father."

"Well, pretend he was someone close to you," I said. "Someone you liked. That way I have a legal justification for not telling the cops about the document."

"And what do I get out of this?" Sarah asked me.

"You get me out of your hair." She glared at me. "It's the only way," I said to her. "It's me or me. Take your pick."

8

By the time I left for Sloane, Sarah and I had fashioned an uneasy truce. She agreed to hire me to investigate her father's murder; and I agreed to stay out of her affairs. Just how that last neat trick was going to work I didn't know. She wasn't happy about the arrangement either. But then annoying someone isn't the surest way to earn their trust.

I couldn't get a handle on Sarah Lovingwell. She was a smart, attractive, self-assured young woman; and she was carrying around the sort of grudge that most folks take a lifetime to work up to—a geniune hatred so implacable that it can't be explained. You have to be hurt beyond forgiveness to reach that plateau of anger. And for the life of me, I couldn't see how dapper, Shavian Daryl Lovingwell could have fathered such a hate.

I was about to step out the door when one of the biggest young men I'd ever seen in my life came striding up the front lawn. He must have been six-foot nine if he was an inch—he had a good half foot on me. But if you can believe it, it wasn't his size that startled me. You've probably seen, in grocery stores and shopping centers, children, six or seven years old, running around in cowboy suits—fancy checked shirts with western piping, blue jeans with a runner down the leg and bunting at the cuff, big leather belts with silver-metal buckles, furry white vests, ten-gallon

Stetsons, and cap guns with mother-of-pearl handles. If you left out the guns and the holsters, that's exactly how this giant was dressed.

"Howdy 'pard," he boomed in a voice that would have made a good bass in a barbershop quartet. He swept the big hat off with a flourish and smiled. "Lester O. Grimes," he said daintily. "Friends call me 'Cowboy.'"

"No kiddin'?" I said. "Stoner. Harry Stoner."

"Is the lady of the house home?" Lester asked.

"Miss Sarah!" I called through the door. "You have a caller."

Sarah came to the door. "Hi, Les," she said. "I'll be with you in a minute."

The Cowboy gave her an "aw, shucks" grin and crooked one foot behind the other. His pointed boots were embossed leather and lethal-looking.

"Y'all from hereabouts?" he drawled.

"Hereabouts is a pretty big place. I'm from Cincinnati, yeah. You?"

"Bloody Basin, Arizona," he said proudly. "It's a mite south of Flagstaff."

"You're pretty far east, aren't you? For a cowboy?"

"I've been doin' a bit of travelin' since I got out of the service. I come up to Ohio last year."

"To work?" I said.

"In a way. Y'all a friend of Sarah's?"

I thought it over for a moment. "You could say that. I'm working for her. I'm a private detective."

"No!" he said, like I'd just told him I had kin in Bloody Basin. "When I was in 'Nam, I knew a fella who wanted to be a private detective. A nosier man I never met. Always stickin' hisself in places he didn't belong." Lester O. Grimes settled back on his bootheels and stared at me with a kind of wry displeasure. "You even look like this fella."

"Coincidence," I said and started for the car.

"No," he said decisively and pushed me back with one paw. "I wouldn't call it no coincidence."

"O.K.," I said. "Tell me about him."

"Not much to tell. It got so that this fella wouldn't leave us alone. And there are times when a man has to have his privacy. So we taught him a lesson."

"Yeah?" I said.

"We killed him," Lester O. Grimes said softly.

62

"You killed him," I said flatly. "That's a mighty hard lesson to forget, isn't it? Good thing I'm not in that guy's shoes."

Grimes laughed heartily. "I'll say. He was practically begging us to finish him at the end." Cowboy made a disgusted face. "Don't like to see that in a man."

"Does this story have a moral?"

Grimes scratched innocently at his blond forelock. "Yeah. I guess you could say it does. Y'see life's kind of like the Army. You got your job to do and your buddy's got his job to do. And people like ol' Roger—that was his name—who insist on messin' where they don't belong—asking questions, talking to cops, taking pictures, maybe—they're just bound and determined to find themselves some trouble. Yessir! And they always do."

"What did you say you did in the Army, Lester?"

"Oh, I wasn't in the Army. I was in the Corps. What they call a weapons specialist. Master Gunnery Sergeant. They're some good ol' boys in the Corps," Lester O. Grimes said. "Yessir, I'd still be in there if they'd of had me."

"Well, nice talking to you."

"My pleasure," he said as I walked past him.

On the way out to Batavia, which is a small community about thirty miles northeast of Cincinnati, I kept trying to picture Lester O. Grimes in a gray overcoat and a green ski mask. But it was like trying to jam a size fourteen foot into a size nine shoe. He wouldn't fit; but his message would. When people start shooting at you and threatening your life, it's hard to miss the point. I'd blundered into something big, nasty, and very private; and the Cowboy and his three-gunned buddy weren't going to let me lose my way again. No sir. They sure weren't.

I was contemplating what that big, nasty, private something might be when I spotted the huge A-shaped administration building of Sloane Labs rising above the pine trees. Like the Gateway Arch in St. Louis or the Mormon Memorial in D.C., Sloane is one of those structures that takes you by surprise. Sixteen stories high, all polished aluminum and tinted glass, it looks vaguely like a pair of enormous hands clasped in prayer. Beside the building, a great circular hillock, like an Indian burial mound, formed a large circuit, maybe four miles in circumference.

And inside this raised oval, I swear, was planted a park, with deer and one hirsute buffalo roaming through the snow-draped pines.

I turned off the highway onto a paved access road that led to the main building. There was a guardhouse about the size of a tollbooth a hundred yards down the road. I gave the guard my name and he waved me toward the visitor's lot. It was a short walk from there to the main concourse, down an avenue planted with leafless ginkos. The lobby, an enormous arena, was planted with ginkos, too, and with a dozen other varieties of ornamental plants and flowering shrubs. They'd regulated the temperature and humidity inside the building so that most of the trees were still in bloom. I half expected to find the receptionist camped on a picnic blanket. Instead she was sitting in a round metal booth at the end of one of the garden trails that wove through the little forest. She had a dreamy, contented look on her face; and she smiled happily at me as I approached her.

"Welcome to Sloane," she said with good cheer. "You're Mr. Stoner, aren't you? Mr. Bidwell will be down in a moment."

I sat down on a sofa, set like a park bench in a square of earth, and listened to the soft music that was being piped in from somewhere above the arbor. There was something a little scarey about this artificial paradise. Maybe it was the thinness of the deception—as if all the trees and grass, the courtesy to nature, could disguise the daily work of atom-smashing and nuclear experiment. Or, maybe, it was the dreamy look on that receptionist's face and the thought that, if you stared long enough and in the right light, those trees and shrubs might actually come to seem like a real forest, the great A-shaped building like a towering herbarium, the four-mile accelerator like a mere pen for the bison and the deer. To me, the place had the shallow charm of a wax museum, only it was nature here preserved on exhibit—as posed and caricatured as a tableau out of history.

Within five minutes, a thin, dapper man of about forty half-walked, half-marched up one of the trails to my bench.

"Louis Bidwell, sir," he said, extending a hand.

There was nothing rustic about Louis Bidwell's looks. His blond hair was cropped in military fashion, short at the back and sides; and he sported an immaculately trimmed mustache that gave his stern Southerner's face a bit of dash. He looked like a young, hard-driving Atlanta business executive, one who had served six years in the Army and was now attached to the Reserves. Good company, a lady's man, a bit of a drinker, and hard as nails. You could see that toughness clearly in his eyes, which were the cold, distant blue of a winter sky.

"We're having a bit of a problem around heah today, Mr. Stoner," he said in that smooth Southern voice. "Apparently some muskrats got into the ventilatin' system of the accelerator."

"Muskrats?"

"Yes, sir. They've colonized a section of the park near the lake."

"There's a lake out there, too?" I said.

"Yes, *sir!*" he said and almost clicked his heels. "We've gone to a good deal of trouble to preserve the natural beauty of this area."

"I think you've improved on it."

"Well, we wanted our personnel to feel as if they were working next to nature and to discourage the notion, which, I'm sorry to say, is all too prevalent about atomic research, that we are somehow tamperin' with nature. The men out heah are no different than you and I, and they're doing important work."

"I'd like to talk to you about one of your personnel," I said. "Daryl Lovingwell."

"A sad thing," Bidwell said sternly. "I've known the Professor intimately for ten years and, in all that time, our relationship was nothing but cordial and sincere. Make no mistake, that kind old man is going to be missed."

"You called Lovingwell on Tuesday morning, about eleven-thirty. Can you tell me what you and he discussed?"

Bidwell gave me a soft, reproachful look. "I don't want you to take what I'm going to say as an insult. But, before I answer that question, I'd like to know what interest you have in the matter."

"Fair enough. At the time of his death I was working for Professor Lovingwell."

"In what capacity?"

"He hired me to recover some papers that were stolen from his safe."

65

Bidwell looked at me uneasily. "You are a private detective?" he asked.

"Yes."

"I see," he said in a voice that made it clear that the fact did not sit well with him. "I take it that you suspect some connection between the theft of the papers you mentioned and the Professor's suicide?"

"I'm not sure. The Professor's daughter has hired me to look into her father's death, which wasn't a suicide, by the way."

"What!" Bidwell said with astonishment. For a second his face hardened into absolute fury. "Are you playing games with me, mister?"

"Lovingwell was murdered," I said. "I've just talked to the police."

"Murdered," he said savagely. He looked quickly around the little forest, as if he were afraid that someone had loosed snakes, as well as muskrats, in his preserve. Then he turned back to me. "You and I *had* better have a little chat, Stoner. Under the circumstances, there are some things you ought to know."

We went up to Bidwell's office. It looked like a high-priced psychiatrist's suite—chrome, glass, and thick-pile rugs. Except that instead of diplomas Bidwell had hung crossed Mausers on the paneled walls.

"Have a seat," he said, gesturing to a chrome-and-leather director's chair in front of his desk. "Do the police have any suspects?"

"Not yet."

"Do you?" he said deferentially.

"I know that the Professor was worried about recovering those papers and that something greatly upset him on Tuesday morning, after you called."

Bidwell looked thoughtfully at a folder on his desk. I tried to make something out of that look, but couldn't decipher it. "He didn't mention any papers to me," he said after a moment. "Our conversation was purely personal." Bidwell blushed as if he'd said a dirty word. "You say you're workin' for his daughter?"

I nodded.

"Well," he said, still reddening. "I'm afraid she was the subject of our talk."

"What about his daughter?"

"This is most awkward," Bidwell said. "But I feel you have the right to know. I believe that Professor Lovingwell was afraid his daughter might do violence to herself or to him."

It was my turn to gawk, blush, and struggle through a sentence. "He told you that Sarah was dangerous?"

"In so many words, yes. Ever since his wife's death seven years ago, that girl's been nothin' but trouble. Daryl came to me several times in the past few years, most recently on Saturday last, to talk it over. You see, I have a daughter who's a bit younger than Sarah, but they...share some of the same problems. I guess that's why we got on so well," he said sternly. And I suddenly realized that that diffidence was his way of disguising affection for a friend. "That man had two crosses to bear—first the wife and then the child. But he wasn't one to complain. Not even when the girl started messin' with radicals and interfering with his work. He said he admired her spirit." Such charity was clearly incomprehensible to Louis Bidwell, who shook his head with disgust. "He'd of been better off stickin' her in a home," he said bitterly. "And the wife, too."

"Why would Sarah 'do violence' to her father?"

Bidwell gave me a "you-tell-me-how-it's-possible" look. "For five years that man nursed his wife through one nervous breakdown after another. Never complained, never asked for help. In spite of all his efforts, she committed suicide seven years ago. Of course it was a terrible blow. And I personally don't think he was ever the same afterward. The worst of it was that Sarah blamed him for her mother's death. She had always been a little unbalanced, like the mother. And the suicide just toppled her over the edge. She started runnin' around with hippies and radicals. Just last Saturday, the Professor came up heah and confessed he'd discovered she'd been takin' drugs. He pretended he wasn't concerned. But I had the feeling, when we got done, that he feared she might do violence. Either to herself or to him."

"Did he say that?"

"In so many words."

"And your call Tuesday morning?"

"Just to follow up on what we'd talked over on Saturday afternoon. He didn't seem upset on the phone. But when

I heard the news of his suicide...I'll be honest, I blamed Sarah."

"But you didn't tell the police that?"

"Out of courtesy to him. I don't think he told another soul what he told me. He was a sensitive and extremely private man. And every time he'd mention Sarah it was only to apologize or excuse her behavior. He loved that girl."

"And now that you know he didn't kill himself, that he was murdered?"

"I honestly don't know," Bidwell said. "It's a terrible thing to think that a daughter would kill her own father."

It was, indeed, a terrible thought. There's mischief and there's crime, and then there are acts that seem to go beyond our conventional notions of mayhem straight to some old, fearful spot in the brain. I remember still, vividly, a custody case that I worked on when I was just starting out. The man and woman fought constantly over the child; then, one afternoon, the wife wrapped the little girl in a gasoline-soaked blanket and left her, blazing, on the husband's porch. I felt that night, when I went home to the Delores, as if I had seen a nightmare seep into the clean day. It's one reason why I could never be a cop. You can only experience so much of that kind of cruelty before it ceases to be a limit—a kind of boundary to what human beings are capable of—and starts to become a law. And when you begin to measure people by that standard, you don't think of them as human beings anymore, but as things—dangerous things.

As a rule I treat other folks as if they were pretty much like me—built according to the same ratio of reason and madness. But even allowing for a bit of mathematical error, the Lovingwells were not like you and me. Whether they belonged in that malignant netherworld where human acts cease to be human, I didn't know. Sarah didn't look like a killer, for what that was worth. Even her implacable hatred could be explained away, since I'd talked with Bidwell. But that's a bad habit—explaining things away. And given the fact that my life had been threatened twice, I didn't want to make the mistake of substituting a prejudice for a fact, even if it were a comforting prejudice. This is a hard world, Harry, I told myself, as I walked back

68

down the avenue of ginkos to the visitor's lot. And it's naive to believe that children always honor their parents, like the good book recommends, although the distance between dishonor and murder was still enough to give me pause.

Bidwell could have been exaggerating his story. Disgust, anger, any number of motives could do that to a man. Of course, he hadn't looked the type to be rattled by death; but he hadn't looked the type to be chummy, either. Yet he had told me a great deal more than I'd expected. Well, more and less. There had been no talk about the document, no mention on his part of Lovingwell's papers, or of the "trouble" Sid McMasters said Lovingwell had been in at the lab. And that was damn curious. Any self-respecting security officer in the world would keep tabs on secret papers going into or out of his establishment, particularly if he'd been having an espionage problem. Bidwell had to know that Lovingwell had checked the document out on Saturday afternoon; yet he'd made no effort to recover it after the Professor's death on Tuesday. Maybe Louis Bidwell wasn't being as candid as he'd wanted to appear. I drove back to town thinking about Bidwell and about what he had and hadn't told me.

9

It didn't take a detective to see there had been trouble at the Lovingwell house when I drove up Middleton at six that night. Squad cars crowded the street, and there was sweet cordite smoke drifting through the dusky air. I parked behind a city ambulance and hopped out of the Pinto. A dozen uniformed police were strutting along the sidewalk between the patrol cars. They had tough, anxious looks on their faces. On the neighboring porches children and parents stood in tight groups, talking actively to each other and, now and again, pointing to the Lovingwell home. In the distance, the scream of a siren floated away toward a hospital or a precinct house. Whatever the problem had been, it was settled now. But my heart was pounding hard as I walked up to one of the patrolmen—a young cop wearing a hard white helmet and carrying a vicious-looking pump shotgun in his hands—and asked him what had happened.

"There was a little trouble here," he said coyly.

"Look," I said. "I work for Sarah Lovingwell and I'm asking you what happened?"

"You work for the girl?" he said. "Maybe you'd better come with me."

He led me through the clump of patrol cars onto the lawn and up the concrete pathway to the front door. There was blood on the stoop. A good deal of it.

71

"Jesus," I said under my breath. "Was anyone killed?"

The cop kept walking. "One of our men is down," he said stiffly. "We don't know how bad, yet."

"The girl?" I said. "Sarah?"

He didn't answer.

We walked through the front door. The scene on the lawn had been a small gathering compared to the convention in the entrance hall. There were so many men in the passageway that I had to stand beside the Chinese cabinet while the cop cleared a path to the living room. Once inside, I spotted Sid McMasters sitting on the buff leather couch and shouted to him.

"Stoner," he said. "Come over here."

"What in hell happened?" I asked him when I'd worked my way to the sofa.

He stared at me grimly. "I sent a squad car up here to pick up the Lovingwell girl. One of her friends didn't want her to come along. There were some words and he started shooting."

"Was it a big guy in cowboy duds?"

Sid gave me a look that straightened my spine. "Just how did you know that?"

"I was here about four hours ago. I saw him then. He was waiting for Sarah."

"Yeah? Well, he shot a patrolman in the stomach. The back-up squad didn't know what was going down inside—some sort of goddamn mix-up—and the son-of-a-bitch got out the back door."

"And the girl?"

"We've got her and the O'Hara boy in the lock-up right now."

"Why did you decide to pick her up, Sid?" I asked him.

"Those pictures you gave us," he said. "We ran makes on all of them and a couple came up dirty. A bombing at a Tennessee nuclear plant."

"And you figured Sarah was part of it?"

"For chrissake, Stoner!" McMasters bellowed. "It was your idea! We don't know if she's part of it or not. All we wanted to do was ask her a few questions when your friend in the cowboy suit blew his stack."

"His name is Grimes," I said. "Lester O. Grimes. He's from a little place called Bloody Basin, Arizona. Served in the Marine Corps in 'Nam as a weapons specialist,

Master Gunnery Sergeant. He came to Ohio about a year ago."

"How the hell do you know that?"

"He told me. He also told me he was going to kill me if I didn't keep away from Sarah, the Friends of Nature, and the police."

"Well, judging by this evening, I'd say he was a man of his word." McMasters gestured to a plainslothesman standing by the door of the study. "You want to tell Collins what you just told me?" he said.

I told the detective what I knew about Lester O. Grimes. When he was through taking down my story, I went looking for Sid again. I found him talking on the phone in the study. When he finished, he looked up at me with the exhausted satisfaction of a man who's heard belated good news.

"This foul-up may turn out all right," he said wearily. "But you're going to be out one customer."

"What do you mean?"

"The Lovingwell girl," he said. "We're going to hold her for the death of her father."

Mrs. Arthur Weinberg was her name.

She lived two doors down from the Lovingwells in another colonial with a red-brick facade and a graceful white frame porch. Her husband taught Romance Languages at the University; and Mrs. Weinberg kept house, save for Tuesday afternoons when she worked as a volunteer at the Clifton Daycare Center. She was a genial woman of about sixty, with a plump, good-natured face and a grandmotherly fondness for Sarah Lovingwell and for all the other "children" who had grown up on her street.

She had wanted to help Sarah when the police came swarming across the lawns and through the backyard arbors in search of rangy Lester Grimes. It was only after talking with the detectives that she realized that she might have made a mistake. "I didn't intend to get her in trouble," she told me when I stopped by the Weinberg house late that night. "It was the last thing on my mind. I won't testify to what I said if it comes to trial."

"There's no reason to blame yourself," I told her. "Sooner or later, the police would have discovered that Sarah's alibi was a lie."

"But that's not why I told them!" she protested. "I thought it was all connected to this evening's shooting. Not to Daryl's death."

What Mrs. Weinberg had told the detectives was this: on Tuesday morning, some time around noon, as she was loading her station wagon with the materials she needed for the Daycare Center, she had looked up and spotted Sarah Lovingwell walking toward the Lovingwell house.

"I waved to her, but she didn't see me. So I went on packing up the car. There was nothing odd about seeing Sarah walking down the street. And, of course, when Daryl...when we found that he was dead, I remember thinking how tragic it must have been for her to walk in and see him lying there. And then I thought...my God, I was present at that terrible moment and didn't even know! There's a disturbing poem in which a man is raking leaves in his yard and rakes up a skeletal hand. I don't think I've ever had it come home to me that brutally—that horror is there, like the hand beneath the leaves." Mrs. Weinberg ducked her head apologetically. "You'll have to excuse my way of talking. It comes from living with a teacher of poetry."

I smiled at her.

"When the detectives came here, I thought their questions were aimed at explaining tonight's trouble. I told them how fond I was of Sarah. What a good girl she had always been. And then that moment just came back to me—well, it had never really left—and I blurted it out, thinking it would prove something about her strength of character. When they started asking me more questions about that afternoon, I knew I had said something wrong; and I didn't say anything else. But it was too late, then. I could tell from the looks on their faces that I had confirmed a terrible suspicion." Mrs. Weinberg looked at me sadly. "She *couldn't* have had anything to do with Daryl's death. I'm certain of it. Why, it's a wonder she survived at all in that household."

"You mean because of her mother's illness and death?" I said.

"That, of course. And other things. You *are* working for her, aren't you?"

I nodded.

"Then you must know how she really felt about her father."

"I know," I said. "But I don't completely understand it."

Mrs. Weinberg smiled at me as if I'd uttered a familiar adage. "No one does. Do you know what I think? I think that he was a little mad."

"Did you know him well?"

She shook her head. "None of us did. He kept almost entirely to himself." She winked mischievously and said behind her hand: "He was a terrible snob, although I suppose that was part of his charm. That and his tweed coats and his briar pipes. And the curious way he had of slipping into and out of an English accent, as if the language were a velvet smoking jacket or a pair of leather slippers. You know how they say of high fashion models that clothes 'hang well' on them? Daryl was like that. Culture, or his Saville Row version of it, hung well on him. At least, on the surface it did."

She looked back through the screen door—to see if her husband was listening—then turned to me with a conspiratorial smile. "Let me be plain with you," she said. "I feel the need to be understood, after being so misunderstood by those policemen. I didn't really like Daryl. There was something wrong with him; and, while Sarah has never told me anything specific in confirmation, her hatred of him is confirmation enough. It's easy to say that she inherited her mother's madness and to attribute her hatred to that. That's how my husband, Arthur, feels. But I don't. Daryl did something to that girl, something unforgivably cruel. An unpardonable sin. And that's why she hates him."

Mrs. Weinberg smiled again. "You don't believe me. I've queered it by talking like a poetry teacher."

"I read," I said testily.

"I meant no offense. It's just that I get enthusiastic about things that other people generally think are fanciful. Read enough poems and you look to the patterns beneath the surfaces. You also begin to see probabilities—the way certain artifacts *have* to fulfill themselves. Daryl Lovingwell was such an artificial creature, so plumped with superficial grace, that I found myself reading him like a poem. And unless my genre expectations are misfounded, he was not at all the man he appeared to be."

75

I shook my head and said, "Let me 'be plain' with you, too. Three days ago Daryl Lovingwell hired me to do a job for him, a job that would have been unnecessary unless, as he claimed, he loved his daughter. Yesterday he died; and Sarah told me, in all candor, that she hated her father and that he hated her. The thing of it is, they were both so damn convincing.

"I've spoken to a man today who knew Lovingwell intimately and he believed that the Professor loved his daughter. He also thought that Sarah might have killed him. There's that, and the police, and Sarah's hatred on the one hand; and on the other, there's you, Mrs. Weinberg, and your intuition."

"And you," she said. "And your intuition."

I laughed. "Yes. And me, too. At least, until the police force me to choose sides."

"There are probably ten thousand reasons," she said, "why I can picture Daryl Lovingwell as something other than the debonair anglophile he pretended to be. Everything from the tone of voice he used when calling Sarah home to supper to the way he stood at the graveside when he buried Claire, his wife. But not one of them would serve as conclusive evidence. And taken together, they would probably tell you more about me than they would about him. I'm sorry. I wish I could be of more help. But I can't give you what you want, Mr. Stoner. Only he could tell you the truth about himself. And he's dead." Mrs. Weinberg looked up Middleton to the Lovingwell house. "I've lived on this street for twenty years; and in all that time I've never seen anything like the past two days."

As I walked off the porch I could hear her asking her husband who it was who had written that poem about the householder who rakes up a severed hand.

I was angry when I walked back to the Lovingwell house. If I had found a stone to kick, I would have sent it flying right through some burgher's picture window. The night was alive with gossip. In every living room of every house in Clifton, someone was talking about Sarah Lovingwell. And by morning the newspapers would have the story, too. Everyone in greater Cincinnati would know, or think they knew, a little bit about Daryl Lovingwell's death. Everyone but me.

The police would start getting anonymous tips. Some less reluctant, less neighborly Rose Weinberg would recall seeing Sarah walking down Middleton at noon on Tuesday. Bidwell would read the morning *Enquirer* and decide that here was where chivalry must end. He or somebody at Sloane would remember the missing document (if there wasn't some dogged little federal cop tailing me already). And the Cincinnati police would put two and two together and ask me to check the figures. That's where you're going to wind up, Harry, I told myself. As a police accountant. And poor misunderstood Sarah L. will get twenty to life. And you'll get a suspension and a light jail sentence. If you're lucky.

If you're not lucky, you'll get a felony murder charge, a criminal espionage charge. Withholding evidence. Abetting a felon. Demonstrating carelessness, sentimentality, and self-destructive impulses. Or, maybe, Lester Grimes will do some addition of his own and invite you to step out into the dusty streets for an old-fashioned shootout. I pressed my coat pocket impulsively. It was there, like a lump of scrap beneath the cloth. But it won't do you any good, Harry, I told myself. Not unless you shoot first. And you're far too fair-minded a gent for that.

It wasn't that I couldn't admit that I might have been wrong about one of the Lovingwells. Like the joke goes, I may be crazy but I'm not stupid. I knew I could be wrong about any number of things. What made me so damn mad was that I still didn't know what right and wrong meant in this affair. Worse, I had the awful feeling that, if it happened the next day that another mild-mannered, sensible-seeming Lovingwell came to me with an oath on his lips and love, like a chocolate stain, on his sleeve, I would probably do the same things and end up in the same spot. What it comes down to in the end is that you hope for the things that you don't get out of life; and I'm so constructed that a doomed love, no matter how doomed, wins my chips every time.

I jerked the car door open, threw myself down on the seat and stared blankly at the Lovingwell house. You couldn't see door or window or gable. Just a black mass, a little darker than the night sky. Goddamn it! I said to myself, I want to find something out! I don't care what it is. I was sick of holding it all in my head, like those chess problems I used to try to solve when I was pretending to be Philip Marlowe. Ten moves and I'd forget who I was, where I was, and what I was doing. The hell with it, I told myself. Tomorrow we go to the police. Let them take care of Sarah Lovingwell. She never wanted your help anyway. And as for Lovingwell *père* . . . like Rose Weinberg had said, he was past caring.

10

I drove up to the Bee and had a steak and a Scotch, a Scotch and another Scotch. I shot the bull with a couple of friends and actually found myself flirting with a blonde schoolgirl who looked vaguely like Kate. She wasn't having any, so I drifted back to the bar. I thought maybe Bullet would show up; but he didn't. And by one o'clock in the morning, I was too loaded to care. I dropped by the schoolgirl's table on my way out, to give her one last try.

"Think I'll take you home with me," I said to her.

"Think again," she snapped.

I was still thinking when I found my car, parked beneath the winter skeleton of a maple tree on Telford. "Big deal college girl," I said as I fiddled with the door.

Something cold and metallic brushed against my cheek.

I didn't even have to look. Not on a dark sidestreet, on a moonless December night. "It's in my pants pocket," I said. "Right rear. I've only got twenty bucks, but it's yours if you want it."

I heard the guy laugh softly. Then I heard him cock the piece. The hair on my arms and on the back of my neck stood on end. "Jesus Christ," I said. "Don't shoot me, buddy. Take the money!"

"I got your permission?" a wry Negro voice returned. He shoved me against the car. "Don't even think about moving."

I spread-eagled against the car door while the gunman picked my pants pocket. He took the wallet out. "Says you're a private detective," he said and laughed. "You best find you a different line of work."

He tossed the empty wallet at my feet and slugged me so hard on the back of the head that my forehead slammed into the car window. I slid down the side of the Pinto and onto the pavement.

Something inside my head seemed to be moving as lamely as a broken limb. "Ow," I groaned. How come you're not blacked out? I thought. I reached for the door handle and started to pull myself up. And then that thing moved again inside my head. Whoah, I told myself. Best wait a bit. I lay back down on the pavement and watched the night sky go in and out of focus. It's a judgment, I thought miserably.

"Hey!" a voice called from across the street. "Hey! Are you O.K.?"

"Wonderful," I said.

"Mister?" the voice repeated.

"You want to give me a hand?" I yelled. And the thing inside my head moved half an inch.

I heard footsteps, then two pairs of hands grabbed my arms.

"Easy, for chrissake," I said.

"What happened?"

"I cut myself shaving. What's it look like? I got mugged."

"You want us to call the cops?"

"No. just get me to my feet."

They lifted me up. I was too dizzy to stand, so I slumped back against the car door and stared goofily at the two boys, college kids, who had helped me out.

"Man, you got a bruise on your forehead," one of them said. "You want us to call an ambulance?"

I touched at the back of my head. "No. I'll be all right."

"You could have a concussion, mister. You ought to see a doctor."

"I said I'd be all right."

The boys looked uncertainly at each other. "O.K., Frank," one of them said. "The man knows what he wants. Let's split."

As they walked off down the sidewalk, I thought, "The

mugger was right—I ought to find another line of work."
I opened the door and sat down on the car seat and stared
at the pavement. My wallet was lying between my feet.
I bent down and picked it up and stared for a minute at
the photostat of my license. Some detective.

It was after two when I got back to the Delores. That
thing in my head had stopped wobbling; and all I felt was
a kind of lassitude that made it hard for me to keep my
eyes open. Judging by the fist fights I'd gotten into in the
Army and as a P.I., I figured the two kids had been right.
I probably did have a mild concussion. I guess the only
reason I hadn't gone to the hospital was that the mugger
had hurt my pride worse than he'd hurt my head.

I made it to the apartment without being slugged or
shot at. And I made it into the bedroom without passing
out. That seemed like enough to hope for out of one night.

I fell asleep as soon as I hit the mattress and slept long
into the morning; and when I woke, I felt as if someone
had braided cornrows in my skull. Around eleven I found
the energy to get out of bed and check the messages on
the answerphone. There was only one and it was terse:
"This is Sarah Lovingwell. I have to see you."

Once they'd talked to Rose Weinberg, the cops hadn't
wasted any time with Sean O'Hara. Before releasing him,
they'd worked on the boy until he admitted he'd been lying
about Sarah's alibi. McMasters filled me in on the rest as
I waited in the courthouse coffee shop for Sarah Lovingwell
to be brought down to the visitor's room on the fourth floor.

"Now he claims he was following you from noon to one,"
McMasters said. "He claims Grimes spotted you taking
pictures on Tuesday morning. Grimes thought you were
a federal snoop. According to O'Hara, Grimes wanted to
kill you on the spot."

"Why didn't he?" I asked him.

"Sarah Lovingwell talked him out of it," Sid said.
"Grimes is a psycho, Harry. He was eased out of the Marine
Corps, after shooting up a hamlet full of friendlies. A newspaperman got wind of it and then something happened to
the newspaperman. The brass had no choice but to give
Grimes the boot. No formal charges were ever pressed
against him. They *liked* Lester Grimes in the Marine

Corps. We had a helluva time getting this much out of them.

"Sarah Lovingwell must have pulled a thorn out of his boot, because O'Hara claims that Grimes would listen to her advice. Only that's all changed since last night. O'Hara says Grimes believes that Sarah set him up. And Grimes is a vindictive son-of-a-bitch. O'Hara is afraid that he'll come gunning for the girl."

"And me?"

"Oh, you're on his list, too. Right up near the top, according to O'Hara."

"How come O'Hara suddenly got so talkative?"

McMasters smiled humorlessly. "He's a snot-nosed kid, Harry. And we were in no mood to mess around last night."

"You worked him over?"

"Wake up and smell the coffee," McMasters said with disgust.

"So why was Grimes worried about federal cops?"

"O'Hara wouldn't say. But those pictures you gave us tell part of the story. And when we busted the club last night, we found a regular armory in the back office. Pistols, grenades, the works."

"You think Lovingwell's death is tied to this business?"

"We don't know. If we can trace the murder weapon to the cache we found on Calhoun Street, we'll be in a better position to say. Right now, we have no idea where the gun came from."

I said, "How much *do* you have on Sarah Lovingwell?"

"We've got a motive," McMasters said. "And we've got a witness who can place her near the scene at twelve on Tuesday. The girl claims she didn't go all the way up to the house, that when she saw her father's car in the driveway she turned around and went back to the club. But even if she's telling the truth and she didn't do the killing herself, she probably knows who did. The lab puts the time of death between twelve and twelve-thirty, and that would be right about the time that Sarah was moseying up to the door. We've also got the fact that she lied to us about being with O'Hara."

I frowned at McMasters. "You don't have a shred of hard evidence. Any lawyer in his right mind would have her out on *habeas* by this afternoon."

"That's true," he said. "She probably will get bailed out tonight. But then we haven't talked to you, yet, Harry."

I pointed innocently at my chest.

"Yeah, you," McMasters said. "You must think I'm an idiot. I've got eyes and half a brain. You've been holding out on me from the start. And I told you—I don't like that. You knew the O'Hara kid was lying. You knew he wasn't with the girl between noon and one. You had to know, because the jerk-off was following you home."

I'd realized it was was there all along; but this was the first time I actually felt the ice beneath my feet.

"All right," I said carefully. "Say I *did* know. I'm still working for the girl."

"The hell. She hates your guts. She thinks it was *you* who set her and the O'Hara kid up."

"Then why does she want to see me?"

McMasters shrugged. "All I know is that after you're done talking with her, you've got an appointment to talk with me. We want to know why she killed her father. And you can tell us."

"Suppose I don't?"

"Then I'll throw you in jail, Harry."

"On what charge?"

"Something'll come to me," McMasters said.

I waited for another twenty minutes in a big, drab anteroom on the eighth floor. The place was as tense and cheerless as a hospital emergency room. Two dozen sad cases waited along with me—nervous, dispirited fathers, mothers, kinfolk. I was vaguely conscious of a pecking order among the old hands. The sort of thing you see at welfare offices—the poor abusing the poor with a heartless gusto. One woman in particular, graying, with large crooked teeth and the cold black eyes of a Negro tough, seemed to be holding court in her corner of the room. But I was too preoccupied with Sarah Lovingwell to pay her much attention, even when she turned to another old hand sitting beside her and said: "That man there has him some trouble."

I laughed to myself. What trouble? There wasn't going to be any trouble. I'd just walk into the visitor's room and tell Sarah L. that I was quitting the case, that I was going to break my word to her father and tell the police about

83

the document. I didn't like it, but McMasters wasn't giving me any other choice.

"Shit," I said under my breath.

The old woman in the corner cackled. She thought *she* was getting to me.

Why the hell had Sarah called me anyway? Judging from what McMasters had said, probably to blow off a little steam. To turn the knife. Or maybe she had phoned me *before* the previous night's fiasco. There was no way to tell from my shoddy answerphone what time a call came in. Maybe there had been something she'd wanted to tell me after that curious, desultory interview on Wednesday afternoon. After I'd blackmailed her into hiring me in the first place.

"Shit," I said again. And the old woman laughed.

It really wasn't very nice, what I was going to do. Extorting Sarah's compliance and then reneging on the agreement as soon as the going got rough. On the other hand, Harry, I told myself, the girl is suspected of murder, of killing the man that you're trying to protect. And Rose Weinberg notwithstanding, Sarah had a motive and she'd been on the scene at the time of the crime. She was a little crazy, to boot. Her own father had feared she might do him violence. It was just self-indulgence, just posturing to pretend that she was an innocent who was being unjustly betrayed.

It would have been self-indulgence, all right, if I'd believed what I was saying to myself. Only I didn't believe that she'd killed her father. I'd told Rose Weinberg I'd remain impartial until the police forced me to take sides. But that was a lie. And she'd known it was a lie. Like Mrs. Weinberg, my intuition said that Sarah Lovingwell was not a killer and that her father was not the man he'd seemed to be. Why in hell hadn't he told me that his daughter hated him? It wasn't a pleasant thing to confess to a stranger, but neither was the fact that he'd suspected his daughter was a thief. He'd hinted urbanely that he and Sarah had had their little disagreements, like every other father and daughter in the world. But if there was one thing that was indisputable about the Lovingwell case, it was the fact that they were *not* an ordinary father and daughter. Why, then, had he disguised Sarah's hatred for him?

An armed guard walked out of the visitor's room and a bell rang. The people in the anteroom lined up before a table and submitted docilely to a search of their coats and handbags. Play it by ear, I decided as I waited to be frisked. Which was just a tired way of saying that the Lovingwells were still a problem that I couldn't solve. The cops patted me down, and I stepped through the door into the visitor's area.

I started down a hall to the main reception room—a big, barren box posted with guards and divided in half by a long wooden table, on either side of which prisoners and their kin sat talking.

"Your name Stoner?" a guard asked me.

"Yeah."

"This way."

He took me by the arm and guided me away from the main hall down a narrow corridor lined with private rooms—cubicles that lawyers used when they wanted to consult with their clients. Since I wasn't a lawyer, the exception struck me as odd. Odd until I walked into the room itself.

It was four-square and as uninspired as a child's wooden block, and along the length of the wall opposite the door a mirror ran from corner to corner. I laughed when I saw myself reflected in it. McMasters wasn't taking any chances. There was probably a microphone, too, hidden under the steel table or under one of the two desk chairs that were parked beneath it.

"Testing, testing," I shouted into the tabletop. "Can you hear all right, Sid?"

I gave the finger to whoever was standing behind the mirror and sat down at the table.

A minute later Sarah Lovingwell walked in.

I'd expected her to look angry when she saw me; I was even prepared to get slapped. But I could see at once that that wasn't going to happen. In her drab prison uniform she looked like a bewildered, overworked waitress. And when she saw my face—a familiar face—she almost smiled. Unless you've been locked in a cell, you can't really appreciate the luxury of an open door or the solace of companionship or the pleasure of simple choice. That half-smile faded almost immediately and was replaced by a tough, unfriendly frown.

85

"Ah," I said. *"That's* the Sarah I've come to know."

"I'm going to skip the name calling," she said coldly. "I called you because I need your help. Your meddling has gotten me into a great deal of trouble and you're the only person who can get me out of it."

"You want me to prove that you didn't kill your father?" I said.

"No."

"What, then?"

"My lawyer is going to post bond this afternoon. Unless I can convince Les that I had nothing to do with what happened last night, he'll kill me."

"You want me to act as a bodyguard?"

Sarah shook her head. "I want you to tell Les that it was your fault, that I had nothing to do with the bust."

I laughed hollowly, pushed back my chair, and got to my feet.

Sarah looked up in confusion. "Where are you going?"

"Where do you think? I heard what you wanted to say and I'm not interested."

"Just what *are* you interested in? Oh, but why ask?" She sat back in her chair and stared at me with fresh assurance. "You're a fascinating type, Mr. Stoner, in a ghoulish way. A man without loyalty, without honor, without friendship. A man who lives like a parasite in the creases of society, feeding on age, disease, and unhappiness. I once told you that I thought you were intelligent. I know now how wrong I was. It's all instinct with you, isn't it? All smell." She leaned forward and looked indifferently at the tabletop. "How much?" she said under her breath. "How much do you want?"

I did a foolish thing. I got angry. "Twenty thousand," I said.

She started as if she'd been slapped. "You're joking?"

"Hell, no," I said. "You understand my type and janissaries come high this year, Miss Lovingwell. I want twenty thousand dollars."

"I don't know if I have that much," she said nervously.

"Sure you do. You've got all of Daddy's money coming to you."

"I have money of my own," she said quickly.

"From where?"

"That's none of your business."

86

"You're wrong, Sarah. If I work for you, everything about you is my business." I sat back down at the table. "Why'd you do it, Sarah? Why'd you kill him? It wasn't for money—that's below your character. That's more in my line, right? So why'd you do it? Revenge? To get back for Momma?"

Sarah groaned as if I'd punched her squarely in the gut. "What do you know about Mother?" she said.

"I know that you blamed your father for her death. Is that why you killed him?"

"I didn't kill him."

"Sure you did. The police have a witness who can place you on the scene at the time of the murder. And when I get through telling them why your father hired me, they'll have a motive, too."

"Don't tell them that!" she said shrilly. "I *have* to get out of here. If you tell them that, they'll never let me go. I'll give you the money you want."

I shook my head. "I don't want to play any more, Sarah. Not for money or honor or fun."

"You're going to tell them?"

"I don't have a choice. McMasters knows I lied to him about your alibi. He knows I'm withholding evidence about your father's death. I'm just not going to risk my neck for you any longer. Because I think you are lying. I think you *did* kill your father."

"I swear I didn't do it," she whispered. All of the outrage and assurance had left her face.

"For what it's worth, I didn't betray you," I said. "Your friend O'Hara told the police that the alibi was a phoney. But before you start thinking up some category to stuff him into, you ought to know that he was beaten up before he confessed."

"I don't believe you," Sarah said.

"It's not in the dialectic, huh? Well, Marx notwithstanding, that's the truth."

Sarah stared forlornly at the mirror behind me. "I need your help," she said in a small, tired voice. "I'm in trouble and I need your help."

It was as if she had pulled a plug inside me. I felt all the anger drain away, and in its place a weak and dangerous pity was sloshing about. I looked away from her and down at the hard grooved rubber inlay of the tabletop.

"Talking to Grimes isn't going to help you," I said. "If he thinks I'm a cop, nothing I say is going to change his mind. He'll kill me, Sarah. And why should I risk my neck for you? I heard all that crap about loyalty and friendship and honor. But you haven't trusted me since we met. Why should I trust you? If I did what you asked me to, I'd just be playing another hunch, a sucker play, which is all I've been doing since your father hired me on Monday." I shook my head. "I'm sorry. But I'm not going to play in the dark any more."

Sarah wiped her eyes and got up from her chair. "Then there's nothing more to say."

She reached for the buzzer by the door, to signal the guard that our conversation was finished.

And then I did another foolish thing. I called her back. "Hold it," I said.

She turned at the door and looked back at me with just the trace of a smile on her face. I nodded at her disgustedly.

"So I'm not a janissary," I said. "You don't have to crow over it."

"I'm hardly crowing," she said. But her smile broadened, and she looked at me with something like gratitude.

"I've waited for two days, I don't suppose another day will hurt. But understand, Sarah, you've got to convince me that you didn't kill your father. You've got to convince me that he was, in fact, the man you've made him out to be. I don't see any middle way. One of you has to be a liar. And remember, if I'm not convinced, I'll tell the police what they want to know."

"I'll convince you," she said.

11

Sid McMasters was waiting in the anteroom with two burly desk sergeants when I walked back out the door.

"Did you get everything settled, Harry?" he asked.

"What's the matter, Sid? Did the mirror fog up or did the microphone go dead?"

"Sure. Make jokes. We heard what you said."

"That's against the law!" I said to him.

"Funny man," one of the desk cops grumbled.

"Let's talk, Harry," McMasters said. "Just the four of us."

"O.K." I sat down on the waiting room bench.

"Not here." McMasters shook his head. "Downstairs."

"How far downstairs, Sid?" I asked him.

"That depends, Harry. On how much you tell us."

"I want to talk to a lawyer."

"You're not under arrest," McMasters said innocently. "You're just cooperating with the police, like every good citizen should."

"I'm not going down to the basement, Sid. If you want to talk, we can talk right here."

McMasters nodded to the other cops, and they walked over and hoisted me to my feet.

"You can't pull this shit. I've got a legal right to keep silent. What Sarah Lovingwell told me is privileged information."

McMasters pretended to chew it over. "Let's talk about it downstairs," he said agreeably.

With the two desk sergeants propping me up, we took the service elevator down to the lobby. The floor numbers were printed in block letters at the verge of each floor, and I counted them off as nervously as if I were descending the levels of Hell. When *ONE* flashed by and the elevator didn't slow down, I knew I was headed for the nth circle—the frozen one—and that McMasters was going to push this thing right over the edge of humor, of practical joking, into a place where kidding becomes a prelude to violence. If it came to that, I'd have to give him something; and I'd have to give it up after a struggle, to convince him that it had been worth waiting for. And that something couldn't be Sarah.

Out of sympathy or lunacy or plain old curiosity I'd given her a reprieve. Just how that was going to work I didn't know. There was no reason to assume that she'd start telling me the truth once she'd gotten what she wanted—which was out of jail. She might go underground, like her friend Grimes; or she just might put a bullet through my head. Didn't think of that one, did you, Harry? I said to myself. But I had thought of it; I just hadn't thought much of it. I simply couldn't believe she was a killer. And in spite of all the parables on appearances and all the hard practical lessons I'd learned in better than ten years of detective work, I'd never yet been that wrong about a client. Of course, I had to be wrong about one of them, father or daughter. But when it comes to a choice between the testimony of a man like Bidwell and that of a woman like Mrs. Weinberg, I always go with the Rose Weinbergs of this world. Perhaps because it's flattering when someone takes detective work seriously, when someone pauses to consider just how much detection goes into knowing anyone at all.

So I couldn't give McMasters Sarah or the document or the reason why her father had hired me. What I could give him was Grimes. Sarah wouldn't like it; but it was the best way, maybe the only way, to keep both of us from ending up dead. Because I was no match for a psychotic ex-Marine with the instincts of a killer. I knew his type from domesticated versions—the men who wall their rooms with rifles, machine guns, and dummy grenades.

Who, if you get on their good side, will take you out back and let you fire off a burst or two from an illegally operative Thompson. And who, invariably, when loaded or sentimental, will let you in on their secret plans, their maelstrom defenses. For they're all Seventh Day Adventists, these gun nuts; they're all millenarians, saving up for that day when apocalypse comes. They're all *prepared*. They've got the fire lines worked out; they've calculated ammunition like a quartermaster. They've built redoubts and shelters and, secretly, they probably know who's going to go first—which member of the family they'll sacrifice in a pinch. It's the most heartless brand of sentimentality you can run up against; and if you believe the shit put out by the gun lobby, it's what makes America great.

Grimes—who probably sat in his rented rooms with a rifle in his lap, trailing straggling school kids and strange Negroes with barrel propped out the bedroom window, squeezing off imaginary rounds in lightning-like bursts—was a wilder and less predictable case. But he'd have that same sentimental streak—killing is kindness—and a helluva lot more expertise. I'd have to do some research on him. Talk to some ex-Marines like Larry Soldi, Bullet's hired man, who could fill me in on just how to defend against a man still fighting wars. Armed with that kind of knowledge and with Sid's help, Grimes could be handled. And handling Grimes would please Sid. Dropping a cop-killer was just about the richest pleasure in his world.

As the elevator pulled to a stop, I tried to calculate exactly how much abuse I ought to take before handing McMasters what he wanted. I half wished I'd had the chance to stop in a john, so I could have stuffed a cushion of toilet tissue in my nose and around my gums. But that would have taken half the fun out of it for Sid, and all of the surprise.

When we got out of the elevator, we walked down a dim hallway into a large empty cellroom. The whole basement had once been used as a keep; now the cells were used as storerooms. Except for the one in which we were standing. The room was absolutely bare—no chairs, no furniture. Just stone walls, gas and water pipes overhead, and a single lamp dangling down like the big white-light lamps hung above the lawn of pool tables. While I was looking around, Sid took off his coat and rolled up his shirt sleeves.

91

The other cops drifted into the shadows outside the pale of the overhead light. There was a stack of phone books in one corner of the room. And one of the desk sergeants walked very deliberately over to them and leaned up against that section of the wall. It was all a little like *No* drama—each gesture calculated to produce its incremental effect. A ritualistic first act, like the unsheathing and wiping of a sacrificial blade. The phone books were a nice touch. No phone, just the books.

That was the way they did it nowadays. Leaded saps and rubber hoses were out. They left marks and, in the heat of the moment, they could do mortal injury. The phone books were an antic compromise. Every criminal knows that he's allowed one phone call and, under the guise of allowing the criminal his rights, the cops kept the phone books on the floor of the interrogation room. If I pushed McMasters hard enough, I'd get a chance to see what they were really used for.

The two desk sergeants would pin my arms back, and Sid would take a phone book and slam me over the head with it until blood ran out of my ears. After ten good shots, my spine would compress and every nerve center would start signaling pain. My legs would throb, my arms would burn. My back would feel as if the vertebrae were cracked. I'd lose control of my bladder, of my bowels. The cops would make me strip, unless Sid was in a really vicious mood, unless he wanted to make me stand ankle-deep in my own waste. I'd seen it happen. Sid knew I'd seen it happen. And he watched me with the cold assurance that I was getting the point. In the white light he looked black-Irish tough— a big, barrel-chested man with red hair, a pasty complexion, and heartless blue eyes. He was enjoying it. I've never known a cop who didn't enjoy making his mark squirm.

"It's working, Sid," I said to him. "I'm scared."

He shrugged. "I would be, too, Harry. You're in a tough spot. It doesn't have to get tougher. You know that. All you have to do is tell me what I want to know."

I swallowed hard. This was the point of departure. After I said "no" once, it was all up to Sid. There were other cops in the room and that made it even harder for him. They knew we were friends, and they'd be watching him.

"I can't do that," I told him. "I have a legal obligation to my client to keep my mouth shut."

McMasters shook his head slightly. He was warning me off.

"I don't want to do this, Stoner," he said. "But you're not giving me any choice."

McMasters reached down to the floor with his left hand, as if he'd dropped something beside him. I followed him with my eyes. He straightened suddenly and brought the back of his right hand up across the bottom of my jaw with a force that made my teeth snap. I rocked backward on my feet and watched the shooters fill my eyes.

"That's just to show you, Harry," he said as I wobbled in front of him. "This isn't a joke. I've got a man in the hospital with a bullet in his spine. So you *are* going to tell me what I want to know. You're going to tell me about Lovingwell and about what he hired you to find out. Or things are going to get very rough very fast. No more song-and-dance. No more confidentiality crap. No more buddy-buddies."

"I can't tell you that."

"The hell," he said.

Sid motioned to the two desk sergeants and both of them ambled out of the shadows. McMasters pushed me back toward the rear wall. It's now or never, Harry, I said to myself.

"Wait a minute, McMasters," I said.

He kept shoving.

"Wait. Goddamn it!"

"What?" he said.

"Maybe we can do some business."

"I'm listening."

"You want Grimes, right? I can give him to you."

McMasters knitted his brow and looked at me with shrewd reserve. He hadn't bitten yet. Maybe I should have taken a few shots in the head before making the offer. But my damn skull was still aching from that run-in with the mugger, and I figured that even a couple of blows might put me in the hospital for a week. Or there was always the chance that, after a couple more punches, I might lose my temper, throw a few punches of my own, and end up in much deeper trouble. There was nothing to do but go ahead with it and try to make it as convincing as I could.

"Listen to me, Sid. I can deliver Grimes to you. The Lovingwell girl is going to try to patch things up with him.

93

Right now he thinks she betrayed him and that means he's going to try to kill her. She thinks she can arrange a meeting and get back in his good graces. I'm supposed to be at the meeting, too. I'm supposed to tell Grimes that Sarah had nothing to do with the bust."

McMasters snorted. "You aren't that stupid, Stoner. The son-of-a-bitch would kill you before you opened your mouth."

"Not if you shoot him first."

McMasters thought it over. "Just when's this meeting supposed to take place?"

"In the next day or two. Grimes has gone underground, but Sarah or one of her friends can get in touch with him." I studied McMaster's face and knew I had him. "It'll pay to let her go, Sid. It's the only way you're going to get Grimes."

"And what's to keep her from going underground, too?" he said.

"Me. I'll keep her in sight."

"She ain't going to like you betraying her again, Harry."

"Well," I said. "A lot of us have to live with things we don't like."

12

I wasn't sure where I stood when McMasters said, "You can go, Harry." So I decided to get some advice.

After cleaning up in the main floor washroom, I walked across the lobby to a phone booth and called Jim Dugan, a lawyer in the Riorley for whom I'd once done a considerable favor. At the time I'd worked for him, Dugan was only a name on an office door. No secretary, no dictaphone. Just a plump, baby-faced Jim, sitting behind a steel desk and gazing up at you with an invincible optimism—as if yours was the case he'd been waiting for all day, all month, all his years as a practicing attorney. He didn't smile at anybody, now. He didn't have to. He had always been a lip-chewer, a mama's boy, and a bit of a liar; his success had only given him the excuse to become himself. But he was a crafty son-of-a-bitch, expert at remembering odd statutes and at fashioning tax loopholes, which made him valuable to the congressman from his district. Jim owed me one; and if I had ever needed an acquaintance with political clout, now was the time.

"I'm in a real fix," I said to him after I'd spent five minutes convincing his secretary that I was a friend. "One of my clients is a suspected felon, and the cops are leaning on me. How far can I push the confidentiality line?"

"Have they sent the case to a grand jury yet?"

"I don't think so. They don't have enough hard evidence. That's why they're leaning on me."

"No grand jury, no summons, Harry," Jim said cheerfully. "It's as simple as that. You don't have anything to worry about until you're called to appear before a panel."

"There are other ways they can screw me. Review boards. Erroneous vag warrants. Parking tickets. You name it."

"How the hell did *you* get involved in something like this? I thought you catered to a quieter trade: Paternity cases, missing persons, minor thefts?"

"So did I, Jim," I said. "This whole business has gone haywire."

"Well, I'm not sure what I can do for you, buddy," he said.

"I know what you can do for me, *buddy*. You can call that s.o.b. in the second district who uses you for a tax shelter and get him to turn off the heat!"

"Hey, Harry," Jim said righteously. "Congressman Giofranconi isn't a switchboard. I can't just patch cords in and out of him. Not if I want to keep his business."

"Jim, I'm not the one who should be saying this, but you owe me."

"O.K.," he said after a minute. "If it gets bad, I'll pull his string for you. But only if it gets bad, Harry."

God bless pork barrel politics! I thought as I hung up the phone.

It was half-past seven according to the clock hanging above the Police Clerk's counter on the other side of the lobby. I walked over to the desk and pressed the service button.

"Can you tell me if a Miss Sarah Lovingwell has posted bond or been released on writ this afternoon?" I asked the clerk—a sour-looking, silver-haired old man in a stained print shirt and black gaberdine slacks.

"The charge?"

"Murder."

He didn't bat an eye, just ran his finger down a work sheet until he came to *Lovingwell, Sarah B.* "Yeah. She was sprung at five-ten. *Habeas*."

"Thanks."

"Think nothing of it," he said drily.

Sarah's release was a good sign. It had gone off on

schedule, which meant that McMasters had bought what I'd proposed. At least until I could deliver Lester O. Grimes. After that ... well, there was always Congressman Giofranconi.

I stepped out of the courthouse into the cold evening air. There was a light dusting of snow on the parkway, and pedestrians were walking pigeon-toed along the sidewalks, skipping over puddles and patches of ice. There's a lesson here, Harry, I said to myself. It's bad weather all over town.

At nine-fifteen I pulled into the Lovingwell driveway and got out of the Pinto. There was a light on the second floor. Sarah's bedroom light. I stared for a minute at the window. There was no sign of expectation. No face pressed against the pane. Nobody tripping eagerly downstairs to greet me. No front door thrown wide in welcome.

Maybe she's changed her mind again, I thought. Like the petal-game—she trusts you, she trusts you not. Maybe you'll walk up there and it'll be the "no peddlers" look and the bum's rush.

"Damn," I said to myself. I was actually nervous. The way you can get at a party when you're not sure of the company, not sure you want to hear this one's lies and that one's gossip.

I might have stood in front of the Pinto until dawn if I hadn't seen the bedroom curtain flutter. It stirred me like a cry for help. I walked quickly up to the door and knocked.

She opened it slowly. Her face was half-hidden by the door, but what I could see of it told me that Sarah Lovingwell wasn't going to be tossing brickbats at me this Thursday evening. She wasn't going to be tossing anything at anyone. In the half-light of the hall she looked wan and exhausted. She also looked very frightened.

"I wasn't sure you were going to come tonight," she said. Her speech was thick and slurred. "I mean I wasn't sure you were going to come at all."

"I said I would, didn't I?"

She laughed freakishly, then shuddered. "People don't always do what they say." If she was high on something, tripped out on soapers, I was in for a rough evening. Maybe even for a quick trip to the emergency room at General.

97

The tremor in her movements, like an old woman's gait, scared me.

"I've been thinking," she said.

"All alone?"

"How else do you think?"

"I meant why didn't you ask a friend to come over and stay with you?"

"Why?" she said. "To celebrate my release? To protect me from Les?" She looked at me with dull-eyed contempt. "Or do you mean to mourn with me over poor Papa?" She waved her hand dismissively, the way she'd done when I'd first spoken with her in the study on the day her father had died. "I didn't feel the need. And, besides, friends are hard to come by tonight. At least, they are for me."

"Do you feel up to talking?"

"Have you given me a choice?"

"I guess not," I said.

"Then, come on. I want to show you something." She turned form the door and walked tipsily upstairs. "I won't bite you," she said over her shoulder.

No, I thought. But I might bite you. Even stoned or fatigued, Sarah was a good-looking young woman. Not beautiful, but erotic in the prim promising way that certain convent girls can be erotic. And I'd been working up to some kind of foolish, romantic gesture for six lonely months. I tried not to think about it; but when I walked into Sarah's bedroom my arm brushed against her breasts or she brushed against my arm, and when I looked at her face I caught a trace of a shallow and quite deliberate smile.

The room was a shambles. Clothes, boxes, papers were strewn everywhere. It looked as if the place had been searched with an unfriendly hand. I sat down on the bed and stared at the mess on the floor.

"Lose something?"

"In a way." Sarah walked to the closet—the one in which I had found Lovingwell's envelope—and picked up a shoe box. "You want to know why I came home on Tuesday morning, don't you? Well, in a way, this is the reason." She carried the box over to the bed and sat down beside me. "He'd taken it from me, and I wanted to get it back before he destroyed it."

I studied Sarah's face for a moment. "Before we get into

this, I think I better tell you that in a few minutes you're going to crash."

"I know," she said hoarsely. "I'm not stoned, if that's what you think. I just couldn't sleep in that cell. I couldn't stop thinking about Les. When I got out, it was like coming down off speed. I lost all my energy."

I wasn't sure I trusted this giddy, exhausted version of Sarah L. She was worn out, all right; and she looked as if she hadn't slept. But there was a movieland factitiousness about the whole business—the unlit house, the disordered room, the dull, ingenuous speech—that reminded me vaguely of the artificial way she had spoken of her father on Wednesday afternoon. She just wasn't flighty enough, I suppose, for someone in the spot she was in. And the smile she had shown me when I'd brushed against her had been as calculated as Greenwich time. Sarah sensed what I was thinking.

"You really don't trust me, do you?" she said.

I didn't answer her.

"Well, I guess I don't blame you. That was a lousy thing I said to you this afternoon. Especially since I found out that you were telling me the truth. I mean about Sean."

"He had a hard time of it," I said.

"So did I. I'm not trying to put you off. I'm just worn out."

Sarah picked up the shoe box and placed it on my lap. "Now it's yours," she said. "I wonder how you're going to like it?"

"What's inside?"

"Mementos. Pictures of my mother." She flipped the lid off the box and sorted through the pictures. "Look at this."

She handed me a yellowed snapshot. It was a picture of a long-faced, rather aristocratic-looking woman, standing before a pond. The photo was of poor quality, but there was no mistaking the resemblance between its subject and Sarah.

"That one was taken in England," she said. "In 1959. Father had gotten a Ford grant, and we spent that year on mother's farm in Bucks."

She looked down into the box and pulled out a second photo.

It was of her mother and father standing together in front of the same pond. Lovingwell looked exactly as he

99

had the last time I'd seen him—deer-stalker cap, ulster coat, his sharp beard making a white V at the lapel. I took a close look at the mother's face. There was something wrong with it. It reminded me of the photographs taken of Virginia Woolf before she committed suicide—an askew face, cheerless and disordered.

I flipped the photograph over. It was dated on the back in faint print—"August, 1972."

"What happened?" I said to Sarah.

"You *see!*" she said triumphantly as if she were at once grateful and content that I had taken her point.

"Yes. Something happened to your mother."

"There's more," Sarah said breathlessly. She began to pull one photo after another out of the shoebox. Some she glanced at before tossing on the floor. When the box was empty she knocked it, too, on the floor, and sat sullenly on the bed. Looking at her, I began to feel a little panicky.

"He *did* it," she said in a hollow voice. "He killed her."

I collected the photos from the floor and stuck them in my coat pocket. "We'll talk about that later," I said. "You need some rest. Do you mind going to my apartment? If your friend Les tries anything, I'd rather be on familiar ground."

"Do I have a choice?" she said again.

"Not if you want my help," I told her.

An unmarked police cruiser followed us over to the Delores. Sid wasn't taking any chances, and, in a way, I was glad. I still didn't have a handle on flighty Sarah L., and the police protection—which was meant as a reminder—felt good. When I'd parked and we'd gotten upstairs to the apartment, I took Sarah into the bedroom and sat her down on the bed.

"I'll sleep on the couch," I said.

"Don't you want to talk?"

"In the morning. You've had a rough day."

Sarah lay back on the mattress. "You think I'm crazy, don't you?"

"Is that what you think?" I asked her.

She closed her eyes. "I don't know. He used to tell me I was crazy. Everybody is, at times, aren't they? He was crazy all the time. Wicked, wicked." Sarah opened her eyes and looked up at me. "You're not going to leave me alone here, are you?"

"I'll be in the other room."

"I'll try to arrange a meeting with Les in the morning."

She curled up under the blanket. I turned off the light, walked into the living room, poured myself a Scotch, and stretched out on the sofa. After downing the drink, I reached over to my coat and took the pictures out of the breast pocket. There were thirty of them—all dated in faint red print. A harmless enough legacy. And yet Sarah claimed that her father had wanted to destroy them. She might, in fact, have killed him to prevent their destruction. And killed him for what? For a picture of her mother beside an oak tree, maybe the tree behind the Lovingwell house? For another picture of Claire Lovingwell seated at a desk, her hand on her chin and her eyes leveled at the camera? Claire in shorts and halter; Claire in a print housedress; Claire, Daryl, and Sarah picnicking on the grass? Why would someone want to destroy a handful of album photographs hidden away in a closet? I thought of what Bidwell had said about Lovingwell and his wife. Maybe the Professor had felt that it was unhealthy for Sarah to dwell on pictures of her suicide mother. Maybe he'd thought that they fueled her hatred of him. The image of that dainty little man alone among all his treasures and of his daughter poring over the past in the upstairs bedroom was ludicrous and unsettling.

13

I hadn't slept well on the couch—a slung leather Danish number that I'd bought on impulse at a furniture store in the Kenwood Mall. Like most Danish furniture it looked more comfortable than it actually was. Once I got it home I realized it was narrow and hard and smelled like a rubber pillow. All night long I kept dreaming that I was about to roll off it onto the floor. I had an aunt who used to recommend putting a chair beside your bed if you were worried about falling off the mattress. I never quite understood the logic—perhaps the chair served as a kind of magical boundary beyond which even the most restless sleeper wouldn't venture. At any rate, at four in the morning, I tried her remedy; and the result was that I started dreaming about rolling off the couch and onto the chair.

At about seven I woke up to find Sarah Lovingwell sitting in the chair and smiling at me.

"Hi," I said sleepily.

"Hi yourself."

"Did you sleep well?"

"I slept like a log," she said blandly. "It's the first good rest I've had since Tuesday night."

Sarah stretched on the chair and I could see her breasts rise against the loose denim of her shirt. She knew I was watching her, too. When she'd finished stretching, she

103

ducked behind her long auburn hair and gave me a coy and sultry look.

"God, you're a strange girl," I said to her.

"I've got you guessing, haven't I?" she said with a wink.

"There isn't much about your family that isn't a matter of guesswork."

"That's us, all right," she said. "The mysterious Lovingwells."

I got up and made some coffee while Sarah rattled the morning *Enquirer.* "Do you feel like talking?" I called to her from the kitchen.

"I suppose you mean about my father?"

"Yep." I carried two cups of coffee into the living room. She was sitting on the couch and, in the morning light, she looked a lot younger and more vulnerable than she had the night before. But even in the morning light there was a certain pugnaciousness about Sarah L. Perhaps it was the way she held her head, tipped back slightly, as if she were reading fine print through invisible bifocals. Her eyes, sea blue and amorous, were cool behind those spectacles and far older than the rest of her face.

"So you want to talk about dear old Dad?" Sarah studied me amusedly. "You have a one-track mind, don't you?"

"Detection is my life," I said to her.

She laughed merrily. "Then this is the big test. Either I convince you that Father was a madman or you go to the police, is that right?" She twisted on the couch and said: "O.K. Where do you want to begin?"

"Let's begin with these," I said, setting the photographs on the coffee table in front of her. "I want you to tell me about the photographs and about what they represented, and let's begin with the first one you showed me last night. The one of your mother standing in front of the pond."

"The pond was on a farm in Bucks," Sarah said. "It was her father's farm. She'd inherited it in 1959. We'd gone to England on a grant, ostensibly for Father to do research but actually to make arrangements about death duties, entry fines. That sort of thing."

"In the picture your mother looks—"

"Sane?" Sarah said. "There's no reason to be embarrassed about it. She was sane, then. My mother was a weak-willed, vain woman; but she did have a genuine feeling for her home. She was very happy when we arrived

104

at the farm. I think she thought of it as a sanctuary or last resort. My mother never quite accepted her marriage as a final condition, or thought of marriage itself as anything more than an escapade. It was as if her entire married life were a kind of preparation for that return home. But then she hadn't bargained on marrying a man as tenacious and uncivilized as Papa."

Sarah plucked a picture of her father from the stack and gazed at it. "I suppose you never really know your parents. They're too close to you, like reading a page of print right in front of your eyes. And with someone like him it was even more difficult because so much of his life was hidden or invested in superficial things—in that moustache and that beard, in the tweed coat with the leather patches on the elbows, in meerschaum pipes and leather hair brushes. He'd grown up with money, and he liked it. So did Mother, but to her it was a kind of security, like the farm or the marriage. To him, it was an ornament of power. I suppose that's one reason why I became a communist, because of his greed." Sarah smiled at me. "I'm a very rich communist, now. Isn't that funny?"

"I don't think the police will find it so funny," I said.

"You're right. But I *do* have money of my own; I wasn't lying to you yesterday. I have a trust fund. It was Mother's last rational act—setting it up and insisting that Father have nothing to do with its administration." Sarah ducked her head and brushed back her long hair with both hands. "Am I being winning enough?" she said with a trace of laughter in her voice. "Doesn't the thought of all that money convince you that I'm safe?"

"Are you trying to bribe me?"

"Are you bribable? If I was more sure of you I'd do it with sex." She shook her hair out and laughed. "I'm being perverse again, aren't I? It's not really fair When I was a girl I was thin with practically no breasts at all. He used to make fun of the way I looked. So I became flirtatious when I grew up." She grinned. "Do you see a pattern developing here?

"I'll tell you a story. When I was eighteen I went to my first formal dance. I went with Sean O'Hara. Before the dance, before Sean picked me up, I was in my bedroom, admiring myself in a mirror. It was my first strapless gown. I'd grown breasts by then. And I felt good looking at myself. Father came in, and when he saw me he kissed me on the cheek. And then he blushed. I looked down and saw that he had a hard-on. It made me feel sensational to know that I had that power over him. After that I went out of my way to expose myself to him, leaving doors open, walking around half-dressed or undressed. You see, in every other way it was me reacting to him.

"Do you think that's queer or terrible? It probably is. I'm not like that in bed, though. I'm really pretty normal."

"You're doing it again, Sarah. And it's making me nervous."

"*Am* I?" she said insouciantly.

I glared at her and said: "Let's get back to that picture of your mother. What happened in England?"

"That's the hard part," Sarah said timidly.

"It's not going to be any easier in McMasters's office or on a witness stand."

"No, it's not going to be easy anywhere."

She drew herself up on the cushion and said, "It was money that started it. Father claimed that we couldn't afford to maintain the farm in Bucks. Maybe he was telling the truth. But with someone like him the truth is always accessory. While we stayed on in Bucks, he was bargaining with a farmer in Devon about selling the property. He never asked her if she *wanted* to sell it—which she didn't. I don't think he ever asked another person what he wanted in this life. He just assumed he knew best. And in the end, he had his way. She didn't have enough character to stand up to him. He sold her patrimony, but she never forgave him for it. And that was the start, if there is a 'start' to the disintegration of a marriage. That fall was the last time they slept in the same room. It was the last time I thought of them as being in love.

"The next year Mother had an affair. Of course I was too young to understand what all the fuss was about. All the shouting and the fighting. But I could feel the hatred in the air like you can feel a storm blowing up. You wouldn't have thought he would have cared—about that kind of betrayal. But he did. You see, it wasn't just the money for him. It was *everything* he touched or could put his hands on. He wanted it all. Like some kind of crazy Midas, who *liked* having the golden touch. She was his

106

property, as much as the house or her farm. He might have given her away, but he'd never let her choose for herself.

"In 1965 Mother had her first nervous breakdown. She had had another affair and it ended badly. She heard voices, hallucinated, said that Father was poisoning her. Of course everyone in the university community was terribly upset." Sarah laughed. "They get upset about those things in academia because so many of them have nervous breakdowns themselves. It's like seeing the handwriting on the wall. When Mother got out of the hospital she looked dreadful. I thought it was a symptom of her illness, like a rash with chickenpox. That it would go away when she got better. I didn't really know what a nervous breakdown was, then.

"But, of course, she didn't get better. Not in that house where he never said a word to her. And she never was the same after that first hospitalization. She wouldn't eat, she slept badly and cried constantly. She had two more nervous breakdowns in the next three years. And each time she suffered the same hallucinations, had the same delusion about Father poisoning her.

"No one believed her. How could they? All you had to do was look at Father to know that he was incapable of something so downright improper. He was so smart, so well-bred, so candid, and so reliable. Did he tell you he hated his job?" Sarah asked. "That if he had been born thirty years later he would have been a hippie? That there was a lot of that sort of thing in his soul?"

I shuddered a little. "Yes, he did."

"Oh, that was one of his favorites. The humble man caught in a world he didn't understand and forced to labor at a job he despised. He was so clever with other people. He had an unerring sense of what they expected of him. And he would play it their way so well that, after awhile, it didn't seem to be their way but his own. It was like a game to him and the stakes were trust."

"Why?" I asked her. "Why would he do that?"

"Hate," she said. "Especially after Mother's infidelity, he had a boundless contempt for other people and a greed for what was precious to them. He would talk about how stupid this one was. How easy it would be to steal his grant, his job, his wife. When he was like that, it was as if he were talking about killing people, about taking their souls from them. He didn't speak that way often. But when he did, in that quaint well-mannered voice...it was terrifying." Sarah looked at me shrewdly. "It's hard to believe, isn't it?"

"Almost impossible," I said.

"But isn't evil always like that? Banal, innocuous-seeming? Daryl Lovingwell just added a little paint, a bit of superficial flash. At heart he was a killer. A sociopath with an inexhaustible sense of having been wronged. Perhaps he had been. In spite of the money, he had had a hard life. Bad childhood. Bad marriage. Bad daughter," she said with a tremor in her voice. "But that doesn't justify...his hate. I don't know how that could be justified. Or explained. I don't know why he killed my mother. Or why he hated me. Perhaps that's why I stuck around—waiting for an answer. Or a resolution."

Neither of us said a word for a second. There didn't seem to be anything left to say, because she hadn't described a man, she'd described a demon, a vice—something smooth, dark, and inexplicable. Men weren't like that, even bad men. And I'd seen enough bad men to know. Yet there was no question that she believed in what she'd said. I'd wanted to believe her, too, for the simple reason that I liked her. But her description was too vague, too uncompromising, too full of smoke. It was a piece of personal mythology—a legend built of years of loveless resentment. And like any legend, whatever truth it contained was hidden away in a nimbus of fears and wishes. I didn't tell her that. I didn't know how. Instead I asked a detective's question—one that had an answer. "Can you prove it? What you said about your mother?"

She shrugged. "How do you prove that someone has been driven insane? It's such common mischief, isn't it? Husbands hating wives, wives hating husbands? Madness seeping in like damp. I know this much; he *was* poisoning her. Perhaps not physically, but mentally. One night when she was frightened she brought me into her bedroom to stay with her. I was fifteen at the time. It was the year before she died. She held me in her arms and said, 'Listen.' At first I didn't hear it. It was so soft and soothing. But what it was saying—" Sarah shivered. "Awful things," she said. "He was whispering to her through the walls—the way children do before they sleep. Talking so reasonably

108

about what he was going to do with her money, about all the things he would buy. If only she'd cooperate, he said. There are pills on the nightstand. There's a bread knife in the pantry, fastened on a magnet beneath the china cabinet. I sharpened it today. In the silverware drawer, a steak knife. In the bathroom, razor blades. Iodine. If only she'd cooperate.

"Now do you understand why I despised him? He'd been doing that to her for years. For years out of greed and hatred he'd been torturing her to death."

Sarah sat back on the couch and stared forlornly at the sheaf of photographs. "I would have killed him myself," she said, "if I wasn't such a coward."

"Who did kill him, Sarah?"

"I don't know."

"But you were there," I said. "You've admitted that you went back to your house around noon."

"I didn't go all the way up the street," she said. "I changed my mind before I got to the house."

"Why?"

"Because he was there. I saw his car in the driveway and decided it wasn't worth a confrontation. He would have lied to me, anyway. I decided to wait until he was gone to search the house for the photographs; so I went back to the club. Then around one Miss Hemann called me up. She seemed so hysterical—I just went."

I sat back on the couch and tried to decide what to make of what Sarah had told me. There had been so many inconsistencies in Daryl Lovingwell's behavior—and in the reports of his behavior—that, sooner or later, I would have begun to think of him as a guilty party. I think I already had begun to do that, though as guilty of what I still wasn't sure. Perhaps, in light of her chilling monologue, simply of having made Sarah's life miserable. In any event, it was time to start turning some of my "intuition" to account. To start taking Sarah (and, to a lesser degree, Rose Weinberg) seriously. It was either that or a return to the ambivalence I'd felt since the start of the case. And from Sarah's description, Daryl Lovingwell was not a man one ought to have felt ambivalent about. Time to take sides, Harry, I said to myself. At least, provisionally. Time to start thinking of the Professor as a man who had more than a little to hide. And to see what could be made of his

109

inconsistencies if I assumed, for the moment, that Sarah had been telling the truth. "That was the second phone call you got that morning," I said to her, talking it out. "The first one was from your father. What did he want?"

"He wanted to know when I was coming home that afternoon."

"I thought you two left each other notes about that sort of thing."

"We did."

"What did you write that morning? Can you remember?"

"I think I told him that I'd be at the club until twelve. And then I'd be coming home before the rally at the museum."

"But you didn't go all the way home, did you?"

"No. Like I said, I chickened out when I saw his car."

"So, your father called at—"

"Eleven-forty."

"Not to find out *when* you'd be coming home. He already knew that. But to find out *if* you'd be coming home."

"Yes, I guess that's true."

"And then he left his office in a rush and asked Miss Hemann not to forward any calls. What does that sound like to you?"

Sarah looked at me cunningly. "Like he was expecting somebody at the house and didn't want me around."

"That's what it looks like," I said. "And it wasn't me he was expecting, so it could have been someone else who had a reason for not wanting to be seen by you. Why would one of your father's associates not want you to see him?"

"Maybe it was a woman," Sarah said quickly. "Wouldn't that be something? If Father had been carrying on an affair behind my back!"

"We've got to be more certain than that if we're going to keep you out of prison."

Sarah smiled at me with pleasure. "Then I passed the test?" she said. "You believed what I told you about Father."

I said, "I believe that you didn't kill him."

"Why?"

"Because I have to believe someone." Which was the absolute truth. I told her. I picked up my cup and walked into the kitchen. "We have two goals now. First, we have

110

to find out who *did* kill your father—that is, if you don't want to take the fall for his death. And second, we have to stay alive to fulfill our first goal; and that means eliminating Lester Grimes."

"What do you mean 'eliminating'?" Sarah said with horror.

"Come over here, Sarah." I took her by the wrist and pulled her to the front window. "You see that gray Plymouth parked across from the lobby?"

She nodded.

"That's an unmarked police car. The men in that car have been assigned to tail you. The only reason you're out of jail at all is that I managed to convince Sid McMasters that you could be more useful to him outside than in."

"What do you mean, 'useful'?"

"McMasters wants Grimes," I said simply.

"So, that's it," she said. "And what makes you think I'll go along with this?"

"I don't know that you will," I said. "I only expect you to think about it. Grimes is bent on revenging himself against you and me. Nothing I say is going to change that. And nothing you want to believe in is going to change that, either. If you want to stay alive, you're going to have to think about it."

"He's my *friend,*" she said between her teeth.

"He's also a psychopathic killer. And no number of principles, good or bad, are going to rule him or convince him of your innocence. He thinks you're a class traitor, Sarah. And he's going to execute you."

Sarah blew air out of her mouth and nodded a kind of concession. "I'll think about it," she said.

14

Sarah didn't feel much like talking to me for the next ten minutes. She sat on the sofa with her chin on her hands and stared at the room the way animals sometimes stare at the bars of their cages. I made a fresh pot of coffee in the kitchen and told myself that it wasn't my fault, that if you play with men like Grimes you're liable to get hurt. But it didn't make me feel happier. I liked the girl. After what she'd told me that morning, I liked her enough not to want to make her life any more painful than it had already been. Which may have been a sneaky way of saying that I wanted out. Or, maybe, that I wanted to make it all better. A friend used to tell me the two were one.

I brought the coffee pot into the living room and set it down on an end table. After a time, Sarah got up and flopped down across from me. I pushed a cup of coffee toward her and she prodded it with a forefinger as if it were alive and dangerous.

"What now?" she said unhappily.

"I'm working for you, ma'am. You tell me."

She worked her jaw noiselessly and looked at me sideways, so that for a moment she looked like a ma'am from Avignon. "What the hell," she said and clapped her hands together. "I can't fight everybody."

I wasn't so sure of that and told her so. Which pleased her.

"I guess I better call Sean and find out whether Les has been in touch with him," she said. "I guess I'd better find out where I stand." She looked at me with a trace of confusion in her blue eyes. "This doesn't mean I'm going to go along with the deal you've arranged. I haven't committed any crimes, yet. I'm not going to compromise myself pointlessly."

"I understand."

"And don't patronize me," she said. "You may not understand it, but my politics are important to me. So are my friends. I wouldn't have survived childhood if it weren't for Sean."

"You two are close?" I asked.

She smiled to herself—a very assured smile. "Would that make a difference to you?"

I hadn't really thought about it, save in passing. Partly because I was out of practice and partly because I hadn't made up my mind about whether or not I was ready to take that kind of chance again. On the surface it seemed too hopelessly complicated by old wounds and new animosities, by distrusts and betrayals. Now it occurred to me, as I watched her smiling that uncanny, Sarah-like smile, that it might make a difference to me. The trouble was I had the uneasy feeling that I could never be completely sure that it would make the same difference to her. Which made me think of Kate, and the letters that weren't being answered.

"What are you thinking about?" she said with a lively grin.

"You don't want to know what I'm thinking about."

"But I do," she said, toying with the top button of her shirt.

"Cut it out, Sarah."

She looked me over for a second, top to toe. I was a little afraid she was about to ask me my sign. "It wouldn't be hard to like you," she said speculatively. "We'd never get along, but it wouldn't be hard to like you."

She sat back in her chair and pondered it like a proposition. "I think I do like you."

"Give it a minute more," I said. "Something'll come to you."

She laughed and pushed back for the coffee table.

"C'mon," she said, standing up. "I want to test out an old adage."

"Which is?"

"Politics make strange bedfellows."

It was my turn to laugh. "You are the strangest damn girl! Just ten minutes ago you wanted to kill me."

"Ten minutes ago I'd forgotten what you did for me last night. Of course, if you aren't interested..." Her voice trailed off and she spun on her heel like an actress making a well-timed exit. Well, Harry? I said to myself. Are you interested? Or are you going to keep on waiting for Kate to call? Oddly enough, it only took me a second to decide.

I caught her by the hand and pulled her down beside me on the armchair. She smelled sweetly of sweat and denim. "Sarah," I said, looking into her eyes. "Do you ever stop acting?"

"Sometimes," she said breathlessly. "Not often. Does it matter?"

I laughed again and slapped her on the rump. "Not at the moment."

She grinned and pulled my head down to her lips.

Sarah was sitting up in bed, Indian-style, her long auburn hair covering her shoulders and the tops of her breasts. Looking at that hard, talented body, I felt like making love to her again.

"Jesus," she said, wide-eyed. "Don't you ever get tired?"

"Someday, Sarah," I said, skimming my fingertips through her hair and over her breasts, "I'll tell you about the last few months. Then, you'll know why I'm not tired at this moment."

She leaned over and kissed me through her hair. "Do you want to make love again?" she whispered.

"I do," I said "But we've got to stop."

She giggled. "Good. Because I'm tired as hell."

While I showered, Sarah made a second breakfast in the kitchen. The smells of bacon and toast drifting through the rooms, the sound of her puttering over the stove, opening and shutting closets, learning where things were, almost moved me to tears. I sat down on the john after I got out of the shower and thought about Kate. That's where Sarah found me.

"Coffee?" She passed a cup through the crack in the

door and peeked in after it. "Hey!" she said, when she saw me sitting, dripping wet, on the toilet. "No towel?"

I stood up and she looked up and down my body and smiled. "You've got nothing to worry about." She put the cup down on the sink and kissed me on the lips.

"You'll get wet," I said.

She threw her head back and laughed. "I don't care." She nuzzled against my chest until her face was slick. "I like the way you smell," she said. "And taste." She ran a sandpapery tongue down my belly, then looked up mischievously.

"We can discuss how I taste later. I've got to get dressed right now."

She made a disappointed face. "All right. But hurry up. I don't want breakfast to go cold, too."

In the living room, Sarah pretended to moon over me. She looked nineteen in the morning light. It made me feel a little guilty for *shtupping* her an hour before.

"Why were you sad just now?" she said as she poured me a cup of coffee.

"I was thinking about someone I know," I said.

"A girl?"

I nodded.

"You still love her?" Sarah asked. "Is that it?"

"You cry when you come. With me, it's the smell of coffee."

"You know I was right—I do *like* you," she said with something like an air of discovery. "For a capitalist pig, you're a decent man. And a good fuck, too."

I looked amusedly at Sarah. "And you've had so much experience."

"You'd be surprised."

"Sean?"

"Jealous, again?"

"Curious," I said. "Tell me about him."

"There's not much to tell," she said. "We've been friends since we were kids. We used to play around with each other—experiment. We still sleep together. But since he's gone radical, he's become militant and monogamous. He doesn't like 'his' lady sleeping with other men. He claims that since the Black Muslim women don't do it, I shouldn't either. As a gesture of solidarity." She laughed. "The truth is he's plain jealous of anybody who looks at me."

"What kind of radical is he?"

"The same kind as I am. A communist. Think of it," Sarah said mysteriously. "You slept with a communist spy."

"Are you?"

She laughed lightly. "Is that what Father told you?"

"He wasn't sure where your politics had led you."

"Politically, I'm a Marxist, but I'm not overly doctrinaire about it. I believe in international communism wherever and however it springs up. Does that bother you?"

"Only when you proselytize. When Sean followed me the day before yesterday, he had company. A thin, black guy with light skin and a goatee."

"Chico," she said. "Chico Robinson. He hangs around the club once in awhile. Chico's a bad dude. He's a Cobra."

"What's a Cobra?"

"It's a special cadre of the Muslims. The Friends have been doing some work with their Avondale chapter, helping them distribute free milk and lunches to neighborhood kids. Chico and Sean became buddies during the operation. They're very tight now. Chico doesn't think much of me. He says I'm soft on discipline."

"And the Cobra business?"

"They're a Muslim sect. I don't know how much of the trash you hear on the streets can be trusted, but the Cobras are said to be enforcers. There's no question that Chico is a mean little man."

"O.K.," I said. "Let's backtrack a little. Two days ago, I was taking pictures of people going in and coming out of the club."

"Why were you doing that?"

"Well, at the time, I thought you were involved in the theft of your father's document. I took the photos to get a notion of the people you were friendly with. I even had the police run makes on the snapshots to see if a real communist spy popped up."

"You did that?" she said angrily.

"Easy, Sarah. I was just doing my job."

"Well, it's a lousy job." She got up from the table and walked into the tiny kitchen. "They knew you were out there," she said after a moment.

"Who?"

"Les and the Weather people. They hang out at the club sometimes. In the back."

"How did they know?"

"Les got a phone call in the club house. Someone must have spotted you from the street."

"What do Weather people do to dumb detectives who take their pictures?"

"They wanted to shoot you. At least, Les did. That's the reason I'm in trouble now. Somehow Les got it in his head that you were a federal agent. Don't ask me how, because I don't know. Anyway, I talked him out of the idea; then he saw you coming out of my house the other day; and when the cops showed up that afternoon, he assumed I'd been lying to him all along."

"That's not very good logic," I said.

"Les is not a logical man."

"What kind of man is he?"

"Tough," she said. "He's been underground for five years, ever since he shot a school superintendent in L.A. Four months ago he drifted into the club. And he's been in and out ever since. He's close to the Weather people and some of the more militant radicals like Sean. They treat him like a hero because of the L.A. thing. But they're afraid of him, too. He can be a very scarey guy."

"How does he feel about you?"

"He used to trust me," she said with heavy irony.

"What happens if you can't get in touch with him or if he won't listen."

"Les is a little crazy, Harry," Sarah said. "Something happened to him during the war. He doesn't talk about it, but Sean knows. When he gets an idea in his head, when he thinks someone's against him or the movement, he just..." Sarah walked down the hall to the bedroom. "I'd better get in touch with Sean. I'd better find out where we stand."

"We?" I said.

"I guess so, Stoner," she said. Sarah brushed the hair back from her face and smiled. "I guess it is *we* from now until this is over. That is, unless you still have any doubts about whether I stole that document and shot poor Papa."

Doubts I had. But not about whether or not she'd killed her father.

* * *

118

While Sarah made her phone calls in the bedroom, I flipped on the Globemaster to one of the few stations that wasn't broadcasting Christmas cheer. With a Brahms quartet playing behind me, I sat back on my Easyboy recliner ($199.95 at Shillito's) and did some more speculating about Lovingwell and his document.

Ever since Wednesday morning I'd been expecting one of Bidwell's charges to pay Sarah a call. The security man would have been polite and businesslike. "Your father checked a top-secret document out of our archives on Saturday afternoon. He was scheduled to return it in two weeks. We're terribly sorry that he's dead, etc. But it's our little secret and we want it back."

So, I asked myself, as I sat in a comfortable chair listening to Brahms and staring through the frosty window at the blue morning sky, how come that hadn't happened? How come Bidwell never even mentioned the document? How come no one cared about it but me?

When you can't answer a question it sometimes helps to rephrase it. So, I asked again, how come no one *knows* about the document but me? Well, I knew why the police, the FBI and Louis Bidwell didn't know about the missing document. Lovingwell hadn't told them it was missing. He'd told me. And for various reasons, I hadn't told anyone but Sarah, who'd claimed she didn't know about it, either. It's embarrassing to keep a secret that no one else is interested in. It's like holding the bag on a snipe hunt or being sent out for a left-handed wrench. It makes you feel foolish, angry, and bitter.

Why would Bidwell delay the recovery of a top-secret document? I asked myself. He could have overlooked it— a remote chance but possible. He could have been waiting a decent interval to ask about it, out of respect for Sarah and the dead man—also remote. He could have sent someone to the Lovingwell home on Wednesday when Sarah had been taken off to jail—less remote but probably impossible, given the fact that he could have subpoenaed her when she was in custody. Or he could have had a reason to conceal his knowledge of the document, which was very possible. Although it didn't seem likely, Lovingwell could have been suspected of espionage; or Sarah could have been under suspicion. Or there was always the chance— the one I myself had proposed to the Professor—that someone else at Sloane (Sarah's erstwhile accomplice) was being investigated and that discussion of the missing document would have jeopardized that investigation. What made the possibility of espionage doubly intriguing was Lovingwell's murder. There had been talk of security leaks at Sloane and of some trouble the Professor might have been in. If he had been meeting with an accomplice on Tuesday afternoon, an accomplice who had some reason to mistrust or to hate or to be done with Daryl Lovingwell, then the killing could be tied to the missing papers. Given the picture Sarah had painted of him, the scenario seemed quite possible. Only, if that were the case, then there was no obvious reason why Lovingwell should have hired me in the first place. And I didn't want to force the facts to fit Sarah's portrait of her father simply because I was attracted to her.

It wouldn't have done any good at that point to ask Bidwell point-blank about the espionage business. He'd give me the same story whether he were lying or telling the truth; and then there would follow that nasty little moment I'd been postponing for several days when the question of how *I* knew about missing secret papers would be raised. Maybe with a vengeance. So, Bidwell was out. At least temporarily. But if I could get my hands on Lovingwell's security file, I could find out part of what I wanted to know. The other part, the vexing question of why I'd been hired, could wait until I settled the espionage issue and the murder itself. That is, unless solving the two somehow resolved the other, which wasn't as comforting a possibility as I might have wished. Hell, we all want things neat. Only in this instance, neatness and symmetry would bring me full circle back to that discomfiting possibility that I thought I'd talked myself out of ten minutes before. The universal law of neatness said that Sarah *was* intimately involved in her father's death and in the disappearance of the document, that our heart-to-heart talk was nothing more than a warm breeze, and that when it had passed the cold, ineluctable climate of hatred and revenge would reassert itself.

Sarah herself startled me out of my reverie by tapping me on the arm. From the look on her face, I could see that something had gone very wrong.

"What is it?" I said. "Did you get in touch with Sean?"

"He's scared, Harry. Les has gone underground again."
She sat down on the arm of my chair and tried not to look
frightened. "Sean says Les told him that he didn't want
to talk, that he's going to kill me."

"Why?" I said. "Why won't he talk?"

She shook her head very slowly. "He's crazy, Harry.
He's really crazy."

I took her hand and she gave me a quick, unhappy
smile. "He's going to do it, Harry. I know him. He's going
to kill me."

"No, he's not."

I patted her hand and walked over to the phone and
dialed McMaster's office.

"What are you doing?" she asked.

"We need some reinforcements, Sarah. I'm going to get
Sid to arrange FBI surveillance."

"FBI!" she said with horror. "My God, he'll really think
I've betrayed him now."

"What do you mean *really?*" I said to her. "Do you want
him to kill you?"

She shook her head again.

"Then we've got to have help."

"The FBI," Sarah said with astonishment. "I don't believe this is happening!"

McMasters wasn't pleased with what I told him, either.

"That kind of blows our deal, doesn't it, Harry? I mean
if the girl can't get in touch with him, why shouldn't I just
put both of you back in jail?"

"For one thing, she's innocent," I said. "And for another
Grimes wants to kill her. If you want him, you'll keep her
on the outside."

"I'll think it over," he said.

McMasters thought it over and called back fifteen minutes later to tell me that the protection had been arranged.
"They're already at your place."

"Am I supposed to contact them?"

"No. Just let things happen."

"Act normal, huh?"

"Your shadow is an agent named Ted Lurman. He's
about six-foot, thirty-five years old, blonde hair. He'll be
wearing a blue pin-stripe suit and he'll have sunglasses
on."

"In December?"

"You tell me, Harry. He's supposed to be in the lobby of the Delores right now. Two other guys, dressed as phone company repairmen, will be coming to the apartment to look after the girl."

"O.K.," I said. "I guess that'll have to do. Is there anything you want to tell me about the Lovingwell case?"

He laughed. "You've got brass. All right, we did uncover a couple of odd things. Over the last few months, Lovingwell had been reorganizing his finances. Converting bonds, selling off stocks. Withdrawing funds from his savings account at Central Trust. He may have been planning a trip of some kind; but we can't connect it up with the murder."

"Maybe he was afraid of someone," I said, thinking of that suppositious accomplice. "Maybe he was planning to get out."

"We thought of that. That fellow O'Hara hasn't been too cooperative—especially after we roughed up his kid. But it seems that he and Lovingwell had some sort of grudge match going on, only it dates back a lot of years."

"What about?"

"You ask a lot of questions for a guy harboring a suspected felon. By the way, the lab has finished with Lovingwell's body. The girl can claim it any time she wants."

"I'll tell her," I said.

While I finished getting dressed, Sarah called her Friends of Nature again.

"What's the word?" I said when I came back into the living room.

"Sean can't get in touch with him until tonight." Sarah looked at me anxiously. "Maybe it's a good thing you called the FBI. Are you going out?"

"I'm going to talk to Michael O'Hara. Beth Hemann, the department secretary, told me that your father wanted to speak to him on Tuesday morning. I'd like to know why. What do you think of O'Hara, by the way?"

Sarah gave me one of her odd, disconcerting looks. But then she was a master of them. "He was good to my mother before she died. She made him executor of her estate and my trust fund. She liked him."

"But you don't."

"He's all right," she said without enthusiasm. "He's run

by his wife—or at least he used to be before they separated—and I don't care much for her. I had the feeling that she was involved with my father at one time."

"Recently?" I said with interest.

Sarah shook her head. "Years ago. Do you want me to come with you to see Mike?"

I thought about Lurman and said, "No. You'll be safe here. Two FBI men dressed as telephone repairmen will come up when I leave. I'll talk to O'Hara, then I'll come back and we can all sit down and plot a little strategy."

"How long are we going to have to put up with this?"

"Until it's over," I told her.

15

Lurman was leaning against a drooping rubber tree in the tiny lobby. He was trying to look inconspicuous in his pin-stripe suit and dark green sunglasses, but he'd only succeeded in looking decent and uncomfortable. When I walked past him, out the front door of the Delores, he counted ten and followed.

There was snow on the pavement from the previous day's storm; and, on Burnet, a woman in a maroon Buick was spinning her wheels in the slush. From the side she looked like a small-town widow—thin, thin-lipped, with a stern irreproachable face. But when she turned my way, she gave me such a pathetic frown that I walked out into the street and started shoving the rear of her car. I almost laughed when I caught sight of Lurman, vacillating in an access of indecision between the lobby and the sidewalk. If he was the FBI's idea of discretion, I was in for an embarrassing afternoon. The woman's car finally broke free of the ice. She waved at me through the rear window and I could see her tight little mouth form the sentence: "God bless you!" After she'd driven off, weaving through the slush and coughing blue exhaust into the morning air, I crooked a finger at hapless Lurman and started down the side stairs that led to the parking lot. Lurman walked very deliberately to a black Chevrolet parked in front of

125

the Delores and stood by the door. He patted the hood a couple of times, in case I hadn't gotten the message.

Once I got the Pinto started, I puttered around to the front of the building, where Lurman pulled out behind me. As we drove away, I could see two telephone repairmen getting out of a second black Chevy. The FBI! I thought.

Because of the snow it took me almost ten minutes to get to Clifton. I kept Lurman in my rearview mirror all the way. We passed McMicken Hall, looking stately in its mantle of snow, crossed Riddle, and headed east down St. Clair. I parked in the underground lot below the Physics Building and waited in the Pinto until Lurman had found a place of his own. I was making jokes about him, but deep-down I was happy to have an armed escort.

Lurman followed me at a decent distance into the Physics Building and down the big, whitewashed hallway to O'Hara's office. When he saw me knock at the department door, he stopped at a marble water fountain and pretended to take a drink.

"Hello," Miss Hemann said as I walked up to her desk. "He's on his way to a meeting with the Chancellor, but he might have a few minutes to spare."

"What makes you so sure I didn't come to talk to you?"

She threw her hand at me and laughed. "Mr. Stoner," she said playfully. "Shall I tell him you're here?"

"Please."

She went into the inner office and came back out a second later. "You can go in," she said.

O'Hara was looking spry and outdoorsy in an open-collared flannel shirt.

"Mr. Stoner!" he boomed. "How's the detective business?"

"Right now, not so good."

"Sorry to hear it," he said. "But don't despair. Being a mathematician, I dabble in statistics and I'd be willing to bet that there's some dirty little crime being committed right now with your name on it."

"Thanks, but I'm booked up. The Lovingwell murder, for instance."

"Are there no policemen? No courts? No grand juries?"

"I was kind of hoping we could skip the sarcasm this trip and talk about your friend."

"What friend?"

126

"You know. That colleague you wouldn't tell any stories about—out of respect."

O'Hara looked at me shrewdly. "Daryl and I didn't get along. It's common knowledge. That doesn't mean I'm going to reveal his private life to every Tom, Dick, and Harry that comes in off the street."

"This Harry's been hired by Sarah Lovingwell to look into her father's death."

O'Hara leaned back in his chair. "Is that right? I've always been fond of Sarah. It's rather a miracle that she survived in one piece, given her father's personality."

I started to say something about his own offspring but let it pass. "Over the last few days I've learned a good deal about Daryl Lovingwell. Most of it contradictory. On the surface he seemed to be a charming and intelligent man."

"He was that, certainly. It's odd how eccentricities can border on neurosis. Much of Daryl's character was poised like that. He sometimes reminded me of a very ornate, highly polished mirror. Brilliant on the surface, but if you scratched through the mica . . . there was a very dark side underneath."

"On the day of his death," I said, "Lovingwell tried to get in touch with you before phoning his daughter. Can you think of a reason why he'd be so anxious to talk?"

"I can think of half a dozen reasons. We went to a faculty party on Sunday and he bent my ear for an hour or so about his work and about Sarah."

"What about Sarah?"

"He was worried about her," O'Hara said. "He was afraid she was slipping off into depression. You know her mother was a depressive. I suppose he saw some of the same symptoms in Sarah. I think it frightened him. But then it was always hard to tell what Daryl really thought about anything." O'Hara seemed to study my face for a second. When he couldn't find what he was looking for, he stared dully at the papers on his desk. "We never hit it off, Daryl and I. He objected to my, shall we say, athleticism. And his quirks always struck me as posed." He looked back up at me and smiled like a jackal. "You say you've spent a few days investigating him? I worked with the man for eight years and never understood him. I don't know if he understood himself. He was a little mad, Daryl Lovingwell."

"You and he had a dispute some years ago?"

O'Hara glared at me, as if I were pushing his good spirits just a bit too far. "The McPhail business is a dead letter. It was only a disagreement over the status of a graduate student. A sad, good-hearted young man. Daryl was unhappy about the outcome, and I'd be lying if I said that academic politics can't get vicious at times. But there was no bad blood between us afterward. At least, no blood that hadn't been bad before."

I thought about what McMasters had told me—about Lovingwell's financial arrangements—and said, "You don't think he would have left the department because of this McPhail business, do you?"

"I told you," he said, coloring. "That was seven years ago. Anyway, Daryl had an endowed chair. He would never have left this department."

"One last question?" I said.

"It'll have to be brief," he said. "I have a meeting to get to."

"The night that Lovingwell talked to you about Sarah, did he mention anything about some missing papers?"

"No." O'Hara got up from his desk and I followed him out of his office. "He mentioned no papers to me," he said as he opened the outer door. "Just Sarah. And now you'll have to excuse me."

He walked briskly down the hall.

"He doesn't seem to like my company," I said to Miss Hemann who was bent over her typewriter.

"That's hardly fair, is it?" she said without looking up. "I did tell you he had an appointment." She stopped typing and eyed me curiously. "Why are you asking him all these things, anyway?"

It was a very good question, for which I didn't have a good answer. And for some reason I wanted to give her a good answer. "It's the job," I said a bit helplessly and then felt embarrassed for having said it.

I sat down on a chair beside the desk and smiled foolishly at her. "It's not just idle curiosity, believe me."

"Oh, I believe you," she said. "But you sound as if you could use some proof yourself."

"It hasn't been my brightest week."

"It hasn't been much of a week for any of us," she said drily.

I leaned back in the chair and stared at the photographs hanging on the wall across from me. "Do *you* have any idea what Professor Lovingwell wanted to talk over with your boss on Tuesday morning?" I asked her.

"Lord, no," she said. "It could have been anything."

I thought of what Sarah had told me and said, "Could it have been about the chairman's wife?"

Beth Hemann blushed bright red. "What in the world do you mean?"

"When people bring the world into it," I said, "they ususally know what is meant."

"I have no idea what you're talking about," she said stiffly. "If anything, Professor Lovingwell probably wanted to talk about his own family. He'd been having problems with his daughter, you know."

Who didn't? I said to myself. Who hadn't he told about Sarah? The pattern was unsettling me. First Bidwell at Sloane. Then O'Hara. And Miss Hemann. And you, too, Harry, I told myself. You, too. In a certain light all our conversations about his daughter could be viewed as admonitory and solicitous. Her impetuousness, her drugs, her communism, her hatred of his work. They all contributed to a picture of a rather desperate and misguided girl. One who could easily steal a document or be made to look as if she had. He hadn't really lied to me—not in any obvious details. But when I thought it over, I realized how much of my original reaction to Sarah had been shaped by comparison to the portrait Lovingwell had drawn. Only I also realized that a lot of my suspicion had been inspired by the portrait Sarah had drawn of him.

Wouldn't it be nice, I thought, if you could know in advance just who was grinding which ax. And why.

I got up from the chair and walked over to the wall hung with photographs. His face was everywhere—finger by his nose and devilish little beard jutting out like a dagger. I studied one of the pictures. It had been taken at a Christmas party. Lovingwell was sitting at the head of the table. The festive party hat on his head made him look like a mischievous elf. There was a blonde woman at his side, also wearing a party-hat and gazing at him with mild amusement. She was a striking-looking woman with a high-cheeked, triangular face, puffed past its prime but still recognizably a smart, stylish face.

"Who's this?" I said to Miss Hemann.

She held a pair of half-frame glasses to her nose and peered at the picture. "That's Mrs. O'Hara."

"What kind of woman is she?" I asked her.

"Awful," Beth Hemann said and clapped a hand to her mouth.

I laughed.

"I shouldn't have said that," she said with another blush. "I have no right to say that."

"Oh, hell, Miss Hemann," I said. "I won't tell anyone."

She pulled sharply at her plain white blouse. "Professor O'Hara won't be back for the rest of the day. So you see there's nothing more I can do for you."

"Oh, Miss Hemann," I said, giving her a wink. "Don't say that, darling. There's no telling what you could do for me."

She smiled. "You're full of blarney, Mr. Stoner."

"Where does Mrs. O'Hara live, Miss Hemann? In Clifton?"

She nodded and gave me an address on Bishop Street. "Are you going to try to talk to Meg?" she said.

I shrugged. "Sooner or later, someone's going to tell me something I want to hear. Why do you ask?"

"I don't like her," she said plainly. "And it would please me if she were involved in Professor Lovingwell's death."

You never really know about other people. What I had thought was a shallow loyalty to her boss was beginning to look something very much like love in this plainspoken, plain-looking young woman. It gave her character and a prettiness born of anger. There was a shape under that drab white wrapper and, given the access of real feeling, it began to swell attractively.

She caught me looking at her and, this time, *she* winked and bit rather charmingly at her lower lip.

"You're a surprising girl, Miss Hemann," I said.

"I like to think so."

"Is there some reason why you think Meg O'Hara might be involved in Lovingwell's death?"

"No," she said. "It just wouldn't surprise me, that's all. She's not a pleasant woman."

"You care a great deal for Professor O'Hara, don't you?"

130

She eyed me coolly. "That hoyden has made his life a shambles. She's ruined his marriage; she's spoiled his son; and now she's taken his home."

"They're divorced?" I asked.

She nodded. "They're about to be. Now I've told you quite enough. And I'd appreciate it if you wouldn't repeat what I've said."

"It'll be our little secret," I promised her.

The O'Hara house on Bishop Street was one of the half-dozen Frank Lloyd Wright originals scattered throughout the city. This was one of his early designs—stolidly nine-teenth-centuryish, but still quite interesting. Beneath the Victorian facade—the round, pillared porch, snow-filled flowerboxes, and massive windows—you could see the twentieth-century mind at work in bold curves and sur-prising planes. The house made me think of Phidias or Rodin or whoever it was who had said of statuary that the design is already there in the stone. Like a half-carved block of marble, the genial, rambling home made a new language of dead proprieties.

It couldn't have been easy to give up a house like that. It wouldn't have been for me. But then O'Hara's divorce didn't really interest me. Meg O'Hara interested me. At least I was interested in what she had to say about Daryl Lovingwell.

She answered the door on the third knock. Blonde, full in the face and upper body. Quite handsome, nevertheless, with a thin crooked mouth like the beak of a tortoise. She was dressed out of Saks—raw silk blouse open at the neck and loose, black slacks that shook like jello when she moved her legs. She asked me what I wanted in a hoarse voice that smelled of whiskey and Sen-Sen. When I told her I was working for Sarah Lovingwell, her puffy eyes plummeted to the welcome mat, as if I'd dropped something untidy at her feet.

"I must look a mess," she said, fussing with her hair. "C'mon in."

I followed her down the front hall to a bright blue sitting room, furnished fussily in ivory orientals and nubby off-white furniture. She seated me on a couch and walked through a door into what must have been the kitchen. A few minutes later she came back out with a silver coffee server on a silver tray. She handed me a bone china demitasse and asked, "Sugar or cream?" She was Daryl Lovingwell's kind of girl, all right.

I told her I didn't want sugar *or* cream, and she nodded with approval. "You like it black," she said. "So do I."

Meg O'Hara sat down opposite me on a wingback chair and looked me over scrupulously. It was one of the few times in my life that I felt like a woman was undressing me with her eyes. "I've never seen a private detective before," she said curiously. "Are they all as good-looking as you?"

"Yes," I said.

She troubled her coffee with a tiny silver spoon and made bedroom eyes at me. "You have a classically handsome face, Mr. Stoner. A little bruised but handsome. Does it bother you that I like the way you look?"

"No. I like the way I look, too."

"Since we're agreed," she said, putting the saucer down on a smoked-glass coffee table, "what say we find out if beauty is skin deep?"

I grinned and thought of Sarah. "What say we skip along to the cigarettes and small talk?"

"As you will," she said casually. "Although I want you to know that I wasn't kidding. Whiskey and fucking aren't laughing matters in this household."

"I wasn't kidding, either. Let's talk first."

"About what?" she said.

"About you and Daryl Lovingwell."

She sat back in her chair with the look of a professor who's just been disappointed by one of his favorite students. "Get out of here," she said.

"That was a quick romance, Mrs. O'Hara," I said. "Do you mind telling me why you want me to go?"

"Yes. I mind."

"Why don't I tell you, then?" I said, moving forward on the couch so I could get a better look at her eyes. It wasn't going to hurt to stir the waters a bit. With a woman of her temper, there was no telling what might pop up. "You were having an affair with Daryl Lovingwell. And he wanted to break it off. He'd grown tired of you. But you didn't want him to leave, did you? The shooting on Tuesday could have been an accident. I'd believe it."

I'd watched her face closely as I'd run through my spiel.

132

She'd shown interest when I'd spoken of the affair, shifting her eyes slightly to the right as right-handed people will do when they're asked a question or are answering one. She was asking herself how much I really knew. But when I got to the accusation of murder, her eyes settled comfortably on mine and her thin, twisted mouth relaxed in a loose, predatory smile. I hadn't struck home. I hadn't even come close. And she knew I was bluffing.

"That's a very interesting story," she said, wetting her lips. "Now let me tell you one of my own. Michael put you up to this. Michael or that twig of a woman he calls a lover. There's nothing he'd like better than to make people think I was a criminal. Suspected murderers don't generally fare well in community property hearings, do they? Well, you go back to Michael, old stick, and tell him your bluff didn't work. He should have known better than to think I could be scared by a faggot detective."

"Trying to blacken your husband's character isn't going to help your case before a judge, Mrs. O'Hara. Your affair with Lovingwell is well-documented."

"I don't know where you've been getting your information, beauty. But my affair with Daryl Lovingwell ended six years ago. And I'll tell you something else. The only reason someone would have killed that man was money. That was all he was interested in, that was all he ever thought about. You go find somebody Daryl was scheming with, you go dig up some dirty plot that involved thousands of dollars and some underhanded deal—you'll find your killer, all right. Now, get the hell back to Michael and tell him he'll have to do better than this. Who the hell are you, anyway?"

"A faggot detective," I said, "working for Sarah Lovingwell."

For a second time, Sarah's name gave her pause. "I have nothing against the girl," she said quickly. "Her mother and I were close friends once."

Allowing me to see anything more than the bitchy, temperamental side of her character had a curious effect on Meg O'Hara. Her face turned bright red beneath the powder and she pounded herself on the legs with clenched fists. It wasn't embarrassment; it was fury. She was enraged at herself for dropping her guard, like a fighter who slaps his own head when he misses a punch. She must have had a lot of enemies in her lifetime, I thought.

She caught me feeling sorry for her and jumped to her feet. "Get the hell out of here!" she shouted. "Get the hell out of my house!"

"It's not yours yet, honey," I said.

"Get out!" she shrieked.

I walked down the hall and back out into the cold December afternoon. I hadn't really learned much—all Meg O'Hara had done was confirm what Sarah had told me about her father's greed. But it *was* a confirmation. And when I added that greed to the missing document and the way he'd been talking about Sarah and the murder itself, it made the espionage idea seem more and more like a good idea.

16

Before returning to the Delores, I drove south on Vine to the Clifton Plaza—a flat, ugly line of shops fronted by a huge parking lot—and pulled in beside Bullet's hi-fi store. Through the picture window I could see Bullet jawing at the register with a customer. Behind them, in the show-room itself, Larry Soldi was wiring a speaker into the console. I waited until Lurman had parked the rear of the lot before getting out of the Pinto.

"Harry!" Bullet said cheerfully as I walked through the door. "Where you been? I've been looking for you in the Bee all week."

"I've got some trouble, Bullet. I need to talk to Larry."

"What am I?" he said. "Chopped liver?"

"This just isn't something you can help me with."

"Larry!" Bullet barked.

Soldi ambled out from the rear of the store—a gaunt, chicken-necked, thirty-year-old white man with a lumpy, cheerful face and the hang-dog posture of the hired man. That was Larry's fate—to play second fiddle throughout his life to the more enterprising soloists like Bullet. He could have had it a lot worse. Bullet was better than a decent employer. But in spite of the fact that he had a good job and seemed happy in his work, Soldi always struck me as a sad case. One of those proverbial types for whom the Army had been the only moment in life that wasn't tainted by the past. I knew Larry enjoyed talking about the war, his voice mellowed when he spoke of it, and the words spilled out energetically, instead of lumbering, as they usually did, out of his throat. But casting him strictly in the role of loser was just an unflattering bit of condescension on my part. It wasn't Larry I felt sorry for in that mood, but the supine and childish part of myself that hated work, and maybe, the very idea of work itself.

I saluted him as he walked up to the register, and he said, "Hey, Harry!"

"Hey, yourself."

"What can I do for you?" he said, tucking his thumbs into his pants' pockets.

"You ever heard of an ex-Marine named Lester Grimes?"

He shook his head.

"Well, the guy's a psychopath. A real shoot-'em-up, gun-totin' maniac. And I want to know how to defend myself against him."

"You can call the cops," Bullet said, reaching for the phone.

"No. I already have police protection. What I need is a profile—a description of the way a gung-ho ex-Marine might go about killing a civilian like me."

"What kind of training did he have?" Soldi said and, already, his voice had taken on assurance.

"He was a weapons specialist."

"That's bad. He'll know how to use automatics and, if he served in 'Nam, he'll know about booby-trapping, too."

"This guy fancies himself a cowboy," I said.

Soldi laughed. "We didn't see a lot of cowboys in my outfit. Unless you can call the recon people cowboys."

"LURPs?" I said.

He nodded. "I only knew one. A guy named Frisco. He'd been in 'Nam since sixty-six. He wore his hair long, like a hippie's. Had a gold earring in his ear. A leather headband. A peace emblem on his fatigue jacket. He'd popped so much dex his teeth had turned black. And I mean *nobody* told Frisco to shape up. Nobody even came close enough to try. The dude always carried two .45s on him, even in camp." Soldi shook his head. "Recon guys were freaky, Harry. You must have seen a few of them, so you know. Every night for months they'd dress up in tiger suits, paint their faces, walk off the LZ and—whoosh!—

they'd be gone into the jungle. They'd be out there in the bush all alone until morning. Doing recon on VC base camps. And killing. Scarey, man. Real scarey. A lot of our own troops used to look away when Frisco'd walk by, because it was like looking at a living dead man, you know. Grunts made jokes about it. Making the sign of the cross after Frisco'd pass by and shit like that. But you can bet your ass they never pulled that crap when he was looking. 'Cause he'd have killed them on the spot and nobody higher up would have said a thing. I hate to say it, but if the dude you're talking about is anything like Frisco, you're in big trouble."

"How would a guy like Frisco come at you?" I said.

"Quick. Probably at night. And he'll be armed to the teeth. There's a chance he'll flip out before he gets to you, 'cause dudes like that were wired like Claymores. Sooner or later they always blew themselves up. That's what happened to Frisco. One day he just walked off into the jungle with a knife in his belt and that was the end of it. Don't try talking to this guy. Dudes like Frisco just don't have anything to say. If you see him before he sees you, my advice is kill him. And make sure the bastard's dead, too, 'cause he'll have lots of juice working for him and he'll have a dozen different ways of wasting you."

I leaned back against the glass counter and rubbed the bridge of my nose. "So all I can hope to do is beat him to the draw."

"I'm sorry, Harry," Soldi said. "But that's the way it is. Guys like that just won't walk into a trap. Man, they used to sit around for hours without moving a muscle, just waiting for the right moment to do their work."

"Well thanks, Larry," I said to him.

Soldi walked back to the rear of the shop and I could almost see the energy draining out of him with each step. Bullet looked at me a long moment and said what I'd been thinking, "Harry, you're in real trouble."

It took me a quarter of an hour to convince Bullet that there was no way he could help me. And at that I wasn't sure he'd really bought what I told him. I didn't like the way he was looking at me as I left the store—like I was a piece of equipment with his own personal five-year warranty on my chest. To be honest, after talking to Larry

Soldi, I didn't like the look of anyone or anything on the mall—the blue-haired woman with a shopping bag on her arm who was gazing into Walgreen's window, the black kids hanging around the liquor store, the Samoyed nosing at some garbage in a wire trash can, and, least of all, Ted Lurman, who was leaning up against his Chevy pretending he was a station chief in Paris. Wake up, man! I almost shouted at him.

It wasn't that Soldi had told me anything I didn't already know. It was just having it confirmed so thoroughly that shook me up. Because if Larry were right, there'd be no percentage in sitting around waiting for Lester to show his hand. He'd have to be tracked down. And then he'd have to be killed. And if I didn't want Sarah and me to end up as casualties in an FBI set-up that backfired, I'd have to make sure the killing was done as coolly and efficiently as possible. That meant I'd have to have some help. I'd have to have access to an informant who could tell me precisely where Grimes was going to be at precisely the right moment.

As I drove back to the Delores I began to form a little plan. If Sarah could get Sean O'Hara and some of the other Friends of Nature to cooperate with us, we might be able to track Grimes down that very night. The trick would be getting O'Hara to play ball. If he wouldn't the FBI could always tail him and his friend Chico Robinson until they led us to Grimes's lair. And once that was over, I could get back to the document and Daryl Lovingwell.

Sarah answered the door when I returned to the apartment. She had wrapped her auburn hair in a plaid scarf. Standing barefoot in her peg-leg jeans and checked shirt, she looked domestic and adorable.

"Hello, lady," I said, kissing her on the lips.

"Hello, man."

"Why so housewifely?" I said as I hung up my coat.

"We have guests."

"And did you have a nice morning?"

Sarah shrugged. "It could have been worse. They could have been Republicans."

The two telephone repairmen were sitting on the living room couch. One of them was about twenty-five, short, with a flushed, pretty, Italian face. He eyed Sarah hungrily as we walked up to them. The other guy was looking straight at me. He was about fifty, stocky, balding, and morose—a big-boned man with the grave, sad-eyed face of a Methodist elder.

"Harry Stoner," I said.

The young one said, "Ed Lionelli. This is my partner, Carl Sturdevant."

"Where's Lurman?" Sturdevant said in a deep, unfriendly voice.

"He was right behind me. I guess he'll be up in a minute."

Sturdevant looked at his watch. "We've got to get cracking," he said. "We've got to make some plans."

I looked at Sturdevant and knew immediately that he was dangerous. A red-baiter. A holdover from the Hoover regime. He was the type who could get Sarah and me killed and feel righteous about it. I started to tell him what he could do with his plans when Lurman knocked at the door. Sarah ushered him into the room, and as he walked past me, he flipped off the dark green glasses and held out his hand.

"Ted Lurman," he said.

"Harry Stoner."

Lurman nodded to Lionelli and Sturdevant and surveyed the room. "You into stereo?"

"No. I just stopped at the store to talk to a friend."

"I used to be," he said. "In the service. Hell, I could pick up a Revox A-700 for six bills in Germany."

"I think they're well over a thousand bucks here," I said.

Lurman smiled. "I know. I sold two of them in New York when I got stateside."

Now, this is more like it, I said to myself. "I thought you guys were all honesty and light."

"We are," he said. "Actually things have kind of loosened up since Hoover broke his promise to himself and died. Isn't that right, Ed?"

Lionelli stared at Sarah and practically licked his lips. "Yeah, we're real loose now."

"Did you get any action on the street?" Sturdevant said. Lurman shook his head.

"Then we'll have to smoke him."

"Hold on," I said.

139

Sturdevant burped in surprise.

"You were saying?" Lurman said.

I sat down on the Easy-Boy and Sarah drifted in behind me. "How much do you know about the way Lester Grimes operates?"

"We know he's a smart, dangerous, and slightly crazy man," Lurman said. "He's good with weapons and he's clever. The job he did on that school superintendent was a work of art."

"How so?"

"He just timed it to perfection. We went back over the scene and we figure he must have sat in front of the building opposite superintendent Bolter's apartment for two or three hours. In broad daylight, mind you. With a machine pistol under his coat. About five Bolter draws the living room curtains and Grimes pulls out the piece, loads it, and shoots him six times before the poor bastard can let go of the drawstring."

"He's that good a shot?" I said.

"Deadly and proficient. We're not sure, but we think he may have killed a narcotics agent in San Francisco, too," Lurman said. "This time, he used a shotgun. At close range."

"A sawed-off?" I said with a shudder.

"Yeah. It's paradoxical. One crime in the style of a Mafia button-man and the other like a barroom brawler."

"What about the 'Cowboy' business?"

"Apparently he's been fascinated with guns and gunmen most of his life. Some of the people we interviewed in California said he liked to switch hats. Some days he was the good guy and some days the bad. Some days he was the town sheriff and others the hot-blooded outlaw. It's not that he's completely looney. He knows that there's more than a little wrong with him; and he's been known to warn friends away when he thinks he's losing control. What he is is a paranoid with a wry sense of humor; and the Cowboy act is a way of dramatizing his own craziness."

"How the hell did someone like him get involved in radical politics?"

"A lot of vets did," Lurman said. "You know men just can't come back home after seeing a lot of death and sit down at the old spot at the table and swallow the same pap. Look who was doing all the sniping in the Miami riots. Lester was involved in the Vets Against the War movement back in the early seventies and drifted from that into more violent protests."

I took a deep breath and glanced up at Sarah. She was staring somberly at Ted Lurman. I touched her hand and she looked down at me. "Do you think you can get in touch with Sean again?"

"Why?"

"We need his help," I said. "Grimes is a trained killer and I don't think he's going to walk into any trap that we set up. He's going to kill us in his own sweet time and maybe these gentlemen will get him after we're dead and maybe they won't. Our only real chance to stay alive is to find Grimes *before* he finds us. And Sean can help us find him."

Sarah knit her brow. "If you expect Sean to betray Les, he won't do it."

"Not even for you?"

"Christ, Harry, that's lousy."

"Yes. It's a choice between lousy and dead."

"Once he finds out that we've thrown in with the FBI, Sean may not even talk to me, much less help me."

"I've got an answer for that one, too. But you're going to hate it."

Sarah stared at me coldly. "You mean lie to him, don't you?"

I nodded. "You don't tell him about the FBI. You don't tell him the real reason we want to find Grimes. You just tell him that you want to make amends with Cowboy. Tell him that you've broken off with me. Set up a time and place for the reconciliation, and we'll go in your place."

"God," Sarah hissed.

"Do you think I would say it if I could think of anything else? Christ, Sarah, it's him or us now."

"I'll think it over," she said tartly and stalked off into the bedroom. I sat back in the chair and lit a cigarette.

"That's your idea?" Lurman asked after a moment.

"That's *the* idea, buddy," I snapped. "There isn't going to be any set-up on this one. No decoys. And that girl isn't going to be involved in the pay-off. When we hunt down Grimes, it's just going to be you, me, and your two friends."

"It's a good idea," Lurman said.

141

I took a deep drag and blew it out. "It's a shitty idea. But if O'Hara plays along, it'll work."

I filled the three agents in on what I knew about Grimes, O'Hara, and Robinson; and we decided that if Sean wouldn't cooperate, we'd split up and follow him and Chico in the hope that one of them would lead us to the Cowboy. While Sturdevant and Lionelli were discussing how the tail should be run, I pulled Lurman into the kitchen and asked him for a favor.

"Do you know a security man named Louis Bidwell?" I said.

"Chief at Sloane?"

I nodded. "I want you to get a copy of Daryl Lovingwell's security file from him."

"Does it have anything to do with Grimes?" Lurman said.

I didn't even have to think about the lie. I just looked him in the eye and said, "Yes."

"All right," Lurman said. "I'll see what I can do."

After setting that wheel in motion, I walked into the bedroom to talk with Sarah. She was stretched out on the blanket, face-down, her head buried in the pillows. When I touched her on the shoulder, she turned over and looked unhappily into my face.

"You think I'm being a shit, don't you?" I said. "That I'm enjoying this?"

"I don't think you enjoy it, but they're my friends. At least, Sean is."

"You still love him?" I asked.

Sarah wiped her eyes with her fingertips and said, "I like him. What does that have to do with it?"

"Nothing," I said. "I guess I was being 'jealous' again." She laughed half-heartedly. "I know it's lousy, but if you don't want to be involved in the violence, it has to be done this way."

"There's violence and there's violence." Sarah sat up on the bed and drew her knees to her chin. "This is a bad thing, Harry. You must feel it, too. I told you before—I don't think I would have survived adolescence without Sean."

"Sarah, the cold truth is that you're not going to survive adulthood without him."

142

"I know," she said. "I'd just like to have the illusion of a choice." She brushed her hair back and got up off the bed. "I'll call him. But I can't lie to him."

"Sarah, you might as well cut your own throat. If O'Hara tells Grimes what we're up to, he'll have the edge."

"Sean won't tell him."

"How can you be so sure?"

"Because he loves me, Harry," she said flatly.

I thought it over. "You'll be trading on his feeling for you."

"How nice of you to put it that way."

"You're the one that wants the illusion of a choice."

"Yes," she said bitterly. "I'll be trading on his feelings. But, at least, I won't be lying about why I'm doing it. And now I better go make that call. If I think about it too much, I'll chicken out."

I left the room, and, a minute later, I could hear her dialing the phone.

When I walked back into the bedroom, Sarah was wearing her scruples on her sleeve. But there was a little human triumph mixed with the remorse.

"He'll meet with us," she said simply.

"When?"

"Tonight. In the lot at Old Coney. You and I are to come alone." Sarah stretched out on the bed and stared at the ceiling. "I ought to feel worse than I do," she said earnestly.

"The hair shirts are in the big bureau, second drawer from the bottom."

She rolled on her side and smirked at me. "It's just that it was too easy. I thought he would be more principled than he was, and now that it's done I'm disappointed in him. He owed it to himself and the movement to refuse me."

"Your father was right," I said with a sigh. "He told me you could never do a thing halfway."

"Him." She waved her hand. "If it wasn't for him, none of this would have happened. No picture-taking, no Cowboy, no FBI."

"No us, either," I said.

Sarah smiled. "Well, I hadn't thought of that," she confessed. "On the other hand, we might have met anyway."

"But would we have made love, anyway?"

143

"It's an interesting question." Sarah rolled over to me, put her hands around my neck, and pressed her forehead against mine. "How does it look from here?"

"Doubtful," I said.

"You're not supposed to look," she said with mock petulance. "You're supposed to commune."

"Is that how the communists do it?"

Sarah butted me hard.

"Ow!" I said.

"Damn it," she said suddenly. "I'm mad!"

"Well, take it out on someone else," I said, rubbing my forehead.

"You know what I think—I think Father planned this whole thing to get me in trouble with Lester."

"You want to hear something strange?" I said. "I found out this morning that your papa told O'Hara that he was worried about your mental health. Two days ago, Louis Bidwell at Sloane told me dear old Dad had told him the same thing."

"I must have been acting crazier than I thought."

I shook my head. "Maybe your father wanted people to think you were crazy. Maybe that's why he hired me."

"Because he thought I was crazy?"

"Crazy enough to steal a top-secret document."

"That damn thing again," she said.

"That damn thing may be the key to this whole mess."

Sarah frowned and, for a second, all the playfulness went out of her face. "Why can't you let it alone, Harry? Isn't Les enough? Why don't you just forget that thing?"

I said, "What would you think if I told you that your father was a spy?"

Sarah gawked at me, then started to laugh. "Father?" she said merrily. "A spy?"

"It fits with all the information I've been able to gather."

"A spy!" Sarah roared.

"Look. Your father told at least two people he thought you were crazy, then he hired me to keep an eye on you. In the meantime, he was converting stocks and bonds into cash—in short, acting like somebody preparing to make a quick getaway. This morning, Meg O'Hara told me that she thought money would be at the bottom of this business. And I think she might be right."

Sarah stopped laughing. "Explain your theory."

It took me a moment to collect my thoughts, because in a way I was explaining the theory to myself, as well. "Say your father had been surreptitiously photographing documents and selling them for cash. Say someone, maybe Bidwell, was catching on. Not to your father, but to whomever your father was working with at the lab. In order to divert suspicion, your father fakes a robbery."

"Fakes it!" Sarah said with astonishment.

"Yeah, I'm pretty sure it was faked. At the time I examined the study I knew something was fishy—only at the time I thought someone was setting your father up."

"Someone meaning me?"

"That's the way it looked. But I didn't know your father then. He was an amazing man."

"Marvelous," Sarah said acidly.

"If I'm right, he showed real genius in planting the original clues—the envelope in your closet, the prints on the safe. They were perfect clues, and I mean that quite literally. Perfectly unsmudged prints, perfect and perfectly available evidence. They were so perfect that he knew they'd be ambiguous and so perfectly ambiguous that he could play them anyway he chose. Or anyway I chose. That's the beauty of it. If I was too dumb to smell a set-up, the clues pointed to you. If I was smart enough to see an unknown hand behind their arrangement, they still pointed to you. It took genius, all right. And a certain degree of malevolence that still astonishes me, in spite of what I've learned about your father's character. If my theory is right, he set you up cold-bloodedly to divert suspicion from himself. While the police and I were busy trying to prove your guilt or innocence, he was preparing to skip the country. Once he'd straightened out the financial side of it, I suppose he would have called Bidwell about the document, reluctantly confessed his suspicions, pointed out that he'd hired a man to look into it, and said that he was going away for a few days to think the matter out. A couple of days would have stretched to a couple of months—while you were cooling off in the slammer—and by the time the lie was unraveled, he'd have disappeared for good."

"And the document?"

"Maybe he planned to sell it, as a final coup before

leaving you holding the bag. Maybe that's why he was killed on Tuesday morning—by whomever he was planning to sell it to."

"That's a gruesome theory, Harry," Sarah said.

"Well, it's the only one I can think of that explains both your father's behavior and Bidwell's. He hired me to keep an eye on you until he was ready to make his escape. At the same time, I was an insurance policy—good p.r. in case anything went wrong and he was found out. We'll know for sure tomorrow. Lurman is going to get your father's security file from Sloane. If he or one of his coworkers were suspected of espionage, it'll show up there."

"You're a clever man," she said.

It sounded a little too "clever" to me, too. Still, it was the best I could come up with. I said, "Let's just hope I'm a clever man who's right."

17

It began to snow around five that afternoon. Big wet flakes that stuck to the sidewalks and the streets. By a quarter of eight, five inches were on the ground and the air was so thick and white I couldn't see twenty feet in front of me.

"It's beautiful," Sarah said as we stood in the lobby, waiting for Sturdevant to bring one of the black Chevies around from the lot.

"For Grimes. Not for us." I turned to Lurman and said, "You and Sturdevant have to stand clear until we've finished talking with O'Hara. He might not see you in the snow, but let's play it safe anyway. You'll let us off on Kellogg and we'll walk up the access road to the main parking lot. That'll give you time to park the car in the Downs lot and position yourselves close to the rendezvous point. If there's a commotion of any kind, I don't want you guys so far away that you won't be able to lend a hand."

"Sean won't betray us," Sarah said confidently.

"Let's hold that thought. As for you—" I turned to Lionelli. "Stick around the Delores in case Grimes tries the back door."

Lionelli nodded.

I took a breath. "O.K. I guess that's everything."

"You have a gun?" Lurman asked me.

"Yeah." I patted my overcoat.

The two agents started for the door.

"We'll be out in a minute," I said. "I want to talk to Sarah alone."

Lurman smiled and Lionelli leered.

"C'mon, Ed," Lurman pulled the other one out the door.

I looked into Sarah's face. She looked pale, tense, and remarkably pretty in the overhead light.

"Well," I said heavily.

Sarah threw her arms around me and kissed me on the lips.

"You'll be O.K.?" I whispered to her.

"Fine."

"And if there's any trouble?"

"There won't be."

I swallowed hard. "Then, let's go."

I took her mittened hand and we walked out of the lobby into the snow-filled street. Sturdevant pulled the Chevy up beside the curb and we piled into the back seat. No one said a word as we drove down Reading to Columbia Parkway and out along the river to Kellogg Avenue.

Up until ten years ago, Coney Island was a flourishing amusement park set in the lowlands on the north bank of the Ohio. Then money men—some of them local—decided to build a glass-and-plastic Disneyland east of the city. Kings Island went up and old Coney was abandoned, except for the huge pool, which was made into a municipal recreation spot. In the wintertime, the grounds were completely deserted, which was why Sean O'Hara had picked them as a rendezvous point. From the entrance on Kellogg Avenue where Lurman had dropped us off, all Sarah and I could see of the park was a latticework of wire fencing and the big snowy parking lot in front of it. Now and then, the wind blew the snow away and a huge corner of building appeared through the haze, nosing out like the prow of a ship through a fog, only to be swallowed up again in the storm. The park was still there—all of it that couldn't be moved or sold or salvaged. The arcades, the malls, the big art deco buildings where the dance bands used to play on hot summer evenings. It made me melancholy to think about those times and oddly fearful, as if Sarah and I were walking through the driving snow into a seedy ghost town, still echoing with the voices of vendors and barkers and the lilt of dance music.

Sarah was frightened, too. She held my hand tightly in hers. And when the wind roared at us, as we picked our way through the unplowed snow—she leaned against me and squeezed my arm. It was a good two hundred yards up the access road to the lot itself. And it wasn't until we were almost on top of it that we saw the van, parked against the cyclone fencing that surrounds the main arcade. I looked back over my shoulder, trying to catch sight of Lurman or Sturdevant. They should have had time to park the Chevy in the River Downs lot and to make their way over the picket fence that separates the race track from the Coney complex. But with the snow blowing so hard, I couldn't see either of them. Just the access road lined with telephone poles and the hillside that fell away on either side of it, dipping down and then back up to Kellogg Avenue. I looked back at the van and caught a whiff of the river, which runs so close behind the amusement park that the whole mall is flooded several times each spring. It smelled rank as death, even in the bitter wind; and it sobered me up immediately. There were only two lights in the lot—big old streetlamps that threw a dim yellow beam on the van and on the snow around it. In the half light, I thought I could see the outline of a man, sitting on the front seat. As we got closer, I could see him more clearly, framed in the front window of the truck.

Sarah and I stopped about twenty yards from the van. The wind was howling so loudly that I had to shout to make myself heard.

"I'll go up."

"No." She shook her head. "I will."

I looked around again, but it was hopeless in the snow. I could barely see the Dodge, much less Lurman, Sturdevant, or rangy Lester Grimes.

"He's expecting *me*, Harry," Sarah shouted over the wind.

I said, "All right. But I'll be right behind you."

Sarah headed for the truck. She walked quickly up to the driver's side door, and I watched her peer through the window. Then something happened to her. She fell against the door and I heard her cry out: "Harry!"

I started to run. From out of nowhere, Lurman and

149

Sturdevant came charging across the lot, their breath hanging in white clouds in front of them.

"Oh, God!" Sarah was shouting. "Oh, God!"

I pulled her away from the window and propped her up against the side of the truck. The snow was swirling around us like a swarm of mosquitoes. I swiped at my eyes and peered through the van window. There was a lacework of blood on the glass, like the web of some red and deadly spider.

"Jesus," I whispered.

Lurman came up beside me.

"O'Hara?" he said.

"He's inside."

Lurman leaned over my shoulder and looked into the cab. He had an ugly, eager look on his all-American face. He was in his element and I realized, as I sank away from the window and down to where Sarah was huddled in the snow, how far out of my own I had drifted. The only thing I could think of was getting the girl back to the safety of the apartment.

"Sarah," I said to her. "We've got to get out of here."

She didn't move. The snow had covered her long auburn hair—she was wimpled with it. I pulled her to her feet and her flesh redounded against mine like an opposing force.

"My fault," she said in a terrifying voice.

I shook her hard and said, "This is *not* your fault. You hear me? *Not* your fault."

She looked at me almost piteously, as if there was something fundamental that I had failed to comprehend. "You don't know," she said in that same ghastly voice. "You don't know. You don't know."

"Get her out of here!" Lurman shouted against the wind. "Take them out of here, Sturdevant!"

Sturdevant bounded ahead of us, up the access road. Sarah continued to stare at me with that same mixture of terror and pity, then she looked back over her shoulder at the van. I jerked her forward. Sturdevant had made fifty yards on us and was tramping, ankle-deep in snow, in the tire tracks that O'Hara's van had made.

I saw him look back at us—his hand raised as if he were about to cry out. And then there was an enormous explosion. A white hot flash of light that shook Sarah and

150

me like a gust of wind and sent us tumbling backward into the snow drifts. Hard clods of dirt rained down on us, sinking into the snow with a quick, sucking sound and peppering the van roof like hailstones. A thin, feculent cloud of smoke drifted across the snowy lot. Stunned, I worked my way to my knees and looked back at the spot where Sturdevant had been standing. A ragged hole, like the hole left when a tree trunk is blasted from the ground, had been gashed in the earth.

"What happened?" I said aloud. I could hear the hysteria in my voice. I looked down at Sarah. She wasn't moving. I leaned over and turned her face-up in the snow. There was a blood-bruise on her forehead and her eyes were rolled back in their sockets.

"Sarah!" I shouted. "Sarah!"

I ripped off a glove and worked my hand beneath her coat. My skin was so cold I couldn't feel a thing. I pulled the hand back out and rubbed her face with snow. Her lips quivered, as if she were trying to wet them, and she moved her head slightly from side to side. "Don't die on me!" I shouted at her. She started to speak, but a trickle of blood stopped her voice. I tried to clear her mouth—to make sure she hadn't swallowed her tongue or bitten it in two. But my hands were too numb and clumsy in the cold. So I wrapped her up in my coat and held her tight until I could hear sirens screaming down Kellogg. A minute later, a hook-and-ladder truck turned onto the access road. Thank God, I thought.

As the fire engine started toward us, Lurman bolted from behind the Dodge and ran, pigeon-toed, across the lot. He stopped about five yards from where Sarah and I were lying and screamed: "Stop! Stop!" The headlights lit the swatch of ground around Sarah and me and around Lurman, who was prancing in the snow, as if he could hold the truck back by main force. When the engine was about a hundred and fifty yards from us, Lurman stopped waving and dove to the ground.

"Get down!" I heard him yell.

I threw myself on top of Sarah and, head bowed, watched the fire engine rumble inexorably up the road through the slow-motion curtain of drifting snow. It was less than a hundred yards away when I realized what was

151

about to happen. And I screamed, "Stop!" although I knew the driver wouldn't hear me.

When one of the massive tires tripped the mines, there was a second flash and repercussion. The cab and front section of the fire engine were actually lifted off the roadbed. And for a second, in midair, the truck looked like a horse rearing on its hind legs. Then it came down with the sounds of a building being struck with a demolition ball—a dull, heart-breaking thud, the crinkling of shattered glass, and the crackle of pipes snapping. The truck turned on its side; then a second explosion rippled through it. The oxygen tanks and the gasoline tank went up in a terrific flash that sent flames towering into the darkness. In the red glow I could see the body of one of the firemen, hanging like a twisted kite from the telephone wires.

"My God," I said.

Lurman got slowly to his feet. His glasses had been snapped and one temple was still dangling from his right ear. "Don't move around!" he called out. "The bastard mined the lot. There may be other charges around us."

"I've got to get Sarah to a hospital!" I shouted back at him.

"I'm telling you he mined the whole fucking lot!" Lurman yelled. "Didn't you see what happened to Sturdevant! Just stay where you are until the police get to you."

I cradled Sarah in my arms. She was still unconscious; and in the eerie light cast by the blazing truck, she looked pale as death.

18

On the way to the hospital she recovered consciousness for long enough to look around her with surprise. At the walls of the ambulance. At the black kid who was holding an oxygen mask to her mouth and whispering sweetly, "Don't move, miss. Don't move." And finally, at me.

I said, "It's all right, Sarah. You're on the way to the hospital now."

By the time we pulled up in front of the emergency room door at Christ's, she was unconscious again. I helped the paramedics get her out of the rear doors and walked beside them through the crowd of white-helmeted police into the emergency room, where a team of doctors took over. I watched them wheel her into surgery, then the room expanded and there were dozens of people around me—young, harried-looking nurses, interns in their blue hospital playsuits, cops of all kinds and jurisdictions and, behind them in the waiting room, the throng of concerned relatives and relations to whom I belonged.

I wandered out to join them, sat down, suddenly exhausted and vaguely conscious that my clothes were wet and bloody from Sarah and the red mist that Sturdevant had become. They looked me over and fell quiet, except for the ones who were crying and the sleepy children stumbling between the plastic chairs. Someone said, "He's one of the men who were trapped in the explosion." It passed quickly through the room that the bloody man by the door had been in the explosion on the river. I could see that a few of them wanted to talk—the ones who were curious without shame and the ones whose husbands had manned that fire truck. I ignored them and tried to fight off the lethargy that had come over me as soon as I sat down. A familiar heaviness in all my limbs, like the heaviness of sleep but duller and irresistible.

I sat there for what felt like hours, unable to move or to think. Waiting for someone to tell me what had happened to Sarah. No one came. After awhile, I got off the chair and walked back out to the nurses' station by the door. The pretty young girl behind the desk eyed me with alarm.

"Where did you come from, sir?" she said. "The doctor will be right with you."

"Where's Sarah Lovingwell? The girl I came in with?"

"Oh, you're Mr. Stoner," she said, looking relieved. "For a moment I didn't know who you were." She was new at her job, I could see that. Just barely out of candy stripes. A youngster who took her charge seriously. "Your friend's still in surgery."

"How long has she been in?" I said with dull terror. My body was beginning to work again. Not fully, yet. Not sharply enough to feel the anguish that part of me knew was there beneath the fatigue.

"Since they brought you in at twelve," she said weakly.

I tried not to think what that could mean. She was the wrong one to ask anyway. Telling me that much had wounded her. I needed one of the old hands. Or one of the residents whose idea of honesty was a brusque indifference to other people's pain. I needed someone who would tell me the truth and not care. I didn't want to see anyone grieving.

"Can I get coffee around here?" I asked her.

"Downstairs," she said. "In the lounge."

I took the stairs instead of the elevator—to make my legs move and my heart pound again. With each step I felt stronger and with each step the anger and fear became harder to contain. I made myself hold it in, pitting my muscles against my gut, parading beside the row of vending machines for above ten minutes. Up and back, sipping

154

coffee that tasted of cardboard and cocoa and telling myself it was going to be all right.

After a time I walked into the lounge itself. A few interns were sitting at the tables—big white lily pads sunk into the concrete floor. Overhead the fixtures dangled in weird geometries, like box kites without their paper skins.

Ten minutes went by, then Lurman entered the room and walked over to the table where I was sitting. "I've been over at General," he said. "After we left, Grimes paid your apartment a visit. We think he was planning to booby-trap it the way he booby-trapped the lot."

"What about Lionelli?"

Lurman sat back in his chair and shook his head. "He's dead, Harry. Grimes blew him away with a shot-gun. Right out on Burnet Avenue."

"Sweet Jesus," I said.

"Poor bastards. This whole damn thing's been a fuck-up from start to finish," Lurman said bitterly. "You know, in the old days they say agents used to duck out of banks during robberies, just so they wouldn't screw up at that kind of high-paced game." He shook his head again. "Can you imagine what the Bureau's going to say about to-night?"

"Can you imagine how little I care?"

He blushed. "I'm sorry. It's just been a bad day. How's Sarah doing?"

"I don't know," I said. "She's been in surgery for two hours."

"It hasn't been a good day," he said again.

For a moment there didn't seem to be anything more either of us *could* say. Two of his partners were dead. Sarah was lying on an operating table somewhere above us. And we had survived to share the guilts that survivors share. And one thing else—the coruscating anger that I'd been holding inside since I'd seen her wheeled into that surgery.

I began to talk to Lurman—to try to explain to him and, I guess, to myself how it had happened that we were now sitting there in that deserted lounge. I told him about Lovingwell, that smooth, eccentric man, about the document that no one had come to claim, about Claire Lovingwell's suicide, about Bidwell and Michael O'Hara. I told

155

him everything except why I was talking in the first place, everything except for how I felt about the girl.

Lurman perked up when I got to the spy business.

"You don't see any connection between your theory and what happened tonight?" he asked me.

I told him, no. "Not unless you want to say that it all began when he hired me." Which was what I'd been saying to myself.

"To find a top-secret document," he said, turning it over with pleasure. "Is that why you wanted me to get Lovingwell's security file?"

I nodded.

"It wouldn't hurt to do a little checking after all," he said. "I'll get in touch with Bidwell for you tomorrow and see what I can find out."

"Good."

"Now, what are we going to do about Grimes?"

"He's not going to have a lot of friends after last night," I said.

"You think he'll skip?"

"He's too crazy for that. He still wants me. He won't leave until it's finished."

Lurman looked me over with a cold, professional eye. "You want out, Harry? No one could blame you after tonight."

"What I want," I said to him, "is for that girl to recover. Then what I want is to kill Lester Grimes."

Lurman gave me a dark, appreciative smile. "We'll get him," he said.

"Not without some help. I'm going to try to get in touch with Chico Robinson tomorrow. Sarah told me he and Sean were close. Maybe that butchering job that Grimes did on his buddy will shake him up."

"After what happened to Sean," Lurman said, "I wouldn't think he'd want any part of this."

"The kid's a Muslim," I said. "He'll have plenty of tough friends and plenty of streetwise contacts. All I want to find out is where Grimes is staying. After that, I'll handle the Cowboy."

At three-thirty that morning a surgeon came down to the waiting room where Lurman and I had migrated and told us that she was out of immediate danger.

Ted made a small grateful noise and I smiled for the first time that night.

"She's suffered a skull fracture," the doctor said. "There was hematoma and we had to remove the clot. Something must have struck her when the bombs went off—a stone, a piece of metal, maybe a piece of bone. Whatever it was, it was traveling like a bullet when it impacted. Understand, she's still in critical condition. Skull injuries are unpredictable. She may start hemorrhaging again. And there's no way to tell how much damage she's already suffered. Not for a few days, at least."

"Can I see her?" I asked him.

He nodded.

We followed him into an elevator and up to the Intensive Care unit on the sixth floor. Halfway down the hall a uniformed cop was seated on a metal stool in front of one of the doors. McMasters still wasn't taking any chances.

"You can't go in, yet," the surgeon said as we walked up to the room. "But you can see her through the window in the door."

I peered inside. She was lying stiffly on the bed. Her head was wrapped in a turban. The flesh around her eyes was a sooty black. Cords ran from different places on her arms and torso to a big bank of monitors and screens.

I was sorry I'd looked. She seemed irreparably wounded lying there, so far from help.

We went back to my apartment. Lurman sacked out on the couch and I tried to get some sleep in the bed. But I kept feeling her beside me, as she'd been the previous morning, and seeing her in that hospital room—wired like a failing motor to that bank of machinery. Before dawn, with the wind shaking the windows in their frames, I got up and called the hospital to check on her condition. It was the same. There wouldn't be an update until nine. I set the alarm for nine-thirty and fell into an exhausted, dreamless sleep.

19

One drunken night many years ago, a friend of mine and I were sitting at a bar talking nonsense and he said to me, in a voice full of liquor and the pompous silliness of the moment, "If you could only choose who you end up caring for." I forget what I said. And he probably would have been happy if I'd forgotten the whole discussion. Because it was one of those mock-epic nights that men treat themselves to instead of to a good cry, and the conversation was filled with that self-satisfying bathos that sounds stirring when you have a few drinks in you and just plain dumb when you don't.

Still, it was a good question. For which I didn't have an answer. And as I sat in bed, with the pale morning light streaming through the dormer window, I wondered if I had chosen the girl or she had chosen me or whether it was just the usual sort of disastrous pairing that scientists attribute to auras and body language and the rarities of scent. It shouldn't have happened—not after the way we'd begun. Not after Kate and Sean. And it might not last after the Lovingwell case was finished. I might not be able to tolerate her theatrical style or she my dogged earnestness. But when I called the hospital and found that she was improving, I felt a rush of affection for Sarah L. and a sense of relief that was not just a matter of guilty conscience or fellow-feeling. She'd made me feel alive again the day before—after six months of emotional hibernation. And I wanted her to be well again. I wanted to *make* her well again. Which, I knew, was dangerous and possibly degradingly sexist. But it was what I wanted early that Saturday morning.

And mixed with the affection or the relief was a terrible sense of anger and a vicious desire to be revenged on Lester Grimes. Of course, I probably knew that it was me I was angry with—I mean, at some level, I knew that I was, in part, to blame. But you don't need a psychiatrist to learn that that kind of guilt gets transferred quickly to another party. And after the way she'd trusted me and confided in me, I felt an awful need to find that other party fast. To find him and to kill him, as he had tried to kill Sarah and me. I guess it was the misplaced confidence, or what had turned out to be misplaced confidence on Sarah's part, that infuriated me the most. After all the betrayals, all the injuries she had apparently endured at the hands of her father and mother, she didn't need the final injustice of Sean O'Hara's death on her conscience. Of course, we all have a life, Harry, I told myself. We all catch our share of the crap. Only the night before somehow went beyond the notion of a "share" toward some sort of dreadful fatality that I couldn't abide and that Sarah couldn't live with. Not and remain sane. So Grimes had to be found; Lovingwell's killer had to be found; and the girl had to be convinced that she was not to blame in either instance. Not for the death of a friend or for having hated a man who might well have deserved her hatred.

I started the day with a sense of mission—dressing and shaving quickly—and found that Lurman, who had less reason, was already dressed and sitting on the recliner.

"I've had better accommodations," he said acidly and stared at the couch as if it were a bed of nails.

"Next time, guard somebody with a bigger apartment."

"How's the girl?" he said.

"Good."

He smiled and sat back on the chair. "I don't suppose you've got anything to eat around here?"

When I said "no," he got to his feet and walked over to the door. "Then allow the FBI to treat you to breakfast. As the saying goes, it's the least we can do."

* * *

160

We drove to a pancake house on Clifton and planned strategy over waffles and coffee. It was a crisp, clean morning. The night's snow was banked high on the curbs. We could see it through the restaurant window, where it sparkled at the feet of the oaks and maples in Burnet Woods.

"At least, we'll have the weather with us today," Lurman said. "At least, we'll be able to see what we're up against."

"I doubt if he'll show today. He'll keep a low profile— for awhile, at least. Maybe by tonight we'll be the ones in control."

"Your idea—about contacting Chico Robinson—you still want to follow through with it?"

I nodded. "I figure you can take the club and the Friends of Nature. And I'll take Chico and the Muslims. Between the two of us, we ought to come up with somebody who's willing to help us find Lester Grimes."

"I don't know about splitting up," Lurman said. "Alone, Harry, you'll make an easy target."

"Not in the West End or in Avondale or wherever the hell the Muslims make their home. A six-foot, nine-inch white man won't be hard to spot on Twelfth Street. Anyway, contacting Robinson is a long enough shot as it is. With an FBI man along, it'll be impossible."

"I still don't like it," he said bluntly and made a serious face to indicate that he'd meant what he said.

I knew that, behind the face, Lurman was telling himself that if I got myself killed the FBI would be out of clay pigeons and he'd probably be out of a job. But that was all right. I'd come across that same combination of decency and self-interest in other cops. It was no different in kind than the back-slapping and back-stabbing that goes on among the personnel of any highly competitive organization. As ambitious men went, Lurman was more likeable and more honest than most. The concern wasn't *all* show. But he was an ambitious man, who'd suffered a bad black eye the night before. And that part of him knew that splitting up would give him some time to mend fences. It would also give him the chance to look into Lovingwell's security file. Nobody loves a spy more dearly than the FBI does; and digging one up, even a dead one, would get Lurman back into grace quicker than prayer.

He searched his soul for a few minutes and stared mood-

161

ily into his coffee cup and finally said, "All right. We'll split up. But, for chrissake, Harry, don't get yourself killed!"

At ten-fifteen I followed Lurman over to the clubhouse on Calhoun. He went in and I stayed out in the Pinto, waiting for Chico Robinson to arrive or depart. It was a long wait in the cold; but around eleven-thirty, he pulled up outside the club in an old Caddy with Hermes as a hood ornament and a side panel that had been stripped and primed in gray. He looked virtually the same as he had on Tuesday afternoon—a light-toned black man in his early twenties with a thin, wispy beard and mean eyes. He was wearing a black arm band over his green combat jacket. And that gave me hope.

Robinson ducked into the club and came scurrying out once he'd spotted Lurman inside. He stood beside the car for a moment, making up his mind, then hopped back in and headed west on McMillan. I followed him in the Pinto at a dead pace, crawling down the street the way security cars do when they make nightly rounds.

Robinson worked his way down McMillan to the Parkway, then south on Liberty into that region of worn houses and low brick projects that is the westside ghetto. As many times as I've driven through it, the place still chilled me. It was a place to chill any good burgher's soul. Cinder lots and broken fencing. Rubbish piles full of pint bottles, cigarette packs, and rotting refuse. The brick tenements not just run-down, but exhausted of hope—like houses in Hell. And, of course, the faces—black and vacant as the abandoned cinder lots. The old-young faces of the boys on Liberty, playing hockey on the ice with sticks and a can. Old men at a busstop whose tired faces had begun to peel away, the way dark paint flecks away from weathered wood. Fearful and fearsome types. The effects or the talents of fear everywhere. Even in the children playing in the snow.

In time I got to the heart of it—Central Avenue at Twelfth Street, like the worst studio mock-up of a slum. Gutted buildings and tired shops, all of them like abandoned kiosks, dotted everywhere on their facades with old posters and snow-matted advertisements. Robinson pulled over in front of one of them and got out. The sign above the door read "Pool." I kept driving, up to a gas station at

Eleventh, where the tough black gas jockeys looked at me as if I'd dropped from a star.

There was a phone booth on the south side of the station. I got out of the Pinto and made my way through the pieces of scrap and snow-covered tires to the booth. Once inside, I felt oddly secure—out of the weather and that other, fiercer weather, like a season within the season, that I felt all around me. I dialed the Hi-Fi Gallery and, when Bullet came on the line, I told him where I was and what I wanted him to do.

He didn't say anything for a minute. "You want me to come down there?"

"That's it," I said.

"How long you been knowing me, Harry?" he said. "Six, seven years? All you ever see is me in the store or me in the bar. Just like a white man. Right? That's the way I wanted it. When I go back down there, man, I go alone. And I don't ever go white."

"It's my life we're talking about, Bullet," I told him.

He thought it over—what it would cost him in pride and credibility against what it could cost me in blood. "I'll meet you at that gas station in ten minutes," he said. "And don't go wanderin' around."

Some of the men inside the pool hall knew Bullet from his football days. They nodded casually to him as he walked by. Then they saw me and their faces filled with hate. There were ten or twelve of them leaning against the walls of the main room, and a half dozen more loitering in the lobby. Robinson might have been there. I couldn't tell. It was so dark and smokey I couldn't see all of their faces and those I did see I didn't look at long.

Bullet said, "Wait out in the lobby, Harry." And walked toward the rear of the main room.

I walked back out to the alcove, where the boys were leaning against the walls. One of them straightened up when he saw me. I turned away and pretended to study an old photo of Elijah Muhammed, and not to see the black kid as he came up behind me.

"Wha'chu doin' here, man?" he said in a quick, sharp, sing-song voice. "Wha'chu want 'round here?"

"He lost his way," one of the kids on the couch said.

"He look like he lost his way," another one said.

163

"Is that right?" the one behind me said. He prodded me in the ribs, hard. "Hey! I'm talkin' to you."

I turned around and looked at him.

He was nineteen, maybe twenty. His hair was braided in corn rows and he was wearing a black dashiki over a pair of jeans. His face was as black as the dashiki, except for the whites of his eyes which were the yellow of raw egg yolk.

"You got a tongue?" he said.

"What do you want me to say?" I asked him.

"Say your prayers," one of them said and they all laughed.

"That's it. Say goodbye, man," the one standing in front of me said. "How much money you got?"

"I'm not giving you any money."

"Oh, you ain't? Well, maybe you change your mind in a minute."

I stared at him. He's just another smart-ass kid, Harry, I told myself. All bluff. Only that's not the way it felt—in that dark, rank room. I put my hand in my coat pocket and he jumped back.

"Wha'chu got in there? You carryin' iron in there? You best not pull no iron around here, man. You dig?"

We stared at each other for another minute, until Bullet came walking back through the door. He had Robinson with him.

"Back off," Bullet said to the black kid.

"Wha'chu mean 'back off,' Tom? I be talking to the dude here."

"Cool it, Lucius," Robinson said.

Lucius looked angrily at Robinson. One of the other boys walked up and took him by the arm. "Let's go, man," he said.

"I be talking to the dude," Lucius said to him.

Robinson walked over to me and said, "Just get the hell out of here."

I walked out into the street, where the air was full of the smell of snow and the spicy incongruous smells of rib joints and chicken shacks. For a second my legs felt rubbery and I was torn with the impulse to run—as fast and as far as I could—away from that dark, dangerous place. A few seconds later, Bullet and Chico Robinson came out the door. We walked quietly through the snow up to the

164

gas station where I'd left my car. A man in a ski mask walked past us. He made me think of the night, four days before, when the gunman had tried to kill me in the Delores lot. In reaction to the rush of fear, I made my voice steady and subdued.

"Are you willing to help?" I asked Robinson. He didn't answer.

We got to my car and piled in. Bullet in back, Robinson on the seat beside me.

"You're a powerful fool comin' down here like this," Robinson said, staring at me the way the gas jockeys had stared. "What you think? You can just walk into this place and nobody be watchin' you? Look over there."

He pointed through the windshield at an old Chevrolet coasting down Central Avenue.

"That's one of our patrol cars, man. They seen you way back on McMillan when you started followin' me. Cobras in that car got them shotguns on the front seat. Po-lice goin' to carry magnums, we goin' to be prepared. And there are ten more of them cars out on the streets. I knew where you was the moment I got back to the hall."

"Can you find Grimes that fast?" I asked him.

"If I wanted to, Jack," he said, "I could find Jimmy-fuckin'-Hoffa."

I didn't know how to make the pitch. In a way it had already been made. Either he felt strongly enough about O'Hara's death to cooperate or he didn't. Banging the drum was just going to offend him.

"Well, where do you stand?" I said again.

"Grimes don't mean nothin' to me. Just another crazy white fucker."

"I don't want you to kill him. I want you to find him."

"The girl," he said. "She dead, too?"

I shook my head.

He got out of the car, slammed the door and walked off down the street. I started to call after him when Bullet clapped me on the arm.

"Just leave it alone, Harry," he said.

165

20

I sat in the Pinto with Bullet for another five minutes, trying to calm down. I was embarrassed with myself for having been afraid in the pool hall. Embarrassed and a little ashamed, because I knew if they hadn't been *black* kids I wouldn't have felt so outmanned. I wanted to apologize to somebody; but Bullet didn't look as if he was in a receptive mood. His heart, or a large part of it, was with those tough kids in the pool hall and, as he got out of the car, he said to me: "Harry, as big as you are, you'd never make it as a nigger. Not for one lonely day."

Lurman wasn't back yet when I got to the apartment.

I made myself some lunch, then called the hospital again and got the same report delivered in the same impatient voice, like a prerecorded message. "She's improved, sir. But she's still on the critical list."

"Has she recovered consciousness, yet?"

The nurse put her hand over the phone. "No," she said when she came back on the line. "She's still in a coma."

"I see."

"That's not unusual," she said in a kinder voice. "Not in cases like this."

I thanked her and hung up.

It was odd. The night before, when it had all come apart so terribly, I'd wanted to hear the truth without any humanity, as nakedly and as fatally as it could be put. That Sunday morning, when it was all coming back together, I wanted to be coddled like a sick man, to be pranked and lied to and made to feel better. I'd begun to think of her as alive again, that was the difference. Where the night before I could only think of her as dead.

At half-past three, Lurman came in. He plopped down across from me at the coffee table and took a bite of my sandwich.

"You talk to Bidwell?" I said.

He shook his head. "But I did talk to Bidwell's aide, Terry Mize."

"And?"

"And Lovingwell wasn't under suspicion of anything. Neither was Sarah or anyone else at Sloane."

I sat back on the chair as if I'd been punched. "No one was suspected?"

"Nope." Lurman ate the rest of my sandwich. "I'll tell you another thing. Lovingwell never checked any top-secret document out of the lab either."

"What!"

At first I didn't think I'd heard him right. But when I asked him again and he repeated it again, I began to suffer a sickening and familiar sense of dislocation.

"He didn't even have a security clearance," Lurman said. "He wasn't working with classified material, so he didn't need one."

"There wasn't any document," I said blankly. Not even hearing myself. Just mouthing the words.

"No document."

"Then why the hell did he hire me!" I almost shouted. "What the hell is going on here?"

Lurman laughed nervously. "Take it easy, Harry."

"My ass."

I got up from the table and stalked into the bedroom and plunked myself down on the bed.

Of course, it made sense. Bidwell wouldn't have been concerned about a document that didn't exist. Nobody would be.

I laughed wretchedly. Only that wasn't true. Lovingwell had been concerned. He'd hired me to recover the goddamn thing! There was no way around that little contradicition except to ignore it. Well, there was. But it took me about ten minutes to find the path.

I began by trying to remember everything that Lovingwell and I had said to each other about the document, from the moment he'd showed up at my office until the day he'd died. The thing was he'd never really told me what the document was about. All he'd done was describe a bunch of papers that looked like top-secret material. Material I was honor-bound not to examine or tell anyone else about.

Lying about the contents of some lost papers seemed like child's play to the man Sarah had described. But if he'd been lying about the document, where did that leave me? Had he really lost something that merely looked like secret papers, something he didn't want anyone to know about, not even the detective he'd hired to recover it? Or had the whole thing been a lie? And if so, why had he lied? What had he stood to gain by implicating his daughter in the theft of nonexistent secret papers?

It wouldn't come clear, like looking at something in front of your nose through a fixed-focus lens. I wasn't standing far enough back. I wasn't seeing all there was to be seen of the Lovingwell case. At that moment I wondered if I ever would.

"You're taking this kind of hard, aren't you?" Lurman called from the living room.

I got up from the bed and walked back to the sofa. "I don't like being used," I said. "Especially when I don't know what I'm being used for."

Lurman shrugged. "These things happen. You get off on a wrong scent and it's hard to get right again. After the spy business petered out, I did some checking up on Lovingwell at the University. Most of the people I talked to seemed to think he was a harmless eccentric. Do you know who Charles McPhail is?"

"I've heard the name," I said. "Why?"

"No reason. One of the assistant deans I talked to mentioned him, that's all. He was apparently the only black spot on Lovingwell's official record. Some kid he'd given a hard time to about seven years ago."

"It's funny they'd remember his name."

"Not so funny," Lurman said. "The kid went loco and ended up killing himself in Daniels Hall."

"Did they say why?"

Lurman shook his head.

Daniels Hall is a large, red-brick dormitory on Jefferson about half a block from campus. Charles McPhail had roomed there for two years, according to the woman in charge of the dorm, before cutting his wrists in his third floor room on the 17th of January 1973. The resident adviser remembered his case well.

"He was a very quiet boy," she said. "Introspective the way many of our students are. And quite meticulous, the way many of them should be. He was, I should say, a model student. Extremely hard-working and absolutely absorbed in his studies."

"Which were?"

"He was in astrophysics, I believe." She checked the card she'd drawn from an old metal file. "Yes. He was a third-year graduate student in the Physics Department at the time of his death."

"Do you have a picture of him?" I said.

She handed me the card. A tiny snapshot was glued to the corner. Charles McPhail had been a rather ascetic-looking young man. Pretty rather than handsome. With a faraway look in his eyes.

"Do you have any idea why he killed himself?" I asked her.

"People always have ideas, Mr. Stoner," she said. "Suicides are like vacuums. Human nature abhors them and rushes in to explain what it can't abide. He didn't want to live—that's probably the only explanation."

I had the feeling that the woman, whose name was Castle, was only too familiar with the tidal-like despairs of unhappy undergraduates.

"Did he leave a note?"

She nodded. "He said he was sorry."

I looked out the window at the leafless trees along Jefferson. "Was there an investigation?"

"Yes," she said. "The coroner held an inquest. The verdict was suicide. There was no mystery about it."

"Did his death have anything to do with Professor Daryl Lovingwell?"

"Tangentially," she said. "I didn't know Professor Lovingwell, but he had a reputation for being very hard-nosed with his students. There was apparently some dispute between him, Professor O'Hara, and the McPhail boy. And Professor Lovingwell took a hard line."

"Do you know the nature of the dispute?"

"I do not," she said. "You might ask Felicia Earle in the Department of English. I believe she was the Physics Department secretary at the time of Charles's death. I think she and her husband were friends of the boy."

I thanked her and walked out of her little office to the dormitory lobby where Lurman was waiting. "Did you find anything?"

"I don't know," I said to him. "I found a dead boy who committed suicide about the same time as Sarah's mother. I don't know if that qualifies as 'anything' or not. I'll find out more on Monday when I talk to a girl named Felicia Earle."

"We better get back to your place," he said, staring at the street. The sun was going down and there were heavy clouds moving in from the northwest.

I said what he was thinking. "Do you think he'll try tonight?"

Lurman looked at me and said, "Who knows?"

It was a very tense evening. Up until twelve I kept hoping that Chico Robinson would call. When he didn't, I settled in for the siege. Lurman sent out for some Chinese food, and he and I sat on the living room floor eating it and jumping at every footstep from the hall.

"There *are* two men outside the apartment," he said.

"There were last night, too."

He didn't say anything.

We finished the chow mein and left the plates on the floor. The FBI had tossed the apartment the evening before to make sure that Grimes hadn't left me any party favors; so the plates didn't make a difference. I stared at the room and thought of Sarah and then of Kate.

"You ever been married, Lurman?" I said.

"Can't see it." He'd made a space for himself on the couch and was leafing through an old hi-fi magazine. "Jesus Christ, this equipment is expensive."

"I almost got married a couple of times," I said, brooding over the shambles my apartment and my life had become in the past few days.

171

"Yeah?" He tossed the magazine on the floor. "What's it feel like?"

"You're not terribly interested in this, are you?"

He threw up his hands like a boxer parrying a combination. "Hey, it's your place! You want to talk about marriage, go right ahead."

"Thanks."

"I almost got married once myself. Right before I went off to college."

"Where was that?" I said.

"Georgetown. I'm from D.C. She was my high school sweetheart. *That* was true love," Lurman said wistfully. "Once you know what you're doing, once you know what it costs, it gets old."

"What happened?"

"She ditched me," he said. "What happened with you?"

"I don't know," I said woefully.

"Women," Lurman said.

There was a very loud noise in the hall. Lurman lept to his feet. The pistol was in his hand before I'd gotten out of my chair.

"Stay away from the door," he said in a low, nervous voice.

I backed against the wall and waited.

Somebody knocked on the front door.

"Ted?" a voice called from the hall. "It's Jesperson."

Lurman let out a sigh of relief and I unclenched my fists. They felt as if I'd been doing exercises with rubber balls. I walked over to the door and opened it.

Jesperson, short, squat, with thin black hair that looked like it was pencilled on his skull, was standing outside. "There's a guy in the lobby says he wants to talk with Stoner."

"What's he look like?" I asked him.

"A big black dude. Must weigh three hundred pounds."

"That'll be Bullet Riley," I said to Lurman. "The man who helped me out this afternoon."

Lurman pocketed his pistol as if it were a briar pipe and said, "Show the man up, Russ."

A few minutes later, Bullet walked into the room. He looked ruffled and angry. As he cleared the door he glanced back over his shoulder, as if he weren't quite sure that the smaller man wasn't standing in his shadow.

172

"Man," he said. "I can't say I think much of your friends."

"Not nice guys like yours?" I said.

"It ain't funny, Harry. One of those crackers 'bout blew my head off down there."

"Sorry, Mr. Riley," Lurman said. "We're all a little edgy after last night."

"That's Agent Lurman, Bullet," I said, nodding at Ted. "My protection."

"Charmed," Bullet said.

We settled down again in the living room; and, after a bit of idle talk about stereos and booze, Bullet cleared his throat and made motions that meant he had something important to say to me. In private.

"Is this pantomime about Chico Robinson?" I said.

He gave me a sour look and nodded.

"Might as well come out with it, then," I said to him. "Lurman's going to hear it, anyway."

"All right. He ain't found Grimes yet. But he's got him a lead. Some junkie in east Walnut Hills who used to be O'Hara's pal in the days of love and peace. Chico thinks he might be able to pin your man down for you by tomorrow night."

"Swell," I said. "Will you be relaying the word?"

"He'll call here. After six tomorrow. Whether he's found Grimes or not."

"I'll be in," I said to him.

21

First thing in the morning I had Lurman drive me up to the University so that I could ask some more questions about Charles McPhail. I wasn't quite sure why I wanted to ask the questions. But with the spy business a dead letter, I needed another angle, and Charley McPhail's death seemed like the most promising possibility. Suicides like Claire Lovingwell's and the McPhail boy's leave very bad memories. Sometimes they leave survivors like Sarah, too. Survivors who live in hate.

I stopped at Christ before going on to the campus, to check on the girl. They wouldn't let me see her, save from behind that window on the sixth floor. And that was one view I never intended to see again. So I told the duty nurse I'd try to get back later in the day and, with Lurman in tow, drove up McMillan to Clifton Avenue and the University complex. I parked on campus, dropped Lurman off at the Student Union, and told him I'd pick him up in an hour. It was a bright blue morning and the sun was shining ferociously on the snowy walks. By the time I got to McMicken Hall, I was squinting from the glare.

Up the wide staircase, on the second floor, was the English Department office. Just a cubbyhole, racked with mailboxes and partitioned off by a short wooden counter. Behind the counter sat Felicia Earle, a short, olive-skinned woman of about thirty, with the bland, abstracted face and long, coal-black hair of a postcard madonna.

Once we'd settled in a rather stuffy coffee room across the hall from her office, she began to tell me the story of her life in a voice as smokey as a slice of provolone. She'd not had a good time of it for the past few years, and it showed in her dress. A sweater out at the elbow, a blue blouse stained red on the breast, torn stockings, drab unironed skirt. In my experience people who don't care how they look are either very idealistic or very angry. As it turned out, Fell Earle was a little of both.

"I want to explain why I'm willing to gossip with you about Charley McPhail," she said, staring down at the dark wood table we were sitting at. "You probably think it's because I liked Charley. But that's not all of it. Look around you, Mr. Stoner. And tell me what you see."

I surveyed the room. It was an ornate, rather tired place, lined with dusty portraits of chairmen and alumni and the kind of sprung furniture you sometimes see in the lobbies of second-rate hotels. It looked rather like a smoking room in a men's club that had seen better days. I told her that and she frowned at the tabletop.

"I see an enormous case of arrested development," she said. "A sanctuary where a lot of frightened people hide from all those terrifying things that come with grown-up life. Things like regular hours, supervised work, a two-week vacation that goes like your twenties, the kind of noisy decisions that drown out the whisper of nouns and the rubbing together of two adjectives. You don't know what I'm talking about, do you?"

"In a way I do. But what makes you think this place is any different from the rest of the world?"

"Oh, but it isn't!" she said. "That's what's so sad. Here we are, putatively surrounded by the best and brightest minds in the city. And as minds go, they're mostly what they pretend to be. It's how they act when their thinking caps are off that offends me so deeply. I've been around this university for ten years, financing my own and my husband's education; so I know whereof I speak. And please believe me, what I'm going to say about Daryl Lovingwell could be said with equal justice about any of the lamed men who poplulate this institution. They don't make very good human beings, scholars. They don't have it in them to care for anything but themselves and their work. What I'm trying to say is that Lovingwell was no worse a bastard than any of his colleagues, just a more conspicuous one. And if you start thinking of what he did to Charley as a special case, you'd be dead wrong."

"When did you work for him?"

"Seven years ago, when he was chairman of the Physics Department. I believe it was seven years ago. At this point it's rather hard to keep all of my time straight. Have you ever done secretarial work, Mr. Stoner?" She looked at me for the first time since we'd sat down in the coffee room. "You see, you don't look up when you type. Just down and to your right." She laughed bitterly. "Like directions to a john. Down and to your right. I guess that sounds self-pitying, but I do have a point to make. You hear a lot of crap when you work in a departmental office. And most of it you hear while hunched over a typewriter with one ear to the dictaphone. Then there's a lot of posturing and preening, a lot of the stiff upper lip thing in the office that makes much of the conversation sound like what you might hear at a lady's tea. They don't really go after each other with razors until they're liquored up or locked in a meeting or in each other's studies. The point is that what I'm going to say can't be documented. That's the reason for this preamble. I can't prove a thing. I can only tell you what I believe on the basis of ten years' experience."

Fell Earle was a conscientious girl. I liked that. Ready talkers rarely make good sense. I prefer the ones who have thought things out. In a way, I prefer the ones with grudges, too. Anger makes a nice focal point, that is, if it's been studied on like a textbook and if it's accessible like Fell Earle's was. I told her that I appreciated her candor and asked her what she'd thought of Daryl Lovingwell.

"There are two types of department chairmen," she said. "One pretends to hate his work, the other to enjoy it. The truth is that both of them thrive on the perquisites of the office. I haven't met a departmental chairman yet who wasn't a secret fascist. Lovingwell was just more open about it. He loved power and he exercised it with panache. But it was the fist inside the velvet glove sort of thing. And eventually it cost him his position. In a way he was lucky it didn't cost him more. I can't prove it, but I believe that Charley was driven to suicide by Daryl Lovingwell."

I could believe it. I suppose, at that point, I was eager to believe it. It made for such a brutal confirmation of all that Sarah had told me. I told her to go on with something like lust in my voice; and she heard it, the eagerness, and looked at me oddly.

"Did you know him?" she said. "Did you know Lovingwell?"

"I knew him," I said, making my voice calmer, more professional. "Tell me about Charley McPhail."

"He was an astrophysicist, working with Mike O'Hara. In seventy-one O'Hara published a series of articles that Charley helped research. They created quite a stir. O'Hara had been cooperating for years with teams in England and at M.I.T. in an effort to validate the big-bang theory of the universe. His articles lent significant support to the theory; in fact, some of his data helped pave the way to the study of background radiation.

"In most respects O'Hara was a decent enough man, innocent of any thought outside his field. But he was very ambitious to consolidate his position within the department, partly, I think, in order to gain supporters for his theories. There had always been a good deal of tension between him and Lovingwell. He was the fair-haired boy and Lovingwell the old hand—the athlete and the tweed coat. When O'Hara's articles came out, the antagonism worsened. Where they had disagreed before in a polite, professional way, they began to go at it no-holds-barred and at every possible occasion, from student parties to meetings of the executive committee. I've seen it happen before, in every department I've worked in, and it's a melancholy thing. People take sides. Talk becomes loose and flagrant. Egos are crushed like cigarette butts.

"Someone started a rumor that Lovingwell was boffing O'Hara's wife, which may have been true. With her, there's no such thing as an accurate body count. Although it was rather amusing to imagine the two of them in bed. She's bitchy, handsome, and hedonistic. He was crabby, supercilious, and about as out-going as hard stool. We figured he kept up a running commentary while they made love, to let her know just how badly she was doing. Then someone else started a rumor that O'Hara had plagiarized his findings from Charley's dissertation, which was what set the whole ugly incident off.

178

"You hear stories all the time about professors lifting their points and paragraphs from students' papers. Two years ago, the English Department almost hired a man named Teague who actually *did* plagiarize most of his work. It was a real black eye for the department and they got out of it as gracelessly as they'd gotten in. Teague had already moved his family here when the tyros found out that he'd lost his job at Cambridge because of the plagiarizing business and canned him on the spot. You see, that's how little attention they pay to each other's work, that's how much unexamined reputation means to them. They're snobs of the worst kind. Teague was famous, so nobody bothered to look at what he'd written.

"When the rumor started about O'Hara's work, Lovingwell took it up like a cause. There would have to be an investigation, he said. There were some public meetings and some incredibly vicious private ones. And poor Charley McPhail found himself caught between two raging egotists out for each other's blood. There's a part of this that I'm not sure about. Whether Charley did, in fact, go to Lovingwell originally to complain in his quiet way about O'Hara's appropriation of his work. Or whether Lovingwell called him on the carpet to browbeat him into a confession. Anyway, he recanted later. Publicly. And apologized to O'Hara. There was something queer about that, too. Because it was Lovingwell who made Charley recant, after he'd gotten him to confess in the first place. After a time, the issue of O'Hara's integrity became secondary. And Charley himself became the issue. Lovingwell failed him twice on his orals and made an ugly scene at a party about Charley's 'weak' character. Charley was a homosexual, and Lovingwell played on that for all it was worth. Which would surprise you in this enlightened place. Eventually, Charley resigned from the Department. And a few weeks later, he cut his wrists in a room in Daniels Hall."

Felicia Earle shook her head sadly. "That's the story of Charley McPhail. Some of it I saw myself. Some of it I got through Leo, my husband, who was Charley's friend. You should talk to him if you want more details. He works at the Gargoyle Record Shop on Calhoun until five-thirty. I'd better warn you, though, he doesn't like talking about it. It still makes my flesh crawl. I must say you don't seem as shocked as I thought you'd be."

"Honey," I said to her. "Nothing you could tell me about Daryl Lovingwell could shock me anymore. What about O'Hara, what do you think of him?"

"Not much anymore. He tries to act tough, but he's run by his wife. Or, at least, he used to be. He drinks a lot, too. And he's a bad sentimental drunk. I've had him on my hands at many a faculty party. I will say this for him, he's got a heart. He took Charley McPhail's death very hard."

"Sounds like a man with a guilty conscience to you?"

She shrugged. "It's possible. But if he had plagiarized Charley's work, Lovingwell would never have let him get away with it. Not in those days. Hell, he would have laid O'Hara's head at the foot of the cyclotron."

"I guess so." I got to my feet. "Thanks, Felicia. You've been a help."

"I feel like a stinker," she said dismally. "In spite of the rancor, I still love what this goddamn place ought to be." She looked mournfully about the room. "Ten years," she said. "And do you know why?"

I shook my head.

"For love. So he could stay a little boy. So he wouldn't have to grow up like the rest of them."

"Your husband?"

She didn't say anything. But the suffering look in her black eyes did.

22

Across campus and up one flight of stairs I found the Gargoyle Record Shop. Two naked rooms with record bins on every wall. Leo Earle, or the guy I took to be Leo Earle, was sitting behind a register by the door. He was a tall young man, in his early thirties, husky, sloppy, and obviously bored with his work. Although he was sitting with his back facing the open room, I could tell that one flap of his shirt was out in back. He was the type. His pants would be falling down periodically, too. He had a broad, boyish face. Wore a light moustache, shaped like a flier's wings. Horn-rimmed glasses. Brown hair that spilled off his scalp, down his neck and curled on his forehead in a love lock. He didn't know me and he figured I wasn't going to buy anthing, so he didn't waste any energy on hellos.

I told him who I was and what I wanted and he gawked at me in disbelief.

"You say you talked to Fell this morning? How do I know that?"

"Give her a call."

"I will," he said.

He eyed me cagily, as if he thought I were going to bolt and run when he put my lie to the test. When I didn't budge, he looked disappointed.

He made the call anyway, cupping his hand over the mouthpiece so I couldn't yell any advice. All I could hear was "some guy," "Charley," and "O.K." When he hung up, he turned to me with a boyish, chastened grin. It was probably the same look he'd been giving Felicia for the last ten years.

"I'm sorry about the confusion," he said, jabbing ineffectually at his loose shirt tail. "How often do you meet a private eye?" He held out his hand, like a real man. And I shook it.

"I did some security work myself one summer," he said avidly.

And I could just see him in his Wells Fargo uniform with an empty gun on his Sam Browne, defending the honor of the all-night grocery the company had stuck him in. It's frightening to think about all the college kids, unemployed salesmen, and self-styled gunsels who are hired for security duty in groceries and five-and-dimes. The general theory is that anybody wearing a badge and a pistol can serve as an intimidating prop—like those decals that security firms hand out with their burglar alarms: "This house is protected by X." But, believe me, a tough with a shotgun under his coat isn't going to fall for a pretty uniform. Which is why the mortality rate in U-Totems is so damn high. Until some real standards of training are established, yokels like Leo Earle are going to continue to get paid minimum wage to be killed and are going to continue to think it's fun.

"You know where the term 'private eye' came from?" he asked.

"Pinkerton."

His face fell. "Yeah. That's right. That was their trademark. An open eye and the motto, 'We never sleep.'"

"Do you think we could get out of here for a while, Leo. I could use some coffee."

"I guess so. There isn't much doing here this morning anyway. I guess it would be all right."

Leo locked up the shop and we went next door to the Hidden Corner—an unprepossessing restaurant that serves some of the best food in the city. I boosted him to a cup of coffee and let him talk for five minutes about his dissertation on the founding of the Royal Society. Then I steered him back to Charley McPhail. It was clearly not a subject he wanted to be steered toward. When I asked him why, he said, "I was there when they found his body."

"I see."

"There are eight pints of blood in the human circulatory system," he said grimly. "And poor Charley had spilled every drop on that damn bed."

Earle shivered in his chair and rubbed the coffee cup as if he were warming his hands over a fire.

"I know it was ugly, Leo. I know he was your friend. But I've got to ask you to do some remembering. A girl's life may depend on it."

It sounded silly, but it was the sort of silliness that impressed Leo Earle. He really was the little boy his wife had said he was. Full of enthusiasms and blank spaces.

"A girl's life?" he said, rolling it on his tongue. "Really?"

"Really," I said with dead earnestness. "I'm not being coy. This is literally a matter of life and death."

Hot dog! Leo said to himself and rubbed his hands on the coffee cup.

"What do you want to know?"

"I want to know why he committed suicide."

Earle sighed painfully. "That's not an easy question to answer."

"I'd like to hear what you think."

"Well, Lovingwell, of course. He was the efficient cause. He and the razor blades Charley used."

"And the final cause?"

Leo looked at me sadly. "You know that Charley was a homosexual?"

I nodded.

"He'd been having an affair with someone on campus. A long-standing thing. When Lovingwell made such a fuss about O'Hara's article and Charley got caught in between, this friend of his dropped him."

"Why?" I said.

"I don't know. Charley would never talk about it. He was a very private man. Very defensive about his personal life. The only reason I know about his lover at all is that Charley got very drunk one night at a faculty party—Lovingwell had been tormenting him with snide remarks—and when I took him home, he started to cry."

Leo squinted at the memory. "It wasn't a pleasant thing to see. He'd always been so much in control, so self-contained. To see him break down like that..."

"Did he ever mention his lover's name?" I said.

183

Earle shook his head. "It wasn't like a confession. It was more of a lament. He just couldn't believe what had happened to his life. After that night he went home for a week or so. His folks live in Batesville, Indiana, I think. When he came back, he seemed to have himself under control. I figured something had happened while he was away. Some sort of reconciliation with his lover. Charley seemed quite ashamed of his outburst when I saw him. He asked me never to mention it again." Earle's boyish face turned red. "I said that I wouldn't. A week later he slashed his wrists in Daniels."

Leo looked up from his coffee cup and frowned savagely. "When I read that Lovingwell had been murdered, do you know what I did?"

"What?"

"I said a prayer that whoever killed him would never be found."

If it hadn't been for Sarah, I think I might have agreed.

23

It was an hour's drive to Batesville. Out I-74, through the sulfur-yellow gorges and huge, forested hills of southern Ohio and then into that flat, pallid Indiana countryside where high power stations and occasional farm houses are the only scenery amid treeless fields of snow. Lurman had come along because it was his job. I could see from the distraction on his face that most of him was looking ahead to nightfall, when the real business of killing or being killed might take place.

Most of me was looking back. Seven years. To two suicides and one vicious man, if he'd been a man—he seemed to me now like an illusion, a trick done with infernal mirrors. I was looking back and thinking about that greed that Sarah and Meg O'Hara had said was his only motive. And not simply a greed for money. But apparently for whatever people held dear. O'Hara's reputation, McPhail's self-esteem. Claire Lovingwell's inheritance. Sarah's damaged love for her dead mother. He'd had a true bully's instinct for the weaknesses of his victims, for the tender spots where their courage failed. Mercilessly, he'd reduced them to death or to impotence; and all the while he'd prospered.

Whatever I found at the McPhail home, it would lead me back to that greedy ghost. How he'd intended to profit, what driving the McPhail boy to suicide had gained him,

I wasn't sure. I only knew that there had to have been some profit. That humilating McPhail, using him against O'Hara, and then forcing him to recant, had gotten Lovingwell something he'd wanted. Some trinket, somebody's soul on a chain. Perhaps his rival's, O'Hara's. Perhaps McPhail's unknown lover. At best, Charley McPhail's parents could tell me precisely why Lovingwell had ruined their son. At worst, they could tell me more about his lover, who might have nursed an old hurt for seven years before salving it in Lovingwell's blood.

It was high noon when we got to the Harrison exit. I dropped down through a stand of leafless oak trees onto a two-lane state road. And about four miles south we hit the first cluster of tract homes, nondescript bungalows and single-story ranch houses that looked as desperately lifeless as trailer parks. We passed through the city proper, four or five blocks of two-story frame buildings, dotted incongruously with the red tile roofs and teepee-tops of fast-food joints. And then into a maple-lined grid of brick houses and snow-covered lawns. I pulled into a gas station and, while a pasty-faced boy in a parka tried to fill the tank and keep warm at the same time, I found a phonebook and looked up McPhail. There was only one listing. On Kearney Street. Number 153.

It was a tiny, two-story bungalow, sided in aluminum and badly in need of repairs. Rust seemed to be everywhere about the house. The cyclone fencing in the front yard was full of it. It came off on my glove when I opened the gate at the foot of the short, snowy walk that lead to the front door. It coated the mailbox and the screens on the square, shaded windows.

Lurman, not a man of delicate sensibility, began to fidget. "I can't take this, Harry," he said. "They're going to be old, and you're going to bring back the reason for all of this." He looked forlornly about the small, untended yard. "It's all too damn familiar. I'm going back to the car."

He walked down the snowy walk and left me standing on the porch. I knocked again.

"Who's there?" a timid voice asked. It could have been a man or a woman. It was that old and out of register. I looked back at the car and thought, you can still call this off, Harry. But she was at the storm door by then. Loose print dress with the frill of her slip trailing at the hemline. Hair white and thin on top. Rouge spots on her cheeks. Lustrous brown eyes that had lost their focus.

"What is it?" she said. "Who do you want?"

"Mrs. McPhail?"

"That's me." She pulled at her dress. "I'm Clovis McPhail."

"Could I come in, Mrs. McPhail? My name is Stoner. I want to talk to you about your son."

"Charley?" she said. "You a friend of Charley's?"

"Not exactly a friend," I said with half a heart.

"What is it you want, mister? Charley's dead. There isn't anything else to say. He's dead, his pop's dead, and I'm still here." She looked past me toward the tired street. "You explain it."

"I can't. I can't explain why your son is dead. Can you help me?"

"Why?" she said flatly. "Why bother? It won't do him any good to explain. It won't do me any good either."

"It might," I said.

She shook her head. "I've been through it too many times. It's been too many years."

"All right, Mrs. McPhail," I said. "I'm sorry I bothered you."

I started down the walk when she called me back.

"You could come in if you want. I don't see that many folks I can afford to scare 'em off. You could come in. For awhile."

The parlor was neat and sweet-smelling. The old mahogany furniture, the sideboards and end tables, were covered with linen doilies. She showed me to a wood rocker with a little quilted cushion on the seat.

"I try to keep it clean," she said, sitting across from me on an old armchair. "Can't do much about the outside. Not since Lou died. But I try to keep it clean in here." She looked at me with naked suspicion, as if she thought I were about to sell her something she didn't want to buy. "Why do you want to talk about Charley? What's this about? Are you with a newspaper or something?"

"I'm a private detective."

That tickled her. "You're joshing me?"

"Nope. It's a poor trade, but mine own."

"Who are you investigating? Charley?"

"No. The death of a man named Lovingwell."

"I know him," she said. "He's the son-of-a-bitch that gave Charley such a hard time. I told Charley to stick up for himself. To tell that bastard he wouldn't do his dirty work for him. But..." She waved her hand, as if she were bidding the idea goodbye once and for all. "He never had anything in here, my boy, Charley." She pressed her stomach and made a sour, disappointed face.

I could see that Clovis McPhail had been a hard woman all of her life. Hard on her son. Probably hard on her husband. In a household where everything was kept just so. It made me dislike her a little.

"He should have gone into a profession. I always told him that. With a profession you know where you stand. You got your feet on the ground. You got money coming in. He wouldn't listen. Just like his old man. He'd go off in a corner somewhere and sulk. What kind of man..." She gave me an abashed look.

"I know about Charley's problem," I said gently.

"He made me sick with it. His friends, too."

"Who were his friends?"

"Kids. Like him."

"Anyone in particular?"

She looked at me shrewdly. "What are you driving at?"

"Charley was having a relationship with someone at the University. The other party broke it off with him right before he died. Do you have any idea who the other man was?"

"I might," she said.

It was becoming a game to her. She had something I wanted and it was not in her nature to give things away for free. In that she reminded me of Daryl Lovingwell. I thought about what she might be after until it became obvious.

"It must be hard living here alone," I said. "On a widow's benefits."

"You don't know the half of it. Lou didn't leave me a penny."

I looked around the room. "You could use a new lamp. That one's about done for."

"A new TV, too."

"What kind of TV were you thinking of?"

She hopped out of the chair. "I got the catalogue upstairs. Sometimes I read through it and circle things I want to buy. I mean if I had the money."

"Why don't you go get it?"

She smiled raffishly and scurried off. When she came back, she had the mail-order catalogue in her hand. She had something else, too. An old envelope. She handed them both to me.

"That," she said, pointing to the envelope, "came the day Charley died. Take a look at it, if you want. If you think it might help."

She was something, all right. A real hardbitten something.

I stuck the catalogue in my coat pocket and examined the envelope. It was postmarked Cincinnati, Ohio, January 17, 1973. There was no return address. Inside was a note typed on onion skin paper. No watermark. "Charley," it read,

Saying I'm sorry that things haven't worked out the way we thought they would is miserably less than you deserve from me. You know I didn't want this to happen. He kept telling me it wouldn't happen. Now I don't know what to do. As long as he has all the cards, I'll just have to do what he wants. Forgive me if you can.

The letter was signed, "Mike."

"He never saw this?" I said.

"No. He never saw it."

"Do you know who Mike is?"

She nodded. "O'Hara. The bastard came sucking around here right after Charley died. Pretended he was paying a condolence call. Lou believed him, but I knew better. He wanted the letter back. But I'd be damned if I'd give it to him. He sends me a few bucks every Christmas. Guess he thinks that'll buy me off. The way I look at it, the son-of-a-bitch owes me a lot more than that for what he did to my son. You can see that from the letter."

I got up from the rocker. "Do you know what Lovingwell wanted from your son? Why he gave Charley such a hard time?"

"Letters," she said. "He made Charley give him some letters. Like that one. Only worse."

189

"From O'Hara?"

"Yes. He didn't want to do it, but my boy Charley never was much on guts. And then Lovingwell told him something that made Charley mad."

"Do you know what it was that made him angry?"

"Nope."

"Can I keep the letter?"

She looked at me slyly. "You got that catalogue good and safe in your pocket?"

I patted my coat.

"Then I guess it'll be all right," she said.

But she thought better of it as I was leaving and made me give her a business card and my word as a gentleman and a scholar that I would hold up my end of the deal. I gave her both, although I couldn't help thinking, as I walked down to the car, what poor credit the word of gentlemen and scholars made in the world I'd uncovered.

24

And so I had a suspect for the first time in better than a week. And a piece of evidence, to boot. It's odd how these things work. I'd gotten off on a wrong track, like Lurman had said the night before. Perhaps because I'd never quite grasped—in spite of all that I'd learned about him—just how singlemindedly vicious Daryl Lovingwell had been. I wouldn't make the same mistake again. I'd gone off fishing for a clue or a lead. And I'd come up with a dead boy who'd committed suicide like Claire Lovingwell and with Michael O'Hara. Smiling Michael O'Hara, who so desperately wanted the world to see him in disguise that he'd abandoned his lover rather than brave public exposure. Now start being a detective, Harry, I said to myself as I walked back down the snowy walk to the car. You've got two dead people, a blackmailer, and a man who's vanity made him a perfect target for extortion. Put them all together and see what you come up with.

It took us another hour to drive back to town, through that chilly countryside shagged with snow. And fifteen more minutes to wend our way up Ludlow to Bishop Street. I parked in front of that handsome Frank Lloyd Wright house and sat quietly for a moment on the car seat, thinking it out, deciding how best to proceed.

"Do you think he's in there?" Lurman said to me. "O'Hara?"

I shook my head. "They're divorced. Or in the process. And it's not the kind of marriage that could be patched up, even by the death of their son."

"Then why bother?"

"It's not O'Hara I want to talk to," I said. "Not yet. Not until I'm sure about why he was being blackmailed."

"What's the mystery?" Lurman said. "It's enough that Lovingwell was blackmailing him, isn't it? And that much is clear from the letter. You've got your motive. What you really ought to be doing is exploding his alibi for Tuesday morning."

"He hasn't got an alibi," I said.

"I thought he was supposed to be at the Faculty Club, having lunch?"

"That's what Beth Hemann said. And Beth Hemann is in love with the bastard. It doesn't make much difference anyway. The Club's off Jefferson on University grounds—only a half-mile from Middleton. He could have made it over there between courses and still made it back in time for dessert."

"Then why not just turn it over to McMasters and be done with it? We've got other problems to take care of. Remember?"

I turned on the car seat and stared at him. "I'm going to say this once, Ted. About a week ago, a man came into my office and hired me to find something that didn't exist. I've got to know why he did that. And I don't want you or McMasters or anyone else telling me how to do my job. You got that?"

"Take it easy, Harry," he said. "I'm on your side."

I got out of the Pinto and walked through the snow up to the big front door. There was a black wreath hung on the brass knocker. I pressed the lighted bell and a few minutes later she answered.

She was drunk again. Much drunker than she'd been two days before. Her face looked raw with grief and whiskey—shapeless as a crushed hat and drained of all that crude energy that had made it seem so smart and vigorous looking. She was wearing a dayrobe and slippers.

"What is it?" she said. "What do you want?"

"To talk," I said.

"No talk. Don't have any talk left. My son—"

Her chin quivered violently and she slapped her right hand across her mouth.

"I know about Sean," I said heavily. "Tonight I'm going to try to do something about the man who killed him."

Her eyes filled with tears. "Won't help."

"I'm not doing it for you. I'm doing it for Sarah. And for myself."

"Sarah?" She swallowed hard. "Is Sarah all right?"

"I don't know," I said. "She was holding her own this morning. But she's still in very bad shape. That's why I have to talk to you."

Meg O'Hara lowered her hand from her mouth and pulled nervously at the neck of her robe. I began to feel a little sick at heart. She wasn't a sympathetic woman—she wasn't the type who courted sympathy. And maybe the tears and the drunk were just for show. Maybe they were her way of working up to a grief that she couldn't really feel. If she were as much like Lovingwell as I suspected, she couldn't feel anything at all—outside of her own needs. But seeing her rubbed raw like that made me suspicious of my own motives. And for a second I was chilled by the thought that I wasn't showing much more humanity than the professor himself. That I'd become greedy, like him—for a truth that wasn't going to satisfy my itch to explain him. Then I thought of the girl, alone in that hospital room. And I went ahead with it.

"Sarah is going to be arrested for her father's murder unless I can prove she's innocent. I need your help to prove that."

"How?" she said. "What help?"

"You said that you were close friends with her mother. I want you to tell me about Claire and your husband."

All of the liquorish grief left Meg O'Hara's face. "You think *Michael* killed Daryl?" She curled her lip as if she would spit. "He didn't have the guts. My husband's half-fag, Mr. Stoner. And I don't mean rough trade, either."

"I know about that," I said. "I still want to know about him and Claire Lovingwell."

She shivered against the wind and pulled the robe tightly against her breast. "All right," she said. "I owe the girl something. Come in."

193

We sat in the parlor again, on the sculpted couch. Only this time there were no tea sets and bedroom eyes. No talk of whiskey and love-making. Just that burned-out woman wrapped primly in her dayrobe and the sound of her voice—vacant, tinged with grief, recounting the distant past as if she were reading from an old, melancholy book.

"We were very close friends, Claire and I. Something alike. Only she didn't have my talent for survival." Meg O'Hara swept her hand across the twill of the sofa seat. "Up until Saturday night, I thought her death was the worst thing that had ever happened to me." She looked into my face. "That's why I took my fling with Daryl after she died—to revenge myself on Michael for what he'd done to her."

I said, "What did he do?"

"He deserted her, Mr. Stoner," Meg O'Hara said. "He deserted her when she needed him most. She and Michael had been having an affair—or their version of one. I knew about it. At that point I didn't care."

"That was very civilized of you."

She laughed. "Would it have been more civilized to live together and to pretend we still loved each other? I would have done anything, sacrificed anything to keep her alive. And for awhile I thought Michael was doing her good. He was very theatrical about it, of course. She was his wounded Beatrice and he was going to save her from the death of madness." Meg O'Hara curled her lip again in disgust. "He was always posturing grandly in his affairs—making them into historical romances, high school dramas that he starred in and directed and produced. He had to be careful, you see, had to make them suitably unreal or someone might have realized what a talentless fake he was. At least that wasn't much of a problem with Claire. She was in such a bad way that he never had to prove himself—sexually. I know for a fact that at the same time he was courting her he was sodomizing a graduate student in the Physics Department. My big, strong husband!"

"Charles McPhail," I said.

She looked surprised. "You know about that, then?"

I nodded. "Why did your husband desert Claire Lovingwell?"

"I don't know," she said. "I don't know if he knew himself. He'd virtually taken charge of her affairs—she'd even

194

made him executor of her estate. Was constantly attendant on her. And then he just stopped. She'd call him, day and night. At first he'd make excuses for not seeing her and then he didn't even bother to answer the phone. A few weeks later, she killed herself."

"But she didn't change her will?" I said.

She shook her head as people do when they're no longer listening to what's being said. "He was still the executor. She'd left it all to Sarah, with the provision that Michael handle the investments and manage the money until Sarah was of age." Meg O'Hara stared off into space. "I've never forgiven him for what he did to Claire. I think that's why we..." She stopped short and sloughed off her mood. "Oh, hell. We do what we do, don't we? I'll tell you this, though. He didn't kill Lovingwell. He just isn't man enough." —

It wasn't until I walked out the door that I realized she'd been defending him all along, as if by making him look weak and indecisive she rendered him incapable of murder. It was one of the oddest testaments to love that I'd ever seen.

The next step was simple enough. Lurman handled it with professional skill, once we'd gotten back to the Delores. A few phone calls to local banks. A few strings pulled with glee, as if he were showing me how an investigation ought to be handled. And by five o'clock we knew for sure what I'd suspected as soon as I saw the love letter. What I guess I should have known days before, when Sarah had first mentioned the trust fund in the same breath with her father's unappeasable greed. He'd been blackmailing O'Hara, all right. But it was Sarah's money—or Claire's—that he'd been after. He hadn't been able to frighten his wife into willing it to him, not with Michael O'Hara acting as her support. So he very deftly knocked that support from under her and, in the same coup, managed to frighten O'Hara—a man who by all appearances was easily frightened—into doing his dirty work for him. After prying the love letters out of McPhail's hands, he'd forced O'Hara to abandon Claire Lovingwell; and after a few weeks of whispered threats, she'd finally lost her nerve and killed herself. McPhail had been eliminated in the same way. And then it was just Daryl and O'Hara and all that money.

"Apparently O'Hara would draw funds out of the trust at regular intervals," Lurman said. "And within a week to ten days, the same amount would show up in Lovingwell's account. They were bleeding her dry, Harry. Of course, the bank is going to do a complete audit, now. But from the size of the sums involved, she was almost broke and didn't know it."

"It doesn't pay to be a commie," I said drily.

"It didn't pay to be Lovingwell's daughter, that's for sure," Lurman said. "Or anybody close to him." He rubbed his hands together. "So now you know."

"Now I know," I said. Only it didn't feel right. It didn't feel a hundred percent. I had a motive, all right. But O'Hara had had seven years of that same motive—seven years to brood over what he'd been forced to do to Charles McPhail and Claire Lovingwell. What had made him decide that seven years and one more day were just too much to bear? And why had Lovingwell hired *me* in the first place? How did Sarah and I fit into the picture? Because we had to fit, I knew that much. Daryl Lovingwell had been too damn meticulous to leave anything to chance.

I pulled the love letter from my jacket pocket and stared at it. "Wouldn't you think," I said to Lurman, "that a man as cautious as Lovingwell would have taken steps to prevent O'Hara from retaliating against him?"

"He had those letters, Harry," Lurman said. "I guess that was his protection."

"What if O'Hara managed to get his hands on those letters?" I said.

"Then why would he need to shoot Lovingwell?"

Why, indeed? I said to myself. What would drive a man with such a thin skin to risk murder?

I got up from the recliner.

Only Michael O'Hara could tell me the answer to that. And I intended that he would. Even if I had to blackmail him myself, even if I had to dangle that last love letter over his head like a sword. I glanced at my watch, which was showing twenty after five, and said, "I'm going out again."

"The hell. You've got to be here to get that call."

"I'll be back in time," I said. "A half-hour is all I'll need."

196

"And if Grimes doesn't want to give you that half-hour, Harry?"

I walked over to the roll-top and pulled the magnum from the top drawer. Lurman looked at it and shook his head.

"Too much weapon," he said with grave authority. "You'd be lucky to get off two shots."

"Not with you along to back me up, old boy."

He looked at his watch and said, "This is really necessary, right?"

I nodded.

"And only a half-hour?"

"At most."

"All right," he said and got to his feet with a groan. "Where are we going this time?"

I pulled out the phone book, thumbed through it until I came to O'Hara, Michael C., and said, "To Ohio Avenue. To O'Hara's home."

It was a tiny apartment off campus, in a building full of tiny apartments. His wife hadn't left him much—that was obvious. And if Lovingwell had been putting on the squeeze, too, the past seven years must have been very grim indeed for Michael O'Hara. I knocked at the wooden door and Miss Hemann answered.

Something about my face or about the way I was standing made her rock back on her feet and stare anxiously into my eyes. "What is it?" she said. "What do you want?"

"I want to talk to O'Hara."

She glanced over her shoulder and said, "He's in a bad way now. Couldn't this wait, Mr. Stoner? Couldn't this wait until his son is buried?"

I shook my head.

"Who is it, Beth?" O'Hara called from the living room.

"It's Mr. Stoner," she said.

There was a dead silence. "Show him in," O'Hara said after a moment.

It was a dreary little flat. Sad enough under any circumstances, but made especially sad by the grief that filled the room. O'Hara was sitting in a baize armchair beside a coiled radiator. There was a bottle of bourbon on the table beside him. The room smelled of bourbon and of heat.

"Mr. Stoner," he said without looking up at me. "I wondered how long it would take you to make this little call. I can't say I approve of your timing. But then you're not a subtle man, are you?"

I didn't know whether it was the grief talking or whether it was something else. A premonition, perhaps, that his past was finally catching up with him. I took the envelope out of my pocket and O'Hara stared at it curiously, as if it were something he recognized but couldn't quite place.

"What is it?" he said. "A letter?"

I nodded. "From you to Charles McPhail."

"Ah!" he said quietly. "I should have guessed."

Miss Hemann stared nervously at me, then at O'Hara. "What is this, Michael? What's this about?"

O'Hara looked up quickly. I could see from the pained expression on his face that the girl didn't know about McPhail or about the other McPhails who had probably replaced him. She didn't know about the blackmail, either. And it mattered to him. After all of the years of lying to himself and to the rest of the world, it still mattered greatly to him that no one knew. I suppose, finally, that it mattered to me, too. But not for his sake. For hers.

"I'll meet with you tomorrow morning," O'Hara said to me in his frigid departmental voice. "At my office. We can discuss this matter then."

It was a peculiar bargain, seeing that I might not be around the next morning to fulfill it—at least, if Grimes had his way I wouldn't. "I'm not sure that will do," I said to him.

He nodded gravely. "I understand. Regardless of what happens, I'll go to the police. I give you my word on that. I would have done so anyway." He glanced quickly at Beth Hemann and said, "Please. One more day won't make a difference to anyone."

"All right," I said. "Tomorrow morning. But understand that the girl is my only concern in this. And that I will go to the police no matter what is said."

"I understand," O'Hara replied.

I didn't like the bargain I'd struck. I'd wanted to hear it all *before* I risked my life against Grimes. But then I'd never championed the truth. In my spavined version of knighthood I was not a Galahad. I was one of that lesser, more impulsive clan—killed early in tournaments or in petty quarrels, over a woman's honor or dishonor. That didn't matter either. Just over a woman, I thought and laughed at myself. Because it wasn't O'Hara I was protecting. His vanity was too corrupt to survive Daryl Lovingwell's furious brand of realism. It was Beth Hemann I'd been thinking of, the loyal Miss Hemann, who loved Michael O'Hara in spite of his lacerating, self-disgusted manhood. I had seen too many sad-eyed sufferers for love's sake in the past week to want to add another to the count.

So I walked out the door and down to the street, where Lurman was waiting in the Pinto, and drove back to the Delores, telling myself as I drove that I'd done the right thing.

25

Lurman and I got back to the Delores at six on the dot. An hour later, Chico Robinson called.

"That you, Stoner?" he said.

I said it was.

"Well listen tight, man. He was staying on the Hill, but he split. Dude he was staying with say he might be in your neighborhood tonight. Maybe pay you a visit, you dig?"

"Yeah."

"He's gone to see a lady friend first. Chick by the name of Linda Green. She lives on Euclid Street."

He gave me an address in Corryville, and I wrote it down and handed it to Ted.

"You be quick and you might catch him there," Robinson said. "But you best be on your toes, dude. 'Cause he's got him a machine pistol and a sawed-off."

I didn't say anything.

"You hear?"

"I heard."

Robinson hung up.

I told Lurman what Chico had said.

"We'll get over there right away," he said excitedly.

Lurman called down to the lot and assembled the rest of his crew in my apartment. We didn't have time to make elaborate plans. He and I were to cover the front of the building. The other six agents the rear and side doors. And that was it. Everyone seemed comfortable with the set-up. Everyone but me.

"This guy's armed to the teeth, Ted. And he knows how to kill. Wouldn't it be smarter to call in a SWAT team?"

It would have been smarter, all right. But it wouldn't have been politic. And I guess I knew that as soon as I'd asked the question. The FBI doesn't like to share their glories or their mistakes with other agencies; it was really that simple, although Lurman tried to make it seem more complicated.

"Euclid Street is right on the border of the University community, Harry," he said testily. "We call in an army and a lot of innocent kids might get hurt. Especially if Grimes is as heavily armed as Robinson said he was. Anyway I don't want to have to bargain for any hostages. I don't want any action inside the building at all. We'll take him when he comes out. And we'll take him clean. No more fuck-ups. No more traps. No more Sturdevants and Lionellis. As soon as any of you makes a positive I.D. and he's out of the building, kill him."

At half-past six we piled into three black Chevies and drove down Taft to Auburn and then north to Euclid Avenue. It was a perfect evening. No snow this time. Nothing to obscure our vision. A night just as cold and clear as glass. We pulled over across from Linda Green's brownstone apartment house at seven; and while the six other agents took their positions around the building, Lurman and I sat silently in the car. For the second time in three days I had the eerie feeling that Ted had become someone else. Someone almost as cool and dangerous as Grimes himself. His face was flushed and when he spoke, it was with a sharp, conspiratorial inflection, as if we were two kids playing games outside an abandoned house. He made me nervous, and so did the old building, which was dotted with tall windows that would make ideal fire lanes if Grimes decided to make a fight of it.

"Here's the way it's going to be," he said. "Take a look at the building."

It was a three-story brownstone with a huge stone stoop in front, fire escapes on either side, and those tall windows arranged in ranks on each wall. A glass door above the stoop led to an alcove lined with mailboxes and buzzers.

Behind the alcove another glass door led to a stairwell and to a hallway that extended to the rear of the building. Looking through both doors I could almost see to the end of the hall. Which meant that anyone coming down the stairs would be fully visible from where we were sitting.

"I've got two men on the north side, two on the south, and two behind the building. We've got the front. We've also got the only view of the lobby. If he doesn't come out the front door, we'll have to let the others know which way he's headed. And quickly." Lurman looked me over as if I were standing in front of him on parade. "You're in on this because you wanted to be and because you deserve to be. But for chrissake, don't go being a hero. Just do what I say and we'll both stand a chance of getting out of this thing alive."

He pointed to a tall maple tree on the east side of the stoop and said, "That's your position. I'll find a spot on the west side. I'll have a walkie-talkie with me to alert the other men in case he doesn't come out the front. Now all I want you to do is stay put until you see him coming out the door. When you've made him, take that cannon of yours and shoot him with it. No questions. No warning. Just shoot. And be careful of the crossfire, because I'll be shooting, too. Just aim carefully and make each shot count. And if he does go down, keep on firing until you're sure he's dead. Until you see his brains on the sidewalk. And don't touch his damn body. He may have booby-trapped his clothes and his weapons. With this guy we just don't know."

"What if one of us gets hit?" I said.

"Won't happen, Harry. This time we got the drop on him."

Lurman smiled icily and held out his hand. "Well, old man, this is it. Just think about what he did to Sarah and pull the trigger."

I shook his hand and we got out of the car and crossed Euclid. Lurman wrapped a scarf around his neck and trotted off toward a telephone pole on the north side of the building. I headed south to the maple tree. By the time I made it there, I was sweating. The tree was set at a slightly oblique angle to the front door, cutting off my view of the hall and the north side fire escape. From where I was

203

posted I wouldn't be able to see Grimes until he came through the inner door into the alcove.

I bothered myself about the angle of vision for five minutes, then leaned against the tree, my right hand on the pistol in my coat pocket, and waited.

An hour passed and there was no action anywhere around the building. I began to wonder if Grimes was inside after all. The thought that he could be somewhere on the loose should have been more disturbing than it was. It probably would have been, if I hadn't been so damn scared already. After leaning against that tree for over an hour and jumping at every sound that came from the sidewalk behind me or from the apartment building in front of me, I would have settled for any resolution. I could see that Lurman was getting antsy, too. From time to time he'd pop out from behind the lamppost where he'd stationed himself and take a long look into the hall.

After another half hour's wait, I was convinced Grimes wasn't in the building. Which suddenly didn't seem so comforting. There was a lot of dark street behind me. A lot of shooting room. And I found myself glancing back over my shoulder more and more regularly. Euclid was lined with parked cars on either side; but there wasn't much traffic, much life, until it intersected with Taft, two blocks to the south. The street lights made a warm, bright cluster at Taft, and I found myself looking toward them, from time to time, with a silly kind of fondness, as if I'd been born and raised on that lonesome streetcorner.

At half-past nine I got tired of pretending I was part of the maple tree and walked over to the sidewalk. A couple of black teenagers, who were passing by, eyed me as if I was Dad's wallet left out on the dresser. They thought better of it after a moment and kept on moving down the street toward Lurman, where they were probably tempted again.

Then an automatic rifle went off somewhere behind the apartment house with a sound like a string of firecrackers exploding in an alley.

The black kids bolted across Euclid. A blue Ford jerked to a stop behind me. Lurman started running down the northside alley to the rear of the apartment. The shooting intensified—first a string of firecrackers, then the garbled popping of handguns and, once, the muted roar of a shot-gun.

I started down the alley after Lurman when I happened to look back at the front of the building. He was just coming out the door—long-legged, hatless, wrapped in a shearling coat. His long, docile face looking the slightest bit perplexed, as if he were trying to make up his mind which way to turn.

"Ted!" I shouted. "He's up here!"

He couldn't hear me. The gunfire was too loud and he was too far down the alleyway. Which meant that Lester O. Grimes had become my problem—alone.

Grimes looked right and left, then stepped off the porch as coolly as if he were off for an evening stroll. I guess he couldn't believe how well his plan had worked. I guess he couldn't believe there was no one out there to greet him. He cinched his coat at the waist, smiled gamely, and started up Euclid toward Taft at a brisk pace.

The whole block seemed to be coming to life. Lights were popping on up and down the street. Faces were plastered against windows. Thrill-seekers were already edging down the block toward the source of all that gunfire. Within a minute or so, a fleet of police cars came thudding through the icy street, their sirens screaming and their blue bubble-tops sprinkling an almost festive light on the snow-draped porches and the cars parked along Euclid. It was pure chaos. And Lester Grimes was walking calmly through its center—secure in the knowledge that in the midst of all that light and sound no one would be paying him a second look.

In a way I was lucky. The confusion would work in my favor, too. And then Lester was playing it so coolly that he might not think to look behind him. And even if he did, he'd have a hell of a time picking me out among all the cops and thrill-seekers streaming down the sidewalk. Just to be safe, I waited until he had about twenty yards on me, then stepped from behind the lamppost, gun in hand, and started up Euclid after him.

Pale, excited faces brushed past me in a blur. But I was concentrating on that tall target sixty feet in front of me. I was going to need to make up some ground, because once he got past Taft and McMillan there would be a lot of dark street in front of him. And then the magnum wouldn't be worth a damn at more than ten or fifteen feet. With a short barrel, it's nowhere near as accurate as a smaller caliber pistol—it can't be fired at all without kicking your arms up ninety degrees. And on the ice, I might well end up on my butt. That meant I was going to get one shot, at best, before Lester returned fire. That meant I had to get as close to him as possible to make that one shot count. Right on top of him if I could manage it, like they teach you at the police academies. Close enough to stick the barrel in his ribs and squeeze the trigger and blow a hole the size of a pie plate in Lester Grimes's belly.

I started to trot.

A half-dozen more people rushed by me, heading up the street to Linda Green's apartment. I didn't see their faces, just that rangy figure bobbing in the distance. The adrenaline was starting up. It made my skin tingle and itch. It brought a cold sweat out on my face and arms and made my heart pound painfully in my chest. My knees felt as if they weren't locking right, as if they might buckle at the very next step.

Easy, Harry, I told myself. Easy.

Another fleet of patrol cars thudded and shrieked down Euclid. I could still hear the roar of gunfire coming from the brownstone, and the air had begun to smell of cordite smoke. It drifted like a fog through the cold air. I could taste it, burning, in my throat.

By the time he got close to Taft, I'd made up twenty feet on him. Not nearly enough. Across the intersection, Euclid became Auburn Avenue—a long, flat residential street, lined on either side with tall brownstones and lit dimly by gas lights. Once he got across that intersection, he'd be home-free. Then it would be like following a wounded lion into the bush. Auburn was a grid of dark alleys and asphalt drives that led between buildings to the old-fashioned slat garages and carriage houses set behind them in unlighted backyards. He could disappear down any one of those alleyways and I would lose him. Unless he'd spotted me, in which case I could suddenly end up very dead. He was heavily armed, I was sure of that. He'd probably left the machine pistol with Linda Green or whoever it was who was creating the noisy diversion that allowed him to escape. But there was still that sawed-off shotgun that Chico Robinson had mentioned. It was probably tucked like a derringer in one huge sleeve of his shearling coat or under the breast where he could jerk it free. And he was a dead-shot, as that school superintendent had learned. He was also slightly crazy, which increased the chances of an ambush if he had spotted me. He wanted to kill me. He'd almost succeeded in the Coney Lot. He wasn't going to miss this time—not at close range, with a sawed-off.

I thought of taking a wild shot at him from where I stood. But there were too many people on the sidewalk. And there were cars on Taft. It would be a ten-to-one shot anyway, from thirty or forty feet.

No, he has to stop, Harry, I told myself. For a minute at least. Either that or you have to follow him into that dark patch of ground on the other side of Taft. I stared at the stoplight, swinging in the breeze at the corner of Taft and Euclid and prayed that it would turn red.

He made it to the corner and the light didn't flicker.

"Change, damn it!" I almost shouted.

He'd just stepped off the curb when it went yellow.

Grimes hesitated a moment, and I thought of how I might die. Vaporized like Sturdevant or locked like the girl in a coma. Then Grimes stepped back up onto the curb. And I cocked the magnum and began to run. All out. Arms chugging. Breath coming in throat-scalding bursts. My heart pounding like someone's fist knocking inside my chest.

There were three people and about thirty-five feet of ground between Lester Grimes and me when that light changed. I made up twenty of those feet and shoved two of those people out of my way in about five seconds. But the third person—a woman in a plaid scarf and heavy wool overcoat who was standing midway and at an oblique angle between me and Grimes—caught sight of the pistol in my right hand and began to scream.

Before I could even raise the revolver, Grimes whirled to his left, tore the shotgun from beneath his coat and fired a single blast of buckshot. The load caught the woman full in the back, lifted her off the sidewalk and sent her flying, head first, through the windshield of a Chevy parked at the top of the street.

Grimes pulled the pump a second time. But I had the magnum braced by then. Arms extended, both hands wrapped on the checked handle, I fired before he could squeeze off a second burst. The magnum roared, sending out a tongue of flame and throwing my arms back so violently that I actually did go down on the icy sidewalk. Hard.

I'd aimed too high and the slug hit him high in front, on the left shoulder. Hit him the way you see big-bore rifle slugs—the 470 Nitro Expresses—bounce against the hides of rhino or of elephant. With a dusty, sick-making explosion. Like I'd thrown a bag of red dirt at him instead of a bullet. It spun him all the way around toward the intersection. And it was only when he was facing away from me that I saw the hole it had made—all the way through his body and out the back of his coat. Jagged, red, the size of a grapefruit. His whole coat was red in back and smoking in the icy air.

Grimes fell forward off the curb and went down to his knees on the pavement. I could see part of his face. Blood was dripping steadily from his mouth and from his nose. There was blood everywhere on the snow and on his coat.

A woman on the other side of Taft had begun to scream, hands on her cheeks and mouth open wide. And several of the thrill seekers had stopped in their tracks and started running up Euclid to where I was sitting on the sidewalk. I could hear their feet on the ice behind me.

"Get back!" I shouted over my shoulder. "Get the hell back."

I looked once at the body of the woman in the wool overcoat, wedged obscenely in the cracked windshield. Then got to my feet.

Grimes was staring at me, over his shoulder.

I pointed the magnum at him and said, "Don't, Grimes." Knowing full well that he was going to do it. Cocking the piece with my left hand because I knew.

"Don't!" I said again.

"Why the hell not?" he said stupidly. His breath was like a red mist.

He moved so quickly it was as if he'd never been hit. Around on his knees, the dull barrels of the shotgun nosing through the opening in his coat. I pulled the trigger again. And he fell back as if he'd broken in two. The shotgun went off with a boom—straight up, in a shower of sparks and smoke. Hitting nothing.

I held the gun on him for another minute. Even though I knew he was dead. Bent back on his knees, the shotgun gleaming in his hands.

26

A police marksman killed Linda Green— Grimes' girl-friend, who'd created the diversion that allowed him to slip out the front door. He killed her with a single shot from an apartment window across from her second-floor room. Before she died, she'd fired over a thousand rounds from the machine pistol Grimes had left with her. And five of those rounds had killed Ted Lurman.

I didn't know that until after a squad car had pulled up at the Taft intersection and an ambulance had come to take what was left of Lester Grimes to the county morgue. The cops in the squad car were nervous and efficient and, once they'd found out whom I'd killed, palsy and sympathetic.

"You *had* to do it. You *had* to do it," one of them kept saying to me, as if he were defending a friend in an imaginary argument.

I kept repeating his words as I walked up Euclid, but I was seeing Grimes' blood frozen in the street and the smoke that had poured from his chest, like the vaporous smoke from a manhole cover. When I made it back to the apartment house and heard that Lurman was dead, I sat down hard on a snow bank beside the alleyway and tried to remember what my life had been like before Lovingwell and Lester O. Grimes had entered it.

"Where'd they take him?" I asked one of the agents.

"Christ Hospital," he said. "We heard you dropped Grimes."

"I shot him," I said.

"Good work. He needed killing." He looked closely at my face and said, "You did what you had to do."

He was a middle-aged man with a tired face and blood-shot eyes. I'd like to think that he meant what he said. Not because it was true, although it was as true as that kind of apology can be. But because a larger part of me than I liked to admit didn't care whether it was true or not. I wasn't feeling guilty about Grimes, just numbed and disgusted and grateful it was done. That's what worried me about what the FBI man had said. Because if he didn't care and I didn't either, then it was just too damn easy to kill a man.

One of the cops drove me to Christ and dropped me at the Emergency Room. They'd already put Lurman on ice. When one of the residents asked me if I wanted to take a look at the body, I asked him why.

He shrugged. "Some people like a last look. It makes them feel like it's over."

I made myself go down to the morgue and take a last look at Lurman, who had been a decent man. But seeing his corpse only made me feel sad and sorry, although that unsettling grief made me think better of myself than I had an hour before.

I checked in on Sarah before going back to the Delores. The duty nurse gave me the only good news of the day. She was out of the coma. She was going to survive a nightmare that was almost ended. All but the very last bit.

Sid McMasters drove me home at three in the morning. He didn't say anything until he got to the front door of the Delores and then he said, "You did a good job."

"I'm not so sure," I said wearily. "What does this mean about Sarah? Where does she stand?"

McMasters looked at me unhappily. "Harry, I've tried to see it every way but the girl. And none of it works. We got a court order to look into Lovingwell's safety deposit box. We cracked it last night, right before you and your FBI friends brought the whole force to Linda Green's apartment. You know what we found inside?"

He handed me a slip of paper.

"I'm going to kill you," it said. *"For what you did to my mother."*

"There were dozens of them," McMasters said.

I looked at the notepaper. "Anybody could have written this."

"They were typed on her typewriter, Harry. And when you take them and how she felt about her father and the fact that she was on the scene at the time of the murder...her best bet is to cop a plea. Insanity. I'd be willing to sit for it, and I've never said that before in my life."

"She didn't kill him, Sid."

"You keep saying that, Harry. But saying isn't proof."

"Lovingwell was blackmailing Michael O'Hara. He'd been blackmailing him for seven years. O'Hara had motive and opportunity."

"Can you prove it?" he said, perking up.

"After this morning I can. I may even get a confession for you."

"Why don't I just pick him up then?"

I shook my head. "He's not going anywhere."

Only that wasn't the reason. After all the lies, after all the divagations, after that bloody night, I was owed the chance to hear the truth about Lovingwell. I'd earned it. What was more, I needed it. And not simply to save Sarah. But to reassure myself. Putting an end to the Lovingwell case was truly putting an end to "it."

"I'll let you know, Sid. By noon."

He thought it over. "All right, Harry. We'll play it your way until noon. Then I want to know exactly what you've got." He sighed heavily. "I guess you've earned that much after what you did tonight."

I got out of the car and started for the lobby.

McMasters leaned across the seat and called me back. "By the way, we found out where the suicide gun came from."

"Where?" I said.

"Lovingwell bought it three months ago. Right about the time these notes started coming in."

27

At nine-thirty the next morning I parked the Pinto on St. Clair and walked under the bare branches of the elms and oaks to the Physics Building on the south side of the street. Miss Hemann wasn't at her desk, but O'Hara was in his office—just as he said he'd be. He asked me to close the door when I walked in and I did. He looked ill in the gray morning light. His face was drawn and there were great scorched circles under his eyes. A pile of letters and documents was sitting on his desk.

"I've been sorting through some of my mementos." he said, passing a hand over the loose papers. "It may be my last opportunity."

He looked up at me. It wasn't a plaintive look. I didn't feel any pity for him and he knew it. It was a look of resentment, as if he held me responsible for McPhail and for Lovingwell and for his son. It was a look I didn't completely understand. I told him again what I knew and what I suspected. He plucked a letter from the pile on his desk.

"Daryl," he said absently. "How does one explain Daryl? How does one account for that much hatred? For that much malevolence? I'm a scientist, Stoner, and I can't answer the question, although I've tried. My God, I can show you, by computation, why space has to be curved. I can debate with you how far quantum physics may imply a deity in the universe. But Daryl..."

I didn't say anything. I wanted to hear him say it in his own way. I wanted to see it come together once and for all. And for his own reasons, he wanted to say it, too. Perhaps because he'd been holding it in for so damn long. He took a deep breath and started to talk.

"In 1973 I became friends with Claire Lovingwell, Daryl's wife. She was in a very bad way and I felt sorry for her. She'd been a handsome woman and very bright. I just couldn't stand to see her go down all alone. We became friends. She confided in me. With my help she made arrangements to rewrite her will. What would have gone to Daryl at her death was set aside in a trust fund for her daughter Sarah. A trust over which Daryl had no control. At least that was the way it was intended to work.

"Of course, at the time, I had no idea how malevolent Daryl could be. His behavior toward Claire while vicious was motivated by a sexual jealousy that was partly understandable. And then she was prone to exaggeration in her mental state. Who knew how much of what she said was true and how much was paranoid delusion?

"So when Charley told me that Lovingwell had approached him about our paper, I thought it was in retaliation for what I'd done for Claire. A fit of pique and jealousy. I didn't think any more of it, then. But I grossly underestimated my man. A serious error for a mathematician. The most serious error of my life.

"Daryl got to Charley. Using his powers as chairman. And using innuendo and lies. He panicked the boy into believing that I was betraying him sexually with Claire. In a moment of fatal weakness he gave Lovingwell those damn letters. And that was it—that was the end. He had me and there was nothing I could do."

I didn't say what I was thinking. That he could have been man enough to brave ridicule and save his friend. Probably the thought had never occurred to him or, if it had, he'd dismissed it with terror. So fragile and fundamental was his vanity.

"What did Lovingwell blackmail you into doing?" I asked him.

He took another deep breath and paused. I could see him thinking it over. Nothing he'd said so far had implicated him in Lovingwell's murder. And he knew that. Nothing he's said so far had taken me an inch beyond what

216

I already knew. He looked at me closely and sighed—an exhausted, curious sigh. Then he looked back at his desk. "You know it anyway. Let it be said that I admitted to it, first.

"After poor Charley was driven to suicide—gotten rid of, really, once he'd served his purpose—Daryl explained to me precisely how my life would be lived and has been lived for the past seven years. I was to be his creature, his Frankenstein. Over and above the extortion money, any piece of blackmail or savagery, any dirty job he wanted done, would fall to me. And you cannot imagine how savage he could be. My first assignment, of course, was Claire's will. She'd rewritten it to put me in charge and left me the discretionary powers to invest the monies as I saw fit. Once Daryl gained control of those letters, the money was virtually his.

"Poor Claire. She'd wanted to cheat him out of that satisfaction. She'd wanted to salvage something for herself and for her daughter. But he won in the end. With my help, he won. By the end of this year he would have gotten all of the trust fund that could be gotten. All of it that wasn't tied up somehow. You see, that's what worried him. Sarah wasn't very conscientious when it came to money. Daryl knew that. But even she would find out that she'd been substantially robbed when the bank informed her that her account showed a balance of zero. Then there would have been an investigation and I would have been exposed. And so would Daryl." O'Hara looked at me sadly. "Something had to be done."

"What?" I said. "What was he going to do?"

O'Hara turned his face away. "Can't you guess?" he said in a thick whisper.

I thought about the pictures Lovingwell had stolen from Sarah's room, about the rumors he'd spread about her depressions, about the ornate house with all its treasures, each one paid for in someone's blood. And I knew. Knew so surely that it disoriented me—a familiar disorientation that I finally identified as the dark remainder of a very bad dream. An oedipal nightmare I had wandered into, years away from my own childhood. "He was going to kill her, wasn't he?" I said, feeling it fully—the ancient monstrousness of it. "The son-of-a-bitch was going to kill her."

217

O'Hara nodded. "He'd been planning it for months. I think, in a way, he'd been planning it since Claire's death."

"How?" I said. "How was he going to kill her?"

"Her mother had been a suicide. Sarah's death would have been arranged to look like the same thing. Daryl had taken steps to prepare for it. Purchased a gun. Stolen some pictures of Claire and Sarah that he was going to plant on her body. Written notes to himself. He'd even cashed in some of his stocks, to refurbish her trust fund, in case anyone decided to look into it after her death. Since she would have died without a will, it would have all come back to him anyway. He told me the entire plan on Tuesday afternoon of last week. He told it with characteristic glee."

"What was your role to be?"

O'Hara blushed. "The executioner, Mr. Stoner. And, of course, afterwards one of the witnesses at the coroner's hearing."

"And what was my role? Why was I hired?"

O'Hara gave me a very odd look, as if I'd said something he hadn't expected me to say. Whatever it was, it made him stop talking and lean back gravely in his desk chair. I didn't like his look. I didn't like the whole aura of reappraisal.

"You don't know why he hired you?" O'Hara said. Then he laughed—a single bark of mordant amusement. "I should have known."

O'Hara reached down to his desk drawer, opened it, and pulled out a small-caliber revolver. I jumped up and he whipped it at me like a teacher's rule. "Just sit," he said sternly.

I did what he said.

We must have sat there for a good five minutes— O'Hara holding the gun on me and staring vacantly at my face. Past my face, really, at something invisible to all the world but him alone.

"You really are a fool, Mr. Stoner," he said abruptly. But his face was still self-absorbed, his voice distant and unreal. "I was right about you all along. I should never have made the mistake of trying to kill you that night in the parking lot. I wouldn't have, you know, if you hadn't come to me so soon after Daryl's death."

I gawked at him. "You? You tried to kill me that night?"

He smiled and his eyes came back into focus on my face.

"Why?" I said.

"Why, the document, of course, Mr. Stoner," he said with eerie amusement. "Don't you remember the document you were hired to find?"

"There was no document," I said uneasily.

"Oh, but there was. I have it right here."

He pulled a sheaf of papers from his desk and floated them over to me. The words TOP SECRET SENSITIVE were printed at the top of each page. I stared dully at the dry, onion-skin paper and began to understand.

"You were supposed to know about these. Daryl told me that you did. He said he'd told you all about me and that you'd expose me if I didn't cooperate with him." O'Hara laughed—a laugh that made me shudder. "And I believed him! Imagine that! After all these years, I believed him when I finally had the upper hand."

"These are the love letters, aren't they?" I said, hefting the sheaf of papers in my hand. "The letters from Mc-Phail?"

O'Hara nodded. "All he did was print TOP SECRET on them and stick them in his safe. Those are what cost Claire her fortune and Charley his life. Those are what he used for seven years to degrade and manipulate me. I *loved* Charley," he said in a whine that made me turn from his face.

I'd seen too many men die in the past week, seen too many victims and too many persecutors. So many that the roles didn't make sense to me anymore. O'Hara didn't make sense to me. Whimpering over a man whose life he could have saved if he'd been willing to face the truth about himself. He still couldn't do it. Just as he couldn't do it the day before, when I'd almost revealed it to Miss Hemann.

And suddenly I realized that that hard-earned vanity was the only motive that would impel O'Hara to kill. Not for money, not for revenge, not even for the memory of poor Charley McPhail. He just didn't have the guts, and that recognition chilled me to the bone.

"How did you get them?" I said—not wanting to hear it. "How did you get your hands on these letters?"

O'Hara brushed the question away with his pistol. "When I told him on Tuesday that it was over, that I had the letters in my hands, he laughed. He said it didn't matter if I had the originals. He said he had photostats. He said he'd told you all about me. He said if I didn't cooperate with him, he would have you prove that she'd stolen them and then expose me."

"Then she really did take them," I said.

But he wasn't listening. "I wanted to help her, but what was I supposed to do? A man like me? In my position? What would people think? What would Meg think? And Beth? And Sean—" His voice broke.

This time I *did* feel sorry for him. For the part of him that only wanted everything to be the way it had been when there were no Lovingwells—father, mother or daughter—to threaten his world.

She had stolen the document, after all. And Lovingwell had hired me for precisely the reason he'd said he had— to recover some papers his daughter had stolen from his safe. Well, not precisely. There had been no doubt in his mind that she'd taken them. It was what she planned to do with them that must have bothered him. And that had been my job—to find out where she'd secreted them. Those papers I was honor-bound not to look at or tell anyone else about. That was how it was supposed to have worked, until he found out on Tuesday morning that she'd already handed them back to O'Hara. Then, I suppose, I became just another prop, a way of bullying O'Hara. Another part of the murder plan, like the threatening letters in his deposit box and the faked evidence of the robbery in the study and the nonsense about Sarah's suicidal tendencies. Faked so cleverly that when it came time to be rid of Sarah L., there wouldn't have been any problems. Lovingwell would tell me that he'd recovered the papers on his own; I'd go my merry way; O'Hara would proceed to murder Sarah; and nobody would ever know what had taken place.

I looked over at O'Hara. His face was calm now.

"What did she bargain for in return for the letters, O'Hara?" I said to him. "What did she want you to do?"

But he wasn't listening. "I'll never get away with this," he said in a quite reasonable tone of voice. "Not here. They'll find out, won't they, Mr. Stoner? Why you've probably seen to it that they'll find out."

I knew what was going to happen. I got out of the chair and walked toward his desk. "Don't," I said as calmly as

220

I could. "Don't, please. It's not worth it. *He* wasn't worth it."

But he still couldn't hear me. A moment later, he couldn't hear anything at all.

28

I didn't see Sarah Lovingwell for almost a month.

McMasters dropped the case against her when he saw the letters and examined the trust fund account. I didn't tell him what Sarah's role had been in securing those letters. Partly because I wasn't sure. Partly because, at that point, I just didn't care. Daryl Lovingwell was dead. O'Hara and his son were dead. Lurman, Sturdevant, Lionelli. Lester Grimes. There had been enough death in that lean, vicious man's wake. He had hired me to protect his daughter and to find the document she'd stolen from him. I'd done both. I'd done my job. The only thing that stuck in my throat was the fact that no one would ever know what a monster he'd been. No one would ever know the evil he had planned. No one would ever know how it had gone wrong. Daryl Lovingwell.

One Sunday afternoon, deep in February's ice, with the church bells ringing outside the windows, she'd come to my apartment to pay me for what I'd done. It wasn't hard to see that she was hurt that I hadn't visited her in the hospital or, later, when she'd gone home.

After a long silence in which we'd looked at each other in that tender, tentative way that old lovers look, she'd asked me in her soft, musky voice why I had abandoned her.

I stared at that prim, pretty face and couldn't tell. And

knew that I never would know. For just a second I wanted to ask her if she *had* killed him. If she'd killed him that Tuesday afternoon after O'Hara had left in a funk. Because O'Hara hadn't really confessed to anything but a miserable and helpless confusion. But I didn't ask her and I didn't tell her that I knew about the letters, either. I knew what she would say—that she hadn't stolen a government document. Which, I suppose, was technically true. Her father had said she believed in equivocation. In a way, that's what I ended up saying in answer to her question—that she was just too clever for me.

She smiled that inscrutable little smile and said, "I'm truly sorry for that."

She walked to the door, looked back once, fondly, at me and my little apartment, and walked out. That was the last time I saw Sarah B(ernice) Lovingwell. The girl who didn't look like she'd caused the trouble.